To Lyn

THE TIP OF THE ICEBERG

Happy reading

THE
TIP OF THE
ICEBERG

DAVID JARVIS

Matador
Unit E2 Airfield Business Park,
Harrison Road, Market Harborough,
Leicestershire. LE16 7UL
Tel: 0116 279 2299
Email: books@troubador.co.uk
Web: www.troubador.co.uk/matador
Twitter: @matadorbooks

ISBN 978 1803135 076

British Library Cataloguing in Publication Data.
A catalogue record for this book is available from the British Library.

Printed and bound by CPI Group (UK) Ltd, Croydon, CR0 4YY
Typeset in 11pt Adobe Garamond Pro by Troubador Publishing Ltd, Leicester, UK

Matador is an imprint of Troubador Publishing Ltd

CHAPTER ONE

It was a map of Antarctica. With a fine, black felt tip, she had meticulously filled it in, being careful not to go into the surrounding sea.

Why had she been remembering this? Turquoise zigzag lines moved gradually to the edge of her vision, behind closed eyelids. They pulsated gently to the rhythm of her breathing. She was sweating and needed to pee. It was pitch black, apart from the fireworks in her head, so it must still be night. Something like the Tommy Hilfiger logo appeared and replaced the flashing, blue-green lines. Anyway, it was time to go shopping. Belinda was late, again. The red, white and ultramarine squares began to fade. She really, really needed to pee.

She tried to turn over in her bed, but she was caught up in the bedclothes. The need to get to the bathroom was overwhelming, and she kicked at the sheets and blankets. It was no wonder that she was so hot. *I need to wake up*, she thought to herself, but couldn't make it happen. As her heartbeat increased, the brighter and more psychedelic the lightshow became. She began to pee and burst into a fit of giggles. Where was Belinda? They should be shopping. The relief swept through her body.

Trying to turn over, she found that her left wrist was chained to the bedstead. *Dreams are so weird, aren't they?* Her right wrist was hurting, but it was free, so she could push herself over to one side, where she bumped into another body. It reacted by kicking furiously and by making a strange mumbling sound.

"Who are you?" she asked, but the words didn't come out right at all, mostly due to the tape across her mouth. Funny that.

Anyway, the flashing lights are beginning to annoy me, she thought to herself. *What's wrong with the word 'anyway', anyway?* She laughed until the snorting through her nose hurt.

The mumbling nearby hadn't stopped. *"Speak clearly or not at all," Mrs Chetwynd is always saying, but English literature is so boring.*

The body alongside kneed her persistently in the thighs.

"Careful! It's wet there." With her free hand she felt for the face. It felt damp and also had tape across the mouth.

The mumbling became frantic.

"Oh, stop it!" she said as she pulled at the tape carefully, so as not to break a nail.

The body vomited in a series of heaves broken by gulps of air.

"Oh charming," she started to say to herself, but it dawned on her that she could take the tape off her own mouth. She rolled on to her back, laughing inside, and pulled it off with her free hand. "*Ouch!*" she shouted.

"Quiet," the body hissed, and then started to gurgle while blowing bubbles.

"Belinda?"

"Angelica?"

"We should be shopping. Hurry up."

They both broke out into suppressed fits of giggles.

CHAPTER TWO

"Angelica … what are you wearing?" Charles Yelland had entered the kitchen to find his sixteen-year-old daughter standing there wearing a pair of lemon-coloured shorts and eating her breakfast.

"They are called hot pants … They were all the rage in 1970 … You probably remember them first time around, don't you?" she replied.

"I wasn't born in 1970."

"Anyway, they are the latest thing."

"What does Belinda think of them?"

"She thinks hot pants are cool."

The word 'oxymoron' came into Charles Yelland's mind, but only stayed there. He was beginning to realise that, despite the expenditure of enormous sums of money on a private education, she was never going to be a rocket scientist. For as long as he could remember, she had been impulsive and with an attention span that could be defined in seconds. He was grateful that her best friend, Belinda, was vaguely sensible and probably the only thing keeping her on the rails – even then, mostly the rails at Harvey Nichols.

"And what's that smell?" Charles asked.

"It's a new coffee thing. It's made from horse chestnuts. Anyway, there's no caffeine or tannin in it, and it makes your hair shiny."

"Angelica, you don't think that some marketing man put those horse chestnuts on the box because *they* are shiny?"

"Look, it says here that it's been clinically proven … and it's traditional."

"You're right … Marketing men have been doing it for years." His observation went right over the top of her very shiny, black hair.

"Anyway, why are you wearing that awful dressing gown? It's not the weekend."

"Do you have to start every sentence with 'anyway'? It happens to be a very important day for me. It's the AGM." He waited for some reaction to appear on her face. "I am chairman, remember? So try not to wind me up too much."

His daughter shrugged and sipped from her mug while scrolling on her phone.

"I don't want raspberry jam down the front of my white shirt," he continued to explain why he was wearing his maroon silk dressing gown.

"You're the only person in the world wearing those shirts and ties. You're so out of date."

"What I look like at the AGM is very important. It's like the horse chestnuts on your box." Nothing registered in her eyes, but he kept going. "I want the attendees to have confidence in me. They want to see conservatism and a sense of style. Not that I am short-selling them in any way."

"So it's OK for you to say 'anyway'?" she said without looking up from her phone.

At that moment, he felt that he had spent his life shouting across a noisy dual carriageway to his daughter. She never seemed to hear and they could never get close.

Maria, his Mexican-born wife, came out of the utility room; she was carrying some bread, which she dropped into the toaster.

Looking at her mother, there was little doubt why Angelica Yelland was so beautiful. Only her pale eyes came from her father, and they were his best feature. How she had managed to end up not inheriting the intelligence of either parent remained a mystery. He had read geography at Warwick University, and Maria had been educated in Switzerland. Surely they must have passed on a few genes? He poured himself some cornflakes while Maria stared down into the top of the toaster.

"I don't know why I eat this organic spelt bread," she declared.

There was a long pause.

"Still, it's good for you," she added.

He pondered this for a moment. "I think 'less bad' would be more accurate." He took a mouthful of orange juice and continued, "Instead of remodifying crops that have been modified out of all recognition over the last 5,000 years, we should have gone back to the originals." There was no bitterness in his voice, unlike in the unsweetened orange juice. "The Romans had it right when …"

But they would never hear the completion of his exposition on early agrarian development.

Charles Yelland was suddenly transfixed and speechless, with a hovering spoonful of cereal in one hand and the newspaper in the other. The single image on one of the middle pages, included to show the best in contemporary photography, had mesmerised him.

"*Where the … did they get that?*"

Angelica looked up, but then went back to texting on her phone.

Maria walked over carrying her cup of coffee. "Oh … it's one of yours, isn't it?"

A dispassionate observer would have seen the beauty in the photograph. An oil rig was silhouetted against a peach-streaked sky. In the far distance, the aquamarine edge of an ice shelf could be seen, giving enormous depth and scale to the view. From a stack on the top of the rig, a bleached yellow-orange flare trailed to a thin smudge of smoke across the sky. In bold letters, the name of Petronello Oil, the Anglo-Spanish company, was emblazoned on the side of the accommodation units.

"Has this stolen your thunder?" Maria asked.

Though a man never short of a word or opinion, nothing came out of Charles's mouth.

"I thought that you were always looking for positive publicity?" she continued.

Still no response.

Angelica had sensed that something was not right and had wandered over. "That's a pretty picture," she said, but her father did not hear her.

He ran his hands through his still-damp, greying hair. "Maria, you cannot imagine the consequences." While she could not be expected to know, even he could never have guessed at the consequences to him, his family, his company and to the wider world.

"Are you sure that you are not overreacting, Charles?" She was treading gingerly. "Photographs of oil rigs are a bit old hat these days. It's better than videos of seabirds covered in oil."

His mind was racing. A sip of coffee seemed to defuse the situation.

"I take it that you were not going to announce any new oil discoveries at the AGM today?" she asked.

"No, I wasn't," he confirmed.

"And now, you will have to?"

"I have a slight problem there."

"But you said that you wanted the share price high over the next few months."

"I do. I do. I need it as high as possible."

She took a closer look at the newspaper article. There was no text accompanying the photograph apart from a caption, which read "Sunrise over the southern ocean highlighted by the gas flare from the Petronello Oil exploration rig the *Advantage*".

"You do still own the *Advantage*, don't you?"

"Yes."

"So what is the problem?"

"It hasn't found oil or gas," he said slowly.

"Ah."

"You see, Maria, it would be quite difficult, given that the *Advantage* is having a major refit on the coast of the Bay of Campeche at the moment."

"So … the newspaper's got the name wrong. So what?" Angelica could not grasp the problem.

"The *Advantage* has never been south of Mexico and, certainly, nowhere near a bloody ice shelf."

***

At that moment, Russell Walker – the Secretary of State for Business, Energy and Industrial Strategy (BEIS) – was not ten miles from the Yelland household, travelling in the back of his chauffeur-driven Jaguar. He was en route from his constituency to a Cabinet meeting at 10.00am that morning. His normally florid face was even redder, thanks to an unknown allergy, and he loosened his tie to free up his collar. The only issue of immediate concern in his ministerial leather box was a proposal to increase by some margin the number and size of offshore windfarms; the environmental pros and cons were finely balanced, and the economic argument was moot. The subject may arise in Cabinet and the Prime Minister would want a discussion before Prime Minister's Questions (PMQs) at 3.00pm. He was a seasoned campaigner, having been a minister for six years, and he was reasonably confident that his job was safe, but the lacklustre performance of the Government after almost two terms was beginning to concern him. Russell Walker knew that you were generally not tripped up by what was in your briefing notes but by breaking news stories and social media speculation. He closed the red leather box – which, bizarrely, matched the colour of his rubicund face – and picked up a newspaper. It opened randomly on the centre pages, and he settled back into his seat somewhere along the M40 in Buckinghamshire.

Five minutes later, he was on the phone to his department speaking to his permanent private secretary (PPS): "John, have you seen one of the photographs in today's papers yet?"

"No, I've just arrived. In which newspapers?" John queried. He repeated the response, which was for the benefit of his secretary who, from his gesticulations, had realised the urgency of finding the newspaper from the pile recently delivered and stacked on her desk.

"I thought that oil exploration in the South Atlantic was a dead duck?" There was no immediate reply from his PPS, who was staring at the photograph for the first time, so Russell Walker continued, "Although I don't suppose dead ducks are an image the oil industry wishes to promote?"

"No … quite. We have had no wind of any discoveries here. I do know that it's Petronello's AGM today. Perhaps Petronello was saving it up."

"My geography's less than perfect, but I didn't think the ice sheets extended up to sixty degrees, and that's where all of the exploration licences have to stop, don't they? Basically within our territorial waters around the Falklands?"

"Yes, they have to be in our territorial waters … As to the extent of ice sheets, I will need to look into it."

"Yes, please check it all out, preferably before the Cabinet meeting, but definitely before PMQs."

"Of course, leave it with me."

***

It had not been a good morning for Sophie Beardsmore – the Secretary of State for the Environment, Food and Rural Affairs – and it was about to get worse. She had tried to open the bedroom curtains of her London flat, only to catapult wooden rings and heavy fabric off the pole onto the floor. She had then eaten (but not enjoyed) a fruits-of-the-forest yoghurt, which tasted of disinfectant; perhaps it was from a coniferous forest? The list of ingredients on the side required degrees in chemistry and Latin. Milk and raspberries were the only two words that she recognised. She was musing on whether raspberries were a forest fruit when her telephone rang. She answered it relieved that it was her mobile and not a Zoom call, given she was not fully dressed.

A plump, self-effacing farmer's daughter who had read biology at Bristol University, she was just about the most popular member of the Cabinet. John Hilton-Verey, known as JHV by his very limited coterie of friends, had once said that there must be a large hole in the hedge through which she had been dragged backwards. Her unmanageable, mousey hair had become a trademark. The public relations advisers had tried to change her appearance, but they eventually came to the conclusion that it was all part of the charm. JHV, who played a very influential behind-the-scenes role for the Government, was in charge of PR. Even a petty and pernicious person like him accepted in the end that Sophie was virtually unchangeable.

"Forget the silk purse, just try to make her into a sow's ear," he had once told his jaded and overworked staff.

On the telephone was the number two at her department, who was about to warn her about the photograph in the newspaper. He had only just been briefed himself by Mervyn Richards, a rather melancholic staff officer to whom the Civil Service and urban living were constant battles.

***

Mervyn Richards was a scientist who had grown up in rural Wales. He was a glaciologist originally – a man of the wide-but-freezing-cold open spaces. His three-year secondment to Whitehall as a special adviser had turned into a prison sentence.

Clattering along on the Underground that morning, Mervyn was supposedly reading a treatise on 'Natural Antifreeze in Mites and Springtails'. In reality, he was daydreaming of happier days at Rothera on the Antarctic peninsula. "Imagine being a scientist on a continent one and half times bigger than the USA, which is run for science by scientists ... and it's land underneath the ice, not like that floating iceberg called the Arctic," he would enthusiastically tell anyone in hearing range.

He loved being mentally and physically isolated from the ills of the inhabited world. Most visitors to Antarctica who stay for more than a month seem to be changed irreversibly and always vow to return. Mervyn had spent almost thirty months in total at various camps and outstations, and he had overwintered twice. Most people are affected by the noise of the wind during months of continuous darkness, but Mervyn had arrived melancholic, which had somehow prepared him mentally; it tended to be the chirpy ones who cracked. It was his melancholia that had indirectly led to his current predicament. At Rothera, he had moaned about everything.

"If you don't like it, change it," they had said.

So he did. He had become a sort of administrator by default, which had led – via the British Antarctic Survey in Cambridge and the Scientific Research Council in Swindon – to Whitehall, where he was the scientific adviser on the approaching fifty-year review of the Antarctic Treaty.

With that acquired skill held by all Underground commuters, he flicked his eyes from his lap to the overhead advertisements without catching anyone's eyes. A new bar of chocolate that would not melt caught his attention. He made a mental note not to take one to Rothera next time. Next time? What he needed was a bar of chocolate that didn't freeze.

Perhaps, they could use some of the research he had just been reading about to produce it? Mind you, in a place where a pot of boiling water thrown into the air freezes before it hits the ground, such chocolate would be sorely tested.

His gaze then fell onto the centre pages of the newspaper, helpfully held at the right angle next to him. Breaking all of the social rules, he asked to see it. If he had been holding the chocolate bar, it would have melted.

CHAPTER THREE

Friday, 26th June was not likely to be a day that Charles Yelland would forget. The dark-grey Mercedes Maybach pulled up under the green glass canopy of a striking new piece of architecture near Victoria Station. The building was state-of-the-art; a sensor automatically triggered a series of events. The main door slid open, and his name appeared on the security guard's monitor. The lift from the twelfth floor was called down, and his usual requirements for the day were entered into the administrative and catering computer. At the separate lift, which only went to his floor, he stared briefly into the lens, which confirmed retinal recognition.

Josephine, his personal assistant, was awaiting his arrival. "Tony is already in the meeting room," was all she said.

He handed her his laptop and stepped through the door. His colleague, who also happened to be married to Charles's sister, was silhouetted against a view towards the gardens of Buckingham Palace. Sometimes, it is hard to begin a conversation. Sometimes, it is unnecessary to speak.

"Who?" is all Charles said.

For the last ten minutes, Tony had been drawing up the surprisingly long list that may provide the answer to that question – *the* question.

"It'll be NorCarbon. Its board think this will send our share price sky high. Then, we will have to deny it, so the share price will plummet, and they will convince their shareholders that a takeover by us is a crazy idea." Tony struggled to keep a wide selection of teeth inside a mouth surrounded by a neat, dark beard. His black-framed glasses were also struggling to stay on the bridge of his long nose.

"Is this a Norwegian thing to do?" Charles asked, "I don't know what Norwegians do anyway, but—"

"They don't want to be taken over. You have to admit that this is ingenious." Tony ran his fingers through his black hair, which stuck up from his scalp from too much hair product.

"But wouldn't the Norwegians get it right?" Charles asked, "Instead of using the wrong damn rig against some Disney ice sheet backdrop?"

"But does it matter? It will force us to deny it at the AGM. If we expose the photograph as a fraud later, so what?" Tony was trying to be pragmatic.

"I'm going to take over that bloody company if it's the last thing I do."

"It must be NorCarbon, Charles. The board knows that Sven Peterson takes over the chair of the European oil producers next month. Its government will be 100 per cent behind NorCarbon, and it gives the opportunity to say there is no way oil will be extracted from their so-called 'Norwegian sector' of Antarctica."

"Kill whales in the Arctic and ban mining in Antarctica. Bloody hypocrites!"

Josephine carried in a tray on which there was a cafetière, cups, saucers and biscuits, which had just been delivered to her office. "There's a call from John at the Department for Business. He'd like you to comment before PMQs."

"Thanks, Jo."

She left as quietly as she had arrived.

"It could be some other Norwegian group. Some ecological, environmental group?" Tony suggested.

"Well … maybe," Charles replied.

"It could be that Greenpeace clone, Sangaia?" Tony slurped the strong coffee, which instantly coated his teeth and made him sweat even more. "It's suspected for years that we've found oil down there," he continued almost under his breath.

"So, what's changed?" Charles asked, "And surely its members would do something dramatic like climb all over Tower Bridge with banners, not ponce up some photograph and send it to the papers."

"It's a lot cheaper." He paused. "Or it could be the other oil companies?"

"Come on, Tony, they would be shooting themselves in the foot. We don't do that to each other. We have enough bloody enemies without that."

"The Argentinians are the other possibility." Tony was moving further down the metaphorical list.

"Don't they ever learn?"

"They claim the contested sector, or most of it, so why not?"

"They can't know whether we have or haven't. We purposely rarely flare any gas or increase activity anywhere in the world when we are exploring." Charles was holding his coffee cup at a dangerous angle.

"They might see it as a way to get back the Falklands and the whole sector?" Tony offered his own idea, which he had been developing in the back of his mind.

"No ... I don't believe it."

There was, however, no certainty in either of their voices.

"Anyway, enough of this." Charles Yelland had clearly adopted his daughter's favourite word. "We don't have much time. Tony, will you check NorCarbon and the Norwegians, and afterwards, check the eco-nuts and the Argies ... and the newspaper. Ring them, but don't frighten the horses, you know ..."

He stood up, drank a mouthful of strong coffee and stared across the air-conditioning units to the back of Buckingham Palace.

"What am I going to say at the AGM and to the minister?"

***

Charles Yelland was a darling of the City. He was seen as a strategist, a cultured maverick and a man of impeccable timing – someone to shake up the oil industry. "Oil may be fossilised, but I don't see why the industry should be," he had once said at a Mansion House luncheon. But all these notions were wrong, even the idea that oil was the distilled juice of dinosaurs rotting in some Jurassic swamp. He was an after-the-event strategist; his good fortune appeared to be the product of careful planning only when viewed through revisionist glasses. He wasn't cultured, but marrying a Swiss-educated Mexican aristocrat's daughter and mixing with her circle had given the impression that he was. His timing was unbelievable but not of his making; he was just lucky. You never hear of the millions who have bought losing lottery tickets. If anyone else gave some chimpanzees a typewriter, they would launch it slack-armed against the concrete walls of the monkey house. If Charles Yelland did the same, they would be composing sonnets while the orangutans next door reconfigured the typewriter into a word processor. When he merged Petroganser Refineries with Tominello Oil, he could not have known that the Italian government was about to collapse, that there would be a devastating earthquake, or of the various indiscretions of the Milanese directors. He just benefitted from the low share price and the need for a fire sale. He had fortuitously chosen the date because he wanted it concluded before he left for a two-week trip to Spain. The City loved it. He formed the third largest oil exploration company in Europe, Petronello Oil, and took over as CEO.

If the bluebird of happiness is going to crap on your shoulder, may she have diarrhoea – and so it was. The neighbour to his Costa del Sol villa was the majority shareholder in Fateema, the Libyan oil company. They had done what every pair of expat neighbours in Spain do: they had ignored each other for months until they had talked rather randomly about something irrelevant; in this case, snooker. They had become friends, and after several games in Charles's underground billiard room, complete with wood panelling, green leather banquettes and signs saying "No Drinks or Food", they were discussing terms and making a merger possible. There were serious difficulties amalgamating the two companies, but after much lateral thinking and many late night sessions potting balls, they had produced the answer. The rest, as they say, is on hooks at the end of the table – if you think laterally.

"Don't become middle class," his father, a lorry driver, had said to him.

"How will I know if I am middle class?" Charles had asked.

"When the fear of losing takes over from the desire to win."

Winning became sufficiently commonplace that he lost all concept of the game and began to feel invincible. He was proud of what he saw reflected in his shaving mirror. Mirrors, however, only reflect what one wants to see in them. He really had not felt threatened by anything – until a harmless-looking photograph of an oil rig appeared in the newspaper.

In a few weeks' time, he would have taken over NorCarbon, and he could have chosen whether to send another exploration rig to join the *Antigone* at around sixty degrees south (he would need to be a little vague here) near the island of Signy in the South Orkney Islands, just outside the internationally recognised boundary of Antarctica. The sectors south of sixty degrees near where Petronello was searching for oil were claimed by Chile, Argentina, Norway and the United Kingdom. These claims had been suspended under the Antarctic Treaty of 1961 and the subsequent Madrid Protocol of 1991, which dealt with environmental protection and the prohibition of mining. Even the ersatz-strategist Charles Yelland had realised that the treaty and protocol were up for renegotiation soon.

***

Just as he had been blissfully unaware of key factors at the time of his takeover of the Italian company, so it was on that fateful day in June. He couldn't have known that the UK had a PM who, only the previous day, had decided that, after one and a half terms, he wanted re-election – contrary to what everyone had been thinking for years. Nor could Charles Yelland have known that the issue of rejoining the EU was about to flare up again. This had never bothered him before, as half his company was in the EU (in Italy and Spain) and half was out (in the UK and – hopefully, if he could get NorCarbon – Norway). Finally, he could not have been aware that JHV had set his sights on a very significant role, which had been promised to him surreptitiously if he could help to engineer the UK back into the EU. JHV, a vehement anti-Brexiteer, thought privately that the days of his PM were numbered and saw himself enjoying a life at a high level in Europe, long after the framed photographs of his friend had been replaced on the walls of the UK's Conservative Clubs and the UK had rejoined the EU. While Charles Yelland had heard of JHV, he had certainly not heard of Mervyn Richards, who would play a much larger role in future events, having been assigned, as he was, to the Government to help review the Antarctic Treaty.

For a man who was meant to be to business what nose clips were to synchronised swimmers, he was about to take on board a lot of water.

***

Mervyn Richards could recite the terms of the Antarctic Treaty like a parrot, even one in the latter stages of psittacosis. The treaty had been enormously successful, which was almost entirely due to the extremely simple but clever mechanism of suspending territorial claims south of the sixty-degree line of latitude for fifty years; it was a brilliant concept that could be written down in a few pages – making it, perhaps, the briefest international document in modern times. It didn't matter which country claimed that one of its explorers had set foot on that particular part of Antarctica, the claim was suspended along with everyone else's. Twelve nations had signed the original agreement that came into force on 23rd June 1961. Since then, very many more had signed up. In 1989, there had been a minerals convention, but it had failed to find a consensus. Nevertheless, the Madrid Protocol was signed in 1991, and that prohibited mineral exploration for fifty years. However, there was now talk that a major review was needed. The whole Antarctic Treaty was in danger of being revoked.

The implied discovery by Petronello, as illustrated by the newspaper photograph, could not have come at a worse time for the delicate negotiations that had just begun. This would really put the cat among the pigeons – or, perhaps, the Caterpillar among the penguins.

Mervyn Richards was writing quietly in his cubbyhole when Sir John Hewlett – PPS at the Department of BEIS, and therefore, his ultimate boss – walked in. They had only met once, as Mervyn was usually instructed by a level-five staff officer called Lawrence, who also stepped into the room with two others.

Mervyn stood up, but he wasn't sure why, so he sat back down. *If only I had my* I-Spy – Civil Servants *book,* he thought to himself, *I could have crossed off half a dozen levels.*

"Thank you for producing the information so rapidly. The paper for the Secretary of State is almost finished. Lawrence and I have a couple of questions, as time is of the essence," Sir John began.

Mervyn picked up his pen for no obvious reason.

"We, the British government, issued the exploration licence to Petronello?"

"Well, strictly speaking, to Petroganser, which became Petronello." Mervyn felt that the walls were moving in on him.

"Quite." Sir John inhaled at least half of the oxygen in the room. "These are un-con-test-ed waters?" He broke the word up into handy, bite-sized chunks.

"Yes, it is north of sixty degrees south, if you see what I mean? And that is outside of the Antarctic Treaty area, but inside British territorial waters off Signy ... South Orkney. Signy is British."

"Was this discovery expected?"

"No, not really. Since the Falklands War, all the other searches to the north have proved to be of little interest."

"Is this discovery going to interest or upset anyone?" Sir John was in full flow, and all of the other visitors stood there looking attentive.

"Well, the Argentinians have another island in South Orkney, so this must mean that there is oil in their waters too, but ..." Mervyn could not suppress his fundamental fear that this might mean there was oil south of Signy, inside the Antarctic Treaty area.

"But ... what?" asked Lawrence, his immediate superior.

"I'm bothered that this means there is oil in the contested sectors of Antarctica, due south of Signy."

"And who claims these sectors?" Sir John resumed the questioning.

"Norway, Argentina, Chile and us," Mervyn listed them slowly.

"All claims are suspended by the treaty until ...?"

"Three years' time appears to be the date being widely discussed." Mervyn could not hide his disgust at the potential dismantling of something he held so dear.

Sir John picked up the newspaper photograph from Mervyn's desk. "Is Petronello the only company down there?"

"Yes, the others have long given up."

"This find could have huge consequences."

Sir John was thinking of his equivalent PPS in the Exchequer, who would be rubbing her hands with glee; the ones from the Foreign, Commonwealth and Development Office and the Ministry of Defence; and the Cabinet Secretary, who could have major international incidents bubbling. He would be talking to them all within minutes. This was how the system worked; these were the famous 'Government circles', which actually more closely resembled a Venn diagram.

"I suppose it's approaching winter down there." Sir John stared at the image. "What do you do when the sea freezes over?"

These were just musings that did not need replies. They left the room amid mumbled thanks.

Mervyn twisted the photograph in his fingers. Something was wrong. It was something that Sir John had said.

Later, while staring at the blue and white tiles above the urinal, he would realise that there should not be any ice visible near the oil rig and certainly not an ice shelf in the background.

CHAPTER FOUR

As each member of the Cabinet arrived, they went through the strange ritual of smiling at the three fixed cameras opposite the shiny, black door of Number Ten, Downing Street. Long gone were the days of individual TV companies getting coverage and packs of paparazzi perched on aluminium stepladders. Now, the BBC covered all the comings and goings on behalf of every network.

Russell Walker carried his papers under his arm and sashayed across the pavement as if he was trying to hold a feather between his buttocks; it would not have been the first time.

Sophie Beardsmore shuffled along the ground, with the soles of her shoes barely leaving the tarmac. Her hair resembled some hideous macramé disaster, and she wore a white dress with a daubed black pattern not unlike the majlis tents of the Bedu. She smiled at each camera, smiled at every policeman and disappeared into the dark interior.

JHV strode purposefully along the pavement, as if rehearsing some lines, posing and smiling with a sincerity that bordered on unctuous. He was sporting a new moustache, which was an attempt to hide his undemonstrative, thin lips. He had foolishly asked his staff how he might improve his image. Pride is a hand-held mirror, and JHV was often hand-held.

There were no special correspondents outside the gates of Downing Street because this should have been a routine Cabinet meeting. Local journalists from Birmingham, Derby and Sunderland would be at the House of Commons later for PMQs, which was to cover a rumoured statement on the globalisation of the car industry; the public gallery would not even be full.

The Cabinet Secretary was already at Number Ten with the PM, preparing to welcome the other ministers. He was the most powerful civil servant. A man who asked for your opinion only having already sown the idea and nurtured it earlier. A man who could take your train of thought and shunt it into sidings before you realised the carriages had been decoupled. He appeared to be of such impartiality and disinterest that he blended into the background, as if his colour balance and contrast had been turned down.

The thirty-seven members of the Cabinet took their places, pouring glasses of water and shuffling papers. It was far too big a forum to make decisions, but this was not a problem as they had been made elsewhere. The Cabinet was a computer-generated façade of political correctness; the optimum blend of ethnic backgrounds, ages, gender, sexual persuasions, geographical distribution, shoe size and myriad other arcane factors. However, this was not a true reflection of society even if they were sitting in a hall of mirrors.

JHV laid out his pad and pens in a preset arrangement; like Stalin, who had required his hotel rooms to be prepared to match his own bedroom perfectly, JHV liked the reassurance of familiarity. He needed to make personal notes on important matters, and this proved difficult given that phones and laptops were not allowed. Sophie Beardsmore never took notes. Why bother? She just highlighted anything important on the minutes when they arrived later. Russell Walker had heard it all before. He rarely took notes, but he might scribble a cryptic reminder to himself. He preferred to wait for the minutes too, but then he would criticise them, aiming to put his spin on matters. It's not what you say, it's what is recorded as what you said.

At 10.45am, the PM reached the point where the unresolved, unassessed consequences of the Petronello discovery appeared on the hastily updated agenda. "One matter we should be prepared for …" was how he began.

When the PM had finished, the Cabinet Secretary gave an understated but purposely vague description of the few known facts. The Secretary of Defence ended the available time by saying that the UK was in no position to fight another Falklands War.

***

"Tony. Tony Dewey. From Petronello. Yes, of course; I'll hold on."

He watched, out of his office window, a Heathrow-bound plane trace a route just inches to the left of its predecessor.

"Hello … Mr Napier?" he enquired once he was taken off hold.

"Speaking."

"I was given your agency's number by the newspaper. I am interested in obtaining permission to use the photograph you provided for today's centre page."

"How and where do you wish to use it?"

"We were thinking for our annual report. Do you have others in the set? We have lots of uses for such images."

"I don't remember others, but the photographer may have more. It is very likely."

"Who is the photographer?"

"Miguel Hernandez from Mexico. He is exclusively contracted to another agency we use, and via it, we are provided with many Central and South American photographs."

"Would you email me your standard contract and give me this other agency's or Miguel's contact details? Petronello will, of course, pay you any appropriate fee for any images we use."

"No problem."

***

Tony Dewey pressed the zoom function using the mouse until the photograph fragmented into a thousand flat, coloured squares. He moved across the screen magnifying and reducing the picture, but he could not see any evidence of touching up. This was not his area of expertise, but he was a mathematician, an economist and a man of patterns. He continued to search, and although not expecting to see the forger's signature, he thought he might find something. Eventually, he did; the blue shadows on the ice sheet in the distance were not on the correct side, but try as he might, he could not find where the flare and smoke stream were added.

The grey shadow cast from the smoke on the support arms of the helipad was perfect. He could not see anything else. Was there something about the name *Adventure* that did not look right? He zoomed in again until there were only fifty or so pixels on the screen; there was consistent gradation – the name had not been changed. This was not a real photograph of the *Antigone* flaring gas off Signy. The ice sheet had been added, presumably to imply that the *Adventure* was in Antarctica and further south. But why not change the name on the side to *Antigone* if you wanted to embarrass Petronello into revealing that it had found oil and gas off South Orkney? Petronello could never deny that the *Antigone* was in the South Atlantic, but proving that the *Adventure* was in Mexico for repairs was easy. The forgers appeared to be giving the company a way out. This was appearing more as a shot across the bows. He rubbed his soft, black beard upwards, so that he could bite it against his bottom lip. Now who would do that to Petronello and why?

If finding the contact details of the photographer had proved straightforward, testing out the environmental organisations was going to be more difficult. He needed to get himself on the inside to ask questions. He used his sister's virtual private network and changed her name by one letter. No one would trace his peregrinations to Petronello. He logged into the Sangaia website.

While it was loading, Jo brought in some confidential economic projections – so confidential that they needed to be on paper. So much for technology in the era of electronic commercial espionage! She was an exceptional support to the board, she was trustworthy and she was very, very well paid. Tony explained to her that he had just logged into Sangaia as Antonia de Rey, offering other photographs of Petronello's oil exploration rig in what he called "the Protected Antarctic Waters". Jo smiled and left him to his devices.

***

Admiral Sir Alexander Price probably thought that the chances of him ever being needed at less than twenty-four hours' notice were pretty slim; one hour's notice was something from the Cold War, fifty years before. He was wrong. Alex Price had not even had time to put his sand wedge away when the helicopter landed at Staunton Grange golf course to whisk him away to a helipad on the top of a Central London building. He was still wearing his golf glove as he walked across the incongruous plastic grass and grabbed the handrail on his way to the lifts. Fortunately, he saluted with his right hand.

Ten minutes later, when he should have been three-putting the ninth green as usual, he found himself in a Whitehall office in London with the Secretary of State for Defence – with whom, fortunately, he was on good terms – and his PPS. It was just after midday.

"Small problem, Alex," declared the Secretary of State for Defence. (Can any culture use understatement to convey the potential enormity of a situation more than the British?)

"Nothing that a basket of balls down the driving range won't put right," stated the admiral. (Would anyone other than the British use humour at a time like this?)

"Have you seen the papers this morning?"

"No."

Copies of the photograph were handed around the table.

"Apparently, it all started with this rather harmless-looking shot of some godforsaken oil rig in this morning's papers," the Secretary of State for Defence began.

"It appears we have discovered oil in the South Atlantic." The PPS wanted to help keep the conversation on track.

"How do we fancy another Falklands War?" the Secretary of State for Defence asked rather provocatively.

"It rather depends on the 'we', doesn't it?" Admiral Price paused. "We British? We Europeans? We … anyone plus the Americans?"

"And that depends on what we are fighting for?"

"Very true." The civil servant wanted them to concentrate on the subject.

"We barely had enough ships in 1982, and we certainly do not have enough now," Admiral Price confirmed.

"At least there now is comprehensive satellite coverage," the Secretary of State for Defence added, remembering the stories of his father.

So, CNN will have twenty-four-hour reporting, the civil servant thought but did not say.

***

To say that a week is a long time in politics is to make a severe overstatement. It was only midday, and the paper on the offshore windfarms was already relegated to the bottom of Russell Walker's heap. He had just been handed some more sheets by his supercilious PPS, Sir John, who was sitting in a chair on the other side of a large, leather-inlaid desk. There was a strong background smell of polish. Between them, to one side on top of the desk, a strange, mechanical device made of brass sat begging comment.

"*What the …?*" would have been most people's comment. It was an orrery, named after one Lord of Cork and Orrery; an elegant clockwork assemblage of cogs and globes representing the solar system. When cranked up, it whirled the planets around the sun like a fairground waltzer. The moon, the size of a mothball, was barely hanging on by the bent piece of wire that connected it to the brightly coloured earth. If Russell Walker had been told why it was on the desk of the Secretary of State for BEIS, it now escaped his memory. Perhaps it represented mechanics, precision and interaction on a global scale? Or perhaps it was on loan from some museum and long forgotten?

Sir John was particularly full of self-importance that morning and was trying to maintain a grave face. 'Saturnine' would have been the perfect word to describe his expression, except that, from where Russell was looking, Sir John's eyes were just to the right of Jupiter.

"The Americans have been in touch." Sir John's voice floated through the ether.

"Are we talking formal or informal?" Russell asked.

"Not informal."

"What does that mean?"

"Well, it was not an informal contact."

No one can predict when someone is going to crack and which small incident will be the one to tip the balance. For various personal reasons, including an earlier allergic reaction and a cramp just above his right kidney, Russell Walker was not in the mood for civil-servant speak. Normally, he would have gone along with it, but not today. He reached across to the side and suspended the recording. The silence was overpowering.

"John … not today, OK? If you value your career and pension, just answer the damn questions."

Sir John looked absolutely shocked. Never in almost twenty years had a minister reacted like this. "I'm terribly sorry, I have been trying …"

"Exactly … so no Civil Service bollocks. All right?"

He switched the recording back on. Sir John just nodded. They were worlds apart – literally, having the orrery between them.

"John, explain to me simply and clearly how the Americans have made contact, what they have said and what you suggest is our reply."

Sir John sipped a glass of water, thought of his almost inviolate pension scheme and swallowed. "We have had a formal letter, via the ambassador, asking us whether we are going to continue to support the Antarctic Treaty's ban on mineral extraction. This is unusual and coincident timing in the extreme. They have had thirty years to ask this question, and it comes in this morning. Informally, the American trade attaché has attended a non-minuted meeting with Douglas, whom you know, at which he asked a series of questions. These ranged from …"

It could have been from the physical pain, an overwhelming sense of impending doom or because he was staring at Mars, but Russell Walker thought the room was spinning. He said nothing and listened to the list of questions.

"… given that only twenty-five per cent of the remaining oil in the world is within the control of very friendly countries, what hope do our economies have against the inevitable commercial and financial blackmail? Secondly, given the ever-stronger environmental lobby, how can we get oil extraction permitted in the relevant Antarctic sector without destroying the treaty? Finally and most pertinently, support for which country would lead to the USA gaining the biggest percentage of the oil from the sectors contested by Argentina, Chile, Norway and the UK? You understand the delicacy, I'm sure."

It was Russell's turn to be dumbfounded. How could a day deteriorate so quickly? He was, however, determined not to give Sir John the advantage. "So, what do you recommend?"

"When US foreign and economic policies are so fundamentally involved, I think this is a matter for the PM to discuss directly with the President."

"Before PMQs?

"Absolutely, if possible. The Cabinet Office, Foreign Office and other departments are all discussing it along these lines."

"When the USA shouts, we all jump?"

Russell rotated the orrery. The moon fell off limply onto the leather surface to be quickly replaced by Sir John.

"This was one of the first manifestations of the planets revolving around the sun and not the earth, wasn't it?" Russell asked.

"Quite," Sir John replied in quintessential civil-servant speak.

CHAPTER FIVE

Maria Yelland had it all, or so it was portrayed in the gossip magazines and on social media, but in reality, like all expats, she suffered from bouts of homesickness. England (and the Spanish Costas) could never provide the forested volcanoes, the screech of the Mariachi bands or her nephews setting off rockets at the fiestas by holding the wooden sticks in their bare hands. Chatting on Zoom to her family in Cuernavaca did not quell her hunger – it only served to heighten it. She missed the smells of the sugar presses, of the polo ponies and even of acrid cigarette smoke. Having the money and the first-class flights every few months did not compensate either – she always wanted more. Charles had bought the enormous villa above the beach in Spain as some sort of replacement. Clearly, he didn't get that, although she spoke Spanish, Spain was not Mexico. The pandemic had made it worse. She had been so tempted to break or bend the rules by flying in a private jet via Bermuda or Greenland, but for what reason? To give her aunts and uncles Covid-19?

Her immediate life consisted of Angelica and Charles. Her daughter had provided some distraction, but however much she loved her, Angelica was not someone to talk to as an intellectual equal. At that moment, she was off with Belinda on some shopping spree and letting the years slip by. Angelica would have trouble locating Mexico in an atlas. She would have trouble locating an atlas.

Maria became lonelier as Charles became more successful. "Why don't you do something? Why don't you buy something? I always pay so ..." was what he frequently said, but all her Mexican ears heard was, "peso". It just made her more homesick and highlighted the gulf between them – somewhat larger than the Gulf of Mexico. She was bored with the bleach and Botox set of rich wives. Apart from the cleaner and the chauffeur, she hardly spoke to anyone else face to face and in the flesh. Everyone else was on a computer screen. She had lamented the passing of the milkman, the post office and the local shops.

Online shopping became her comfort, and the more she ordered, the more she sent back. At their house in Buckinghamshire, Stanley drove the local courier van and became a daily visitor; he was on a year out before university. As always, he drove in an arc around the gravel of the driveway in his sleek, grey van; as he did so, a spaniel in the house ran from room to room, barking and skidding on the polished floors.

Maria – dressed in a short, black jacket and tight, white trousers – opened the door. "Good morning, Stanley. What have I ordered now?"

He handed her a compact, padded envelope, which she placed on the hall table. She indicated the two return-to-sender envelopes under the long mirror.

"Have you ever been to Mexico, Stanley?" She was speaking to his reflection.

"No. No, I've not travelled much." He did not know whether to look at her directly or at her reflection in the mirror.

"You should travel; it broadens the mind."

"And empties the wallet," he added.

She switched her eyes so that she was looking directly at him. He was left staring at her sideview in the mirror. She always flirted with him, and he found himself looking – in a bizarre, voyeuristic way – up and down her body. She continued to face him, watching his eye movement; she enjoyed it.

He snapped back to the real Maria.

"Don't worry about money; it cannot buy you happiness," she stated, trotting out the usual platitudes.

"Maybe not, but it can make a happy man happier."

She stepped a pace nearer to him. "Good looking and clever boys should not be driving delivery vans."

He instinctively pulled the two envelopes closer to his chest and swivelled on the doorstep. "We all have to start somewhere," he spluttered.

"Then why start at the bottom?" She stepped outside and closed the front door behind her.

He wondered what she would do next. Every week, she became more provocative and teasing.

She followed him to his van. "Have you ever made love in the back, Stanley?"

"No. I … no."

"Do you ever deliver beds?" she arched her immaculate eyebrows over her very dark, smiling eyes.

"Well …" He had carried mattresses over the months, jammed up against the side. He thought about her and a mattress. His heart thumped, but mainly because it couldn't decide whether his young blood should go to his reddening cheeks or to his groin. He threw the two padded envelopes onto the passenger seat to avoid opening up the back.

"Remember, Stanley, you don't have to start at the bottom." With that, she walked past him towards her waiting car.

It might be cheap and vicarious, but at least the emotional contact was real and was on her terms.

For his part, Stanley was beginning to fantasise in the security of his cab as he drove away. Too much extrapolation makes you go blind. He was finding it all a painful experience, especially from using his accelerator foot while he had an erection.

Stanley, however, was only a sexual stepping stone for Maria that lunchtime.

For a few years, it had seemed a wide river to cross, as she paced up and down her side of the bank in sexual frustration. Guilt, loyalty and self-doubt in equal measure had confined her to peering through the trees at a watery expanse of Amazonian proportions. The loyalty had disappeared unnoticed. The flirting had restored some self-confidence, but the guilt, or fear of feeling guilty, still remained. The voices in her head now cancelled each other out. She was cruising in neutral. It would take only a small incident or opportunity for her to be across those stepping stones to the greener pastures on the other side.

***

If Stanley had unwittingly helped her a small way out from the water's edge, Rod the photographer was about to give her a helping hand up (or should that be down?) the slippery slope opposite. She was driven into the small, 1960s shopping precinct in Chalfont St James, and she got out in front of the launderette. Who in Buckinghamshire these days could not afford a washing machine? Whether the sharp smell of chemicals was coming from the dry cleaning operation or from Rod's dark room was debatable. It could be an inflammatory cocktail. In her head, she had passed the point of no return, so what she did with her body no longer counted.

Even the wedding portraits in the window did not throw her as she stepped into Rod Cameron Specialist Photography ("established 1643" was written in smaller letters underneath). She turned over the sign on the inside of the door – which said "Gone to get some bulbs … back in a flash" – and walked into the shop, behind the counter and through the black curtain into his studio. She did not know if she was about to cross the Styx or the Rubicon or was about to drift down the Swannee River.

So this was the fabled grass that is always greener? A photographer's back room? She wondered how it would develop; she was in the right place.

Rod's work space was where he earned his real money. There were images everywhere of test tubes, piston arms and dissected amphibians. He specialised in photographing science subjects for books and advertisements; he was an artist who promoted science. Leonardo da Vinci would have been proud of him.

Maria tried to calm herself down, but a nerve rash was prickling under her white blouse. She was forty-eight years old and glad that her young lover-to-be would see her for the first time in a semi-dark room suffused by the glow of a red light above his lab door. A red light? Has ever an object had two such contrasting cultural associations?

***

Mervyn Richards had often wandered lonely as a child over vales and hills – that is why he became a geologist and, subsequently, a glaciologist. It may also explain why he was so introspective and distant. As he grew older, he had come to the conclusion that it wasn't the world but the people in it who depressed him. Given the choice between a milling crowd or a host of golden daffodils, he would take the plants every time (and not just because he was Welsh). He may have spent long periods alone on a million square miles of ice and rock, but he had never felt lonely. He had a very short fuse, so it was best that any interaction with humans was kept to a minimum.

That morning, he had never been so popular; it almost brought a smile to his face. Over seventy emails were waiting for him by 11.30am. They fell firmly into two camps. Half of his friends were scientists and environmentalists out there in the commercial world, paid for by corporations. The other half were scientists and environmentalists protecting the world *from* commerce. His communications that morning really did come from the two extremes. Opinions were polarised – literally. As with so much to do with Antarctica, there was no middle ground. Everything was black or white, ice or water, summer or winter. He began to see a large problem looming out of the mist, and nine-tenths of it was below the surface.

Mervyn did the same thing that he always did when he reached a crisis point: he went out, bought a doughnut and telephoned his mother in Swansea (the doughnut part was optional). She was a woman who looked permanently startled; this was because life constantly surprised her. With her poor memory, she would be hard pressed to play a goldfish at snap.

Mervyn was an only child. (Perhaps she had others and had forgotten where she had left them. Who knows?) She had not been a good mother. It had all been a bit stressful, but her one strength was that she had always been there for Mervyn. When he telephoned at critical moments in his life, usually when he was about to explode, he never reached an answerphone. The fact that she couldn't remember if he was in Rothera or Rhayader did not matter.

"Mervyn, how are you, my dear?"

"Fine, Mam." He made the word sound warm and engulfing as only the Welsh can.

"I'm burning the toast; well, practically."

"It's a bit late for breakfast, Mam?"

"No, I'm making breadcrumbs … for a recipe."

"What recipe's that then?"

"Had-dock bake." She filleted the syllables.

Mervyn thought about this. "Why you cooking 'addock bake, Mam?"

"It's for the elder's dinner at the Baptist church, Mervyn." She made the word Mervyn go up and down like the Mumbles lifeboat.

He completely forgot his own problems and came up with so many questions that they were scrambling to reach the surface first. "Mam, you in the Baptists, then?"

"Of course I am. I do the cleaning."

"Is that with Uncle Cledwyn?"

"Yes. He's a minister."

"What's he doing these days?"

"He's making the profiteroles."

Within minutes, Mervyn had entered a prosaic soap opera and had forgotten his own mounting problems; this was why he did it. While chatting to his mother, his subconscious had a few minutes to put his own problems into some sort of order, and his blood pressure could reduce.

**

Sophie Beardsmore was a simple soul, and this was her strength. Despite this, her intellect was multilayered and capable of retaining and analysing information of prodigious complexity. When she was chewing over something particularly deep, she wouldn't hum, whistle or drum her fingers; instead, she would find herself counting. Leaving the Cabinet meeting, she had descended the stairs counting each step in her head. Outside, it had been the number of pigeons, the paving slabs and the members of the press who were beginning to congregate. Counting on this scale meant that something was seriously bothering her.

She was the Secretary of State for the Environment, Food and Rural Affairs, and although Antarctica did not technically come under her department, she had heard virtually nothing about Antarctica since she had been in office. Even the emerging idea of a review of the treaty in three years' time had not been mentioned. She began to smell a rat. It was a powerful smell, and she had a very good idea about the source; she had always thought that he looked like a rodent. *In a city, you are never more than five feet from a rat, they say, and in politics, it's even closer,* she thought to herself before she counted the people on the open deck of the tour bus stopped temporarily outside Downing Street.

A little later, back in her office, an assistant brought in lunch on a tray. It was chicken and sweetcorn soup with doorstops of malted bread. Sophie thought that she could smell rat for the second time that morning, but it might have been the association of rats and granaries. She needed to eat, even though it was barely midday, because she was about to chair a meeting of coastal county chief executives vying for the limited flood alleviation funds available following decades of gently rising sea level and ever more violent storms. She was one of the few pragmatic people who favoured abandoning a few thousand hectares in places such as East Anglia in order to concentrate the money where it could have maximum long-term effect. The coast of Norfolk was doomed whether it was this winter or the next. Spending a few million pounds was not, as she regretted saying on one occasion, a drop in the ocean.

She counted a precise number of pieces of sweetcorn onto her spoon and contemplated that morning's Cabinet meeting. This oil discovery was unbelievably convenient. Her suspicions were growing, but she was unsure who exactly was party to whatever it was – a game or a conspiracy?

Sophie direct-dialled her department, and Molly, Sir Michael Asplund's secretary answered immediately.

"Shall I get Sir Michael to call you right back?" Molly enquired.

"No, that won't be necessary, Molly. You can probably give me the answer yourself. Who's in charge of reviewing the Antarctic Treaty at BEIS?"

"Lawrence O'Brien."

"What level is he?"

"Five."

"How many staff does he have actually preparing the review?"

"Well, I'm not entirely sure, but they have one special secondment to deal with purely scientific matters relating to Antarctica."

"What's his name?"

"Mervyn Richards."

"May I speak to him?"

"Shall I get him to call you back?"

Sophie was always impressed by the seemingly effortless way in which Molly directed all communication through Sir Michael. If Sophie said nothing, it would be Sir Michael, her PPS, and not the person she wanted to speak to who would telephone her back ten minutes later.

"What's his direct-dial number? Does he have one?"

"I'll have to look it up." This was Molly's last try. Any more side-stepping would be over the line.

"I'll wait." Game, set and match.

"It's 2374."

"Will you put me through?"

"Of course." Molly was visualising Sir Michael's face.

***

"Mervyn Richards?" Sophie enquired.

"Yes."

"Hello, this is Sophie Beardsmore ... Secretary of State for the Environment, Food and Rural Affairs," she added a little pointlessly.

Mervyn almost choked on his egg sandwich. He did not receive calls from ministers. "Hello. How are you?" He heard himself ask out of embarrassment.

"I'm a bit confused. I understand that you know all about

Antarctica and the review of the treaty?"

"Well … I'm supposed to." He gripped his free hand into a tight fist, as everything he said sounded wrong.

"Did you write the briefing paper I have received this morning?"

"Yes, well … the factual bits."

"I have a lot more questions that I would like answered."

"Well, I'm sure that Sir Michael—"

"No. No, there's no need to involve him. You see, I have some concerns about recent events, and I would welcome some unbiased answers."

"You're not the only one." His nails were digging into the palm of his hand.

"You have concerns as well or you would welcome unbiased answers?"

"I have concerns."

"Will you come to my flat tonight? I would prefer to discuss this over a cup of tea and off the record."

***

Maria Yelland was stretched out, leaning on one elbow. She was luxuriating in a post-coital state of suspended animation. Time was standing still. She was crudely wrapped in a black, velvet drape (which was used for backgrounds) over her unbuttoned white blouse. Below the waist, she was not wearing anything. Rod Cameron, by contrast, was standing in a state of pre-climactic animated suspension. His heart was pounding, and he was having trouble packing everything back into his trousers that had previously fitted comfortably.

"I thought that you'd turned the sign over on the door?" he asked.

"I did."

"It must be a friend. I'll get rid of them. Wait here." He pushed his way (bending forwards for several reasons) through the curtain to the front of the shop.

Wait here? She looked like a nun in a *Penthouse* centre spread, so she was unlikely to walk off down the High Street. The last time she was dressed as a nun was at finishing school in Switzerland. The hills were, indeed, alive with the sound of music and the panting of an adolescent lonely goatherd. Thirty or more years on, with her pale-brown skin, black wrap and white blouse, she looked like a painting by Juan Gris. The few thoughts she was having were in Spanish, mostly from her childhood, as if the period with Charles had never happened. The years of emptiness had ended. She had come quietly. She had come of age. She sat up and tossed back her black hair. She let the cloth fall from her body such that her skin was bathed in a red glow, moving her from Gris to Gaugin. Maria looked about the room. Regret and Guilt must be hiding somewhere, but at the moment they were doing a good job. It was probably a game of hide and seek. She saw that Rod had folded up his sweater, just like Charles would have done. Guilt was clearly not such a good player as Regret.

She listened to the timbre of the conversation muffled by the heavy curtain, and it became increasingly animated. It did not sound like a customer. She stood up and began to get dressed. Her few clothes were where they had landed. A white shoe was embedded in the top of her open handbag. Once dressed, it was as if it had never happened. How could it have happened? She was out shopping on a weekday morning.

Maria picked up her handbag and switched her mobile back on. Regret was indeed a better player, but was about to reveal itself in a momentous way. While she had been pulling at the black velvet curtain and cursing the Catholic saints of her childhood all the way to her climax, she had missed the most important phone call of her life.

CHAPTER SIX

Charles had also been cursing at that precise moment. He was stuck in a traffic jam en route to the conference centre on the South Bank. The AGM was forty minutes away, but he wanted a little time to prepare himself, time to think.

In his office, he had decided upon his course of action with Tony, who would probably fly to Norway very soon to further negotiations with NorCarbon. Charles needed to deny finding oil and to denounce the photograph as a fraud. The share price would drop, but not, he hoped, enough to prevent him buying NorCarbon. There really was no choice. He could not risk the almost certain exposure by somebody that the photograph was a fake. Then what would he say? The share price would really plummet. This could even be the faker's ploy.

He wanted control of NorCarbon before he discussed any potential oil finds anywhere in the world, because there were other sensitive matters he wanted dealt with first. He was naturally impulsive, but he would always choose the time and date to go public after very careful assessments of a whole range of political, economic and environmental factors – or so he had been briefed by Tony. Charles Yelland was still not a strategist at heart.

Why should he worry? How could he lose if the world believed that he had discovered the largest oil field in the world? It didn't mean that he had to start extracting it immediately. Getting permission to extract was always a little difficult. He had it under control. His horoscope in the newspaper had it absolutely right. Mercury, the winged messenger, was in some sort of alignment with Saturn, the bringer of wisdom. He would learn something today that would change his life. "*Too bloody right!*" as his father used to say. Unfortunately for Charles Yelland, it was not as a consequence of the photograph in his newspaper.

His phone rang.

"Yelland."

"Please do not say anything, Mr Yelland. We have your daughter. If you wish to see her again alive, you will do the following—"

"Who is this?"

"At the AGM, you will confirm that you have found oil in the Antarctic."

"What?"

"I will repeat it one more time. At the AGM, you will confirm that you have found oil in the Antarctic."

"What? How do I know that I can trust you?"

"You cannot. You do as we say, and we release your daughter, and if you do not…"

"*Where is Angelica?*" he began to scream down the phone.

"She is safe, Mr Yelland … That is, if you do as we say and do not ring the police or try to contact anyone."

The line went dead and left him listening to an annoying synthetic burr.

Charles Yelland sat there stunned as Central London roared past him on all sides. He had not even noticed that the traffic was moving again. He raised his phone and dialled Angelica's number.

As soon as it was answered, he cried, "Angelica! Angelica!"

"I warned you not to contact anyone. You will not get another chance." The line was cut once more.

Charles Yelland activated the intercom and asked his chauffeur to pull up at the end of a side street a few hundred yards before the conference centre. He got out of the car without putting on his jacket and walked up the concrete steps of the Thames embankment. It was a warm summer day, and the acrid exhaust emissions competed with the indefinable background smells of the river. The sun was casting strong shadows, and there was a businesslike feel to the city. Charles, however, felt numb, and his senses detected none of this. He was angry and frustrated, with a desperate urge to lash out or blame someone. His wealth only served to highlight the hopelessness of his situation; there was nothing he could do. Nothing he could do to guarantee Angelica's release, that is. Once he had announced to the AGM what they wanted him to say, would they release her? Why would they? Could she identify them? He prayed that she had not seen them and had been blindfolded the whole time. The shareholders did not bother him. This played into his hands as he now had a reason for announcing Petronello's discovery off Signy that would push the share price right up. With his head buzzing, he approached a new building with huge façades of dark-brown chromatic glass, each pane an abstract study of amoeboid oily shapes. Leaning on the limestone balustrade, he peered down at the river, which was covered by a film of oil beneath him. Everywhere he looked, he found the damn stuff.

And at breakfast, he had thought that the day could not get any worse.

He thought of Angelica in her hot pants, remembered the smell of her strange coffee and pictured her shiny, black hair. She couldn't be kidnapped, surely? Some internal defence mechanism tried to persuade him that she was still out shopping. *At least,* he tried to reassure himself, *they have demanded something I can deliver. Anyway, I really need to think about how I am going to change my speech.* He heard himself start the sentence with 'anyway', and his eyes began to brim with tears. He would be able to keep it together for the AGM, but it was a very thin veneer of bonhomie that he would be wearing. With a full intake of breath that almost hurt, he turned from the river.

His footsteps ricocheted off the low concrete walls as he retraced his route back to his car. Luis, his rather stocky chauffeur, turned off the radio, but he could not get out quickly enough to open and hold the door before Charles had slid into the back.

"Once more into the breach," is what came out of Charles's mouth, but it was not what he was thinking, and Luis was very unlikely to get the reference.

In the two minutes it took to arrive at the venue, Charles had made three decisions: Firstly, he would announce the discovery because he had no other choice. Secondly, he would give the kidnappers one hour after the AGM to release Angelica or he would go to the police. There was nothing they could do realistically before the AGM, and he hoped they would not be needed; it would be better if no one else knew. From today, he would increase security for his whole family. His final decision was to use as much of the many hundreds of millions he was worth to track down the kidnappers. For Charles Yelland, this would be as close to a strategy as he would ever devise.

Monty, a rather neurotic man with staring eyes, who was dressed in a dinner jacket, opened the rear door to the car. Charles was ushered in through the stage door and along a depressing, roughcast concrete corridor. Monty guided him up some stairs with a bony arm protruding from his black jacket; his constant fretting having consumed any fat his body had ever managed to lay down for the future.

"Everything is the same as last year, as you requested. Podium. Lectern. Lighting. Actually, the only difference is that the display behind you rolls automatically, but if you want to ad lib, there is a button marked 'Pause'. One push for 'Pause', and one more push for 'Restart'. I'll show you when we are on stage before the curtains open," Monty explained.

"Just give me two minutes in the dressing room."

"Of course, of course. In here."

"Where's Tony?"

"He's in the VIP lounge, calming them all down. The main auditorium is absolutely buzzing. They're all working out how to spend their millions."

Once alone in the over-lit room, Charles combed his hair and straightened his tie. He had not forewarned Tony, who would be expecting him to denounce the photograph and not to admit to any discovery, despite the wild speculation all morning. At that moment, he was probably dampening down the enthusiasm of the bankers and pension-fund managers in anticipation of his chairman's speech. Tony would be shocked, but he would understand – even if it might make him look a bit stupid. Tony was his brother-in-law; he had been a loving husband to Charles's sister, Geraldine, and blood is thicker than, well, oil?

A couple of other things that had been concerning him were bubbling to the surface. It was as he was switching off the light that one slight concern came to the fore. Several months ago, he had agreed to an idea for the presentation that had seemed innovative at the time, but it was so reliant on technology that perhaps, on reflection, it was a bit risky. Cameras on five drones flying above Petronello's main areas of operation or exploration would be beamed to the AGM by satellite so that the shareholders could see real-time images from the North Sea, Arabian Gulf, Mexico, Trinidad and the South Atlantic. For all of the rigs, it had been agreed that there would be no flaring of gas today. He was still nervous.

By the time he reached the green room, he had remembered the second thing that was bothering him: he remembered the name of a very successful private investigator his closest friend had used a couple of years ago. "Kingdom, Mike Kingdom …" Fortunately, he stopped himself before misquoting Shakespeare twice in quick succession.

Monty was waiting for Charles as he arrived at the green room. Monty's permanently outstretched arm made him look as if he had an invisible dancing partner. "Mr Yelland. Shall we go?"

The noise from the other side of the curtains was unbelievable as the compere continued his warm up. Charles was shown the controls at the lectern, with Monty pirouetting, two-stepping and leaving the stage. A raucous fanfare blasted everyone into near silence, and a well-known TV newsreader, who was approaching retirement, made a few bland introductory statements and introduced the chairman. The curtains swept back across the stage, and Charles Yelland was confronted by the blur of a thousand cheering faces. TV cameras beamed the AGM around the world. The live images of the North Sea on a dull day appeared behind his head.

***

It was 7.30am in Washington DC, and the President of the USA was sitting there wearing an open-necked, green shirt and sipping a cappuccino. A large Stars and Stripes flag was incongruously rolled up against what looked like a kitchen cabinet, or so it appeared on the video link. The British PM was wearing a burgundy cardigan, and his wavy, white hair looked a little bohemian.

"Good afternoon to you," the President opened the conversation.

"Good morning."

"I apologise for the coffee and muffin, but they woke me early."

"You go ahead, Conrad. I may have to resort to a gin and tonic myself before we've finished."

"So might I." He sipped his coffee. "Victor, until 6.00am this morning, I could only find Antarctica on a map because it was coloured white and was at the bottom of the page. I don't know about you, but it was not high on my list of priorities."

"It wasn't even on my list of priorities, apart from general environmental concerns."

"I know what you mean, but I've gotta say that the USA running out of gas *is* somewhere near the top."

"I can understand that."

"I have more people looking at alternative energy sources than I've had Big Macs. None of them is going to fill that gap any time soon. And I don't like being held hostage by the Arabs and the Russians."

"I understand all that, Conrad."

The President took a mouthful of blueberry muffin and brushed the crumbs from his lips. Something appeared to be moving in the President's lap, and the PM was relieved to see that it was Banjo the Basset hound and not an intern.

"Is everything I've been told true? Have your guys found oil?" Conrad asked.

"I believe so. We are still checking."

"And we are talking north of this magic sixty-degree line of latitude?"

"Again, I believe so."

"So it's all in British waters?"

"Well, I understand that Signy is a British island in the South Orkney group, but its neighbour is Orcadas, which is Argentinian."

"And you two are not fighting over that?"

"Well, yes and no. It makes a change, I know, but they are mostly still contesting the Falklands."

"Judging from the way the lines are humming, do I take it that we are talking of a big oil field?"

"You probably know as much as me, but I think the speculation is getting out of hand."

"May I add to that speculation for a couple of minutes? It would not be unreasonable to assume that this oil field does not miraculously stop at the sixty-degree line?"

"I agree."

"What if it extends some way south of that line?"

"Conrad, if it's anything like here, you will have been briefed by every government agency in the USA on the consequences of such a theoretical development."

"I have been."

"I expect the advice falls into two camps. On the one side, protect the environment, avoid international conflict, re-ratify the Antarctic Treaty and leave the oil in the ground for future generations."

"I've had that one."

"On the other side, this is probably the last great oilfield on earth, the technology has improved immeasurably since the 1991 Madrid Protocol was signed, and both the USA and the UK need oil."

"Looks like we have a matching hand."

"Except that the oil may be in the British sector of Antarctica," Victor continued.

"Which is contested by three other nations, as I understand it, and suspended for so many years."

"Quite so."

"I know I'm piling the hypotheticals a bit high here, but what if the USA supported the British claim and supported controlled extraction subject to the most stringent regulations, etc. ... You know the rest of the words."

"I'm sure that we would be absolutely delighted."

"How delighted, Victor?"

"It would be up to the British government to license the extraction, of course. Some licences could go to American companies, I am sure."

"What about this Petronello? Doesn't it have the blanket licence to extract?"

"Only exploration licences with options, I expect, and Conrad, I do not know the small print, but trust me, there will be small print."

"Are you ready for that gin and tonic?"

"Are you proposing a toast?"

"How about, ''Til hell freezes over'?"

***

"… which almost completes what I have to say about the Bay of Campeche off Mexico, except that in the live view behind me you will see, I hope, one of our exploration rigs." Charles paused to look over his shoulder.

The restlessness in the auditorium was tangible. The shareholders were only interested in hearing one thing. They all knew that their chairman could announce that all the rigs in the North Sea and Arabian Gulf had turned upside down, but as long as he said that substantial oil had been discovered in the South Atlantic, the shares would rocket.

Only one man in the vast room was sweating profusely and waiting for the bomb to drop. Tony Dewey was sitting in the VIP box with half the key merchant bankers of London and Frankfurt. He pressed his head back into the large, comfortable chair ostensibly to listen better through the small speakers in the upholstered wings. He had tried his hardest to play down the photograph, but not to discount the possibility of future oil and gas discoveries. It was a thin tightrope to walk, and he felt like he was out over the Grand Canyon, looking down into the void below. He wiped the sweat from his beard and gripped the armrest.

"The exploration rig you see is the *Adventure*," stated the steady voice, echoing around the hall.

There was no reaction because hardly anyone was listening to the detail. They were all clutching their annual reports or imagining buying that villa in Majorca.

Here we go, thought Tony, not unlike when he had reached the crest on Disney's latest stomach-turning ride in Orlando with his eldest son.

"This is the *Adventure*, which many of you will have seen in this morning's newspaper, photographed off Signy." Charles paused again, and some of his audience began turning their heads to seek reassurance from their neighbours. "I am sorry to tell you, but the photograph is a fake. To use a cliché, it is fake news."

You could have heard a pin drop. The silence was deafening. The clichés were stacking up.

Tony looked tentatively around the hall. The press box was the first fault line to break. It became the epicentre of frenzied activity. Gradually, murmuring waves of discontent and disbelief drifted across the floor, building up into a tsunami of cynicism that smashed against the podium on which Charles Yelland looked marooned. Tony admired the way that his brother-in-law was standing his ground and letting the swell abate. After all, this was only a temporary setback. As long as the share price did not plummet too low, they would acquire NorCarbon, and in their own time, explore the possibilities, if any, of developing a field around the sixty-degree line. Tony's secret agenda involved having a Norwegian company, so that if there were objections to the expansion in the sector, Petronello had a second base covered. The Argentinians, he could do nothing about, and the Chileans were a neutral player who would probably concede, given enough money. Tony's strategy meant that this AGM was a dose of medicine they needed to take. He had agreed with Charles that they should end the presentation on an upbeat assessment of the future possibilities in the South Atlantic and leave it at that. He prepared himself for the inevitable questions once Charles had finished.

"Ladies and gentlemen, please do not jump to conclusions. Please hear me out. Some of our enemies have tried to use the photograph to steal our thunder and muddy the waters, if you'll allow me to mix my metaphors. It would have been dishonest of me not to point this out to you. However, I do have some excellent news for you all."

The presentation screen behind him began its transfer to the South Atlantic, with coverage from the drone of the *Antigone* rig.

What the shareholders saw was a rubber dinghy from the Sangaia ship *Harmony* discharging people in frog suits onto the rig supports with a large, flapping and unreadable banner. What they heard was Charles Yelland saying that he was happy to confirm that Petronello had, indeed, found oil off Signy, north of the sixty-degree latitude.

There was pandemonium. It took people minutes to work out if they had won or lost. It would take Tony Dewey a lot longer.

CHAPTER SEVEN

The PM was having a working lunch at Number Ten, Downing Street prior to the afternoon's PMQs. With him were JHV and one of his oleaginous spin doctors, who had once been something big in a newspaper; perhaps, like Harry Ramsden's extra-large cod. The high-ceilinged room and dark, striped Georgian wallpaper gave a formality to the meal that was probably neither intended nor desirable. They were sitting at one end of a long walnut table, laid with silver cutlery and Waterford cut glass, looking as if it had fallen from the small chandelier above. JHV, despite his strong right wrist, was having trouble cutting through the meat on his plate – his elbows were raised. With the dark sauce removed, the meat was dry and sinewy. Whichever animal it came from had probably survived on Noah's ark because nothing else wanted to eat it.

"What meat is this?" JHV asked.

"Ostrich," confirmed the PM.

"Ostrich? If this is ostrich, then I'm a monkey's uncle." JHV was adding nothing to the conversation except an interesting take on evolution.

"Simon, I hope that you are enjoying the wine? It's from down your way, south Somerset, isn't it?" the PM asked, turning around to face the butler, who nodded.

JHV took a swig of the over-oaked yellow liquid and used it to swallow the chewy meat.

"With the recent run of hot summers, these wines are really quite passable," the PM noted.

In a urinary sense, perhaps, JHV thought to himself.

A man in a shiny, dark-blue suit, which was frayed at the cuffs, entered the room and bent over to the ear of the PM. JHV smiled thinly at Simon, the spin doctor, and reconfigured the food on his plate to make it look as if he had consumed plenty. This was an impossible task, as a partly eaten meal always looks more than when it was served.

"Ostrich is low in cholesterol," Simon said quietly.

"Never eat anything that looks as if is wearing tights and false eyelashes," JHV whispered.

"Well, that's as expected." The PM had just learnt that Petronello had confirmed the discovery of oil in the South Atlantic at its AGM.

"What did the President have to say earlier?" enquired JHV.

"He said that the USA would go along with whichever country of the four claiming the sectors gave them the biggest percentage of the oil and its production."

"You are joking?"

"Well, that is the short version."

The other two stared at the PM.

"Imagine if we didn't have our Special Relationship?" he continued.

"That's blackmail." Simon did not need to use much spin.

"Let's get real. Without the USA, we will not be extracting any oil. We cannot take on Argentina and/or Chile." The PM was adamant.

JHV had been scrupulously careful not to be seen as a rampant Europhile, but he always used a naturally occurring opportunity. "You don't think that this is a chance for us to team up with the Norwegians who also control the sector?"

"What? To take on the South Americans? What with? Viking longships and broadswords? We need the Americans, because with them, there would be no war … and even if there was to be, we might stand a chance of winning it," the PM continued, "I'm not sure what's got into the Norwegians. They think about joining the EU when everyone's leaving and try to join OPEC when their own oil reserves are dwindling."

"I suppose a joint venture of the four countries is out of the question? You know? It's better to have twenty-five per cent of something than 100 percent of nothing," Simon suggested, entering the fray, "and we wouldn't have to involve the Americans?"

"We couldn't concede anything to the Argentinians," the PM said, and then helped himself to more bread, "I am sure that any concession would bring the Falklands back into play."

JHV did not like the way this was going; he wanted it more Europe- than USA-orientated. If in doubt, ask for more information. "Do we know if there is substantial oil south of sixty degrees? Nobody is really contesting north of this line, apart from the Argentinians and, under the UN, they are on thin …" He never finished the sentence because he was so pleased with himself.

The strange, anaemic-looking man in the blue suit and tie re-entered the room, this time with a sheet of paper.

The PM – looking slightly foppish with his over-long white hair and high-collared, yellow shirt – twisted the paper in his fingers like a magician with a playing card.

"Apparently, our Secret Squirrels have been monitoring the chairman of Petronello this morning. He hasn't reported it, but his daughter has been kidnapped. Their only demand was that he confirm that he had found oil at the AGM."

"What?" the two table guests asked in unison. One wondering about the kidnap and the other wondering who authorised the surveillance.

"Unbelievable, isn't it? Have the bastards found oil or not?"

***

"Where are you, Miles?"

"Do you want exact coordinates?"

"No, you idiot."

"We are at Outstation Twelve on the ice, somewhere a few hundred yards above the Weddel Sea."

Mervyn was staring with envy and awe at his old friend in some portable cabin in Antarctica. The real-time pictures shrank the world to fit in the grip of the human hand. "God, I wish I was with you."

"So do we; no one's done the sodding washing up for weeks, and someone needs to climb up the transmitter and de-ice it."

"How's the ice drilling?"

"We are back to the time of Christ."

"Any surprises?" Mervyn asked genuinely.

"Well, we haven't hit frankincense and myrrh, if that's what you mean."

"No, really."

"It's going well. We have the atmosphere gas log of every year for the last two millennia."

"You can't imagine how envious I am."

"Yes, but I bet it's a damn sight more comfortable where you are?"

"What? An office in Whitehall?"

"Yes, but you can go down the pub tonight, drink beer and eat pork scratchings."

"Oh no, don't mention pork scratchings!" a voice cried out for mercy in the background.

"Unfortunately, I can't tonight," Mervyn stated.

"You haven't found some sad Welsh tart who's daft enough to put up with you, have you?"

"Not quite."

"*The Secretary of State?*" The three voices could almost be heard in London from their bleak outpost halfway around the world.

"Yes, she wants to see me tonight," Mervyn explained.

"*Give her one from me, Mervyn,*" a voice shouted from off camera. "*On second thoughts, give her two.*"

"Actually … how old is she?" Miles asked, "I'm not that desperate. I'm only stuck on an ice sheet for two months with two of the ugliest humans since the Neanderthals."

"And don't leave the Zoom camera on. We don't want to watch," came a voice in the background.

"Mervyn, just remember the Antarctic Rules: just wash your face, hands and hairy bits," Miles suggested.

"Lads, what do you think she wants?" Mervyn asked.

"The same as all women; a good looking, funny man like you to take her to a restaurant. What with the white stick and the dog, she probably doesn't get out much."

"Lads, now come on."

"OK, OK; she probably wants to hear it from the horse's mouth."

"Shall I tell her everything?"

"Why not? It's your one big chance."

"What about the ice sheet?"

"Sure, why not? At this precise moment …" Miles leant out of view to check a reading. "… It is twelve inches north of when we started talking to you."

"Has the southern edge fractured?"

"It is floating northwards … yet another ice floe the size of Belgium."

"Let's hope there isn't a Belgian driving it!" a voice called out, identified only by a puff of breath visible to the left.

"It should be about the size of the Isle of Wight by the time it hits South Orkney," said Miles.

"And what's the latest prediction on the size of land that will be revealed?" Mervyn asked in his Welsh lilt.

"You can tell your new girlfriend that, for the first time in 13,000 years, an area the size of England will not be covered by ice this summer … and when the sun shines, who knows?"

"A great place for oil production?"

"You give it to her straight, Mervyn—"

Fortunately and appropriately, the line went snowy and died.

***

Charles Yelland was being swept up the stairs to the VIP lounge on waves of backslapping adulation and general euphoria. He had already worn out one smile and replaced it with another. He was a Russian doll of emotions, not knowing how many layers down the smiling would be replaced by anger, bewilderment and frustration. The sooner he could leave the building, the better. At least Monty was excited. He was standing at the top of the stairs with both arms outstretched like a scarecrow.

"This way, Mr Yelland; you deserve a drink … *Make way for the chair!*" he shouted above the throng. "Brilliant, Charles; brilliant."

So it continued to the door of the VIP Lounge.

This should have been one of the best days of his commercial life. To stand up and announce that you are making great progress searching for the last great oilfield on earth should have been a pleasure. Instead, he was fretting about Angelica, with no idea how he was managing to perform at the AGM. He had the immediate problem of facing Tony and, soon afterwards, his wife. *Shit! She doesn't know yet.* His nerves were at breaking point, but one thing at a time. He tried to push thoughts of Angelica to the back of his mind, but he could not stop wondering how far away she was from where he was standing. Trivial and happy memories of her childhood flooded back, despite the fact that they had never really been close. It was with Maria that she had any sort of bond.

Once past the bizarre bronze statue of Prince William in the pose of a maître d'hôtel, he was presented with a tableau of smiling faces. However, projecting from the bas-relief, all he saw were the buck teeth and beard of his brother-in-law. A glass of champagne was thrust into his hand by an unseen waiter, by Monty or perhaps even by Prince William. Two of the German bankers were the first to step forwards. The one with the wide box jacket, speaking from somewhere at the back of his throat, offered his congratulations. Charles allowed a polite amount of time to receive and acknowledge the plaudits. Only then did he ask for two minutes with Tony, "to discuss important arrangements".

It is hard to whisper aggressively. Even more so when you are trying to control your body language. "What the ...?" Tony asked.

"Tony, trust me, I had to. Angelica's been kidnapped," Charles explained.

"You ... she what?"

"Go along with me. I had no choice."

"When?"

"About twenty minutes before I got here."

"Have you told the police?"

"No, not yet ... I'll explain later. I hope that she will be released in the next hour. They didn't want money. They just wanted the oil discovery to be announced."

Tony looked stunned, but he was nothing if not practical. "Have you changed the press release?"

"Shit! No. Will you telephone Jo?"

"What should it say?"

"Just that we have found oil."

How could that sound so anticlimactic?

***

Seconds later, out on the empty terrace overlooking the Thames, Tony was calling the wonderful Josephine. "Jo? Tony. I'll explain later, but Charles decided to announce that we found oil off Signy at the AGM."

"OK." This was unflappability at its most flightless and grounded.

"The latest press release condemns the photograph as a fake, but confirms hopeful investigations?" he asked.

"Yes."

"Will you do an update that confirms limited discovery of oil north of sixty degrees south, as announced at the AGM?"

"Yes."

"And make the words leap out. This had better be clear to everyone." This was said to the woman who was his knowledge of all fonts.

***

Was the thumping music for real or was it in Angelica's head? She couldn't tell.

"Can you hear music?" she whispered to the prone body she could feel next to her.

There was no response from Belinda. *Perhaps she has left the dream. That happens in dreams, you know?*

The fluorescent zigzags had returned, and they were not helping her developing headache. Her right wrist throbbed as well.

This was not a great shopping trip; the changing rooms were too dark. She reached up with her free hand and moved a curtain. Instead of shop assistants and rails of clothes, she saw daylight. The blue sky was bright, but she could not lift herself enough to see out. Reality cut into her dream in transitory flashes of awareness, like sparks from a bonfire, only to fade to black. She was in a room, and they were both on a double bed, tangled up in the blankets. She glanced at the chain holding her wrist and knew that this was not right, but the thought disappeared. Belinda was motionless and lying on her side, both her wrists were still manacled.

There was no thumping music. It was the rhythm of her heartbeat pumping blood around her body.

She lost her train of thought. Where were the assistants? The smell was terrible. Didn't they clean these motorway toilets every hour? A memory of Reading Services flashed into her consciousness, but it took the form of a drive-in movie.

"I want to get out of the car? Why won't you let me get out of the car?"

It was a crap film, and she passed out again.

CHAPTER EIGHT

"Does the Prime Minister agree that, given the environmental catastrophes of the first decades of this century, the last thing we should be doing at the moment is contemplating messing up the last great wilderness on earth?"

"What is the Right Honourable gentleman opposite talking about? We, on this side of the House, are not 'contemplating messing up' Antarctica. All we know is that some oil has been found near a latitude of sixty degrees south. Oil and gas have been extracted for the last sixty years from sixty degrees *north* – that is to say, from the North Sea, west of Shetland – without any damage to the Arctic. Perhaps the Right Honourable gentleman is scaremongering, as usual?"

"Here! Here!" The MPs on the green benches behind Victor, the PM, stood and cheered. PMQs always created a febrile atmosphere in the House of Commons.

"Are there not political as well as environmental questions

to be asked? What about the Antarctic Treaty review? What about the contested sectors *north* of sixty degrees south?"

"I think that the Right Honourable gentleman means south of sixty degrees south. Perhaps he should sit down before he gets himself into hot water, which would be quite difficult discussing Antarctica."

Loud guffaws echoed around the chamber.

"While my sense of direction may have let me down, my sense of responsibility has not. Can he reassure the House that no extraction licences will be issued without the full support of this House and our international colleagues?"

"No one has applied for any extraction licences. When and if they do, they will be considered on their merits. The Right Honourable gentleman need not trouble himself," concluded the PM.

"Mr Jack Middleton!" The Speaker of the House of Commons called out an MP's name.

"Mr Speaker, if I could pour oil on troubled waters, perhaps we could all concentrate on the problems of the day, rather than hypothetical ones in the distant future on the other side of the earth." There was much hooting, and the MP for Derby South continued, "The proposed consolidation of the car industry …"

***

Charles Yelland turned on the screen in the rear of his car and checked yet again that he had full coverage on his mobile phone; he did not want to miss any calls. The M40 motorway slid down into a wooded cutting, giving the false impression that he had left the suburbs of London. Within twenty minutes, he would be home, ready to deal with his daughter's release. The rushing of blood in his ears resonated with the tyre noise on the road surface outside. He was in a padded cell going mad from frustration and anger.

He had not telephoned Maria. He was hoping that Angelica's release would preclude him having to put Maria through this torture. This was such an odd time of day to return that he had no idea whether she would be home or not. It would probably be for the best if she were to come back later from some shopping trip to find the matter resolved. Charles rehearsed a few weak reasons for his early arrival home in case she was in. The motorway trees gave way to soft birch woodland, and the roads narrowed from six lanes to two. He lifted his palm from where it had been resting to find that it was damp.

He leapt as his mobile rang, and he fumbled to press the green icon. It was a major investor wishing him well. His heart was still pounding as the tyres crossed from tarmac onto gravel.

***

Maria was wallowing in a double jacuzzi beneath a blanket of creamy bubbles. Late afternoon was not her usual time for a bath, but it seemed the natural way to prolong the sensual feelings that were still passing through her body, and also as a way to cleanse herself of all traces of her earlier liaison. In her sexually heightened state, she was watching the screen on one of the four mirrored walls in her enormous bathroom, finding every male presenter or actor surprisingly attractive. The layer of fragrant bubbles served to cushion her from the outside world and to conceal any trace of her reawakened interest.

A persistent bell rang throughout the house, triggered by the opening of the main gates. She sat upright, sending a wave across the jacuzzi and sliding up the surrounds. The backwash met itself in the centre and swept back and forth; a diminishing panic looking for an escape. She grabbed a towel, dried her hands hurriedly and looked at her phone. She turned on the coverage of the external cameras, only to see her husband's chauffeur reversing the car towards the garage block. She stood up quickly, the white foam slipping down her bright-red skin. Whether from guilt, embarrassment, sexual arousal or the hot water, her capillaries had decided that they needed to spend some time near the surface of her body.

He must not find me like this, she thought to herself. *Why shouldn't he find me like this?* She argued internally. *Why shouldn't I take a relaxing bath? Because he will put two and two together!* The prosecution and defence battled it out in her head. *What if he wants sex? Why would he want sex? But why is he home mid-afternoon?*

She towelled herself down roughly and slipped on a thick dressing gown. Maria stared at her many reflections in the mirrored walls. Each and every one of her could not have looked more guilty as she repeatedly grew smaller, disappearing into the distance, even if the word 'guilty' had been tattooed on her forehead. She saw a jar on the shelf and saw an escape. By the time Charles was calling up the stairs, her face had been daubed in foul-smelling, green paste. "Hide all of your embarrassing blemishes," the jar proclaimed. Just hiding the embarrassment would do fine.

"This is a surprise," Maria declared.

"So this is what you do all afternoon. If I had known,

I would have worn fancy dress." He deliberately kept the conversation light.

"What brings you home? Was the AGM all right?"

He had rehearsed the reply to the point where it could never be said convincingly. "Yes, fine. I'm waiting for an important call. I can deal with it just as easily here as at the office."

It did not sound convincing. *He must know about Rod,* she thought, and then went redder under the green mask.

"I'm going to have a drink. I'll take any incoming calls," he said.

Does he think Rod is going to phone? Maria mumbled something about leaving the mask on for twenty minutes, and then retreated into her mirrored hell.

He went into the kitchen and placed his mobile on the work surface; it would not leave his side until he had confirmation Angelica was free. She would probably need picking up, he had thought, so he had arranged for his chauffeur to wait in the staff room above the garage. He poured himself a glass of Châteauneuf-du-Pape and scoured the cabinets for snacks to stave off his growing hunger. When the call came in, he almost regurgitated the wine and nuts.

"Yelland."

"Mr Charles Yelland?" the caller asked.

"Speaking."

"This is the Great Western Hospital, Swindon. Paramedics have just brought in your daughter, Angelica. Please don't worry, Mr Yelland; she is all right, but she seems to be under the influence of drugs at the moment. Your name came up as next of kin."

"What? OK. Thanks ... I'll ... we'll be there as soon as possible ... It'll take over an hour ..."

"Please drive carefully, Mr Yelland. She is asleep at the moment. Her life is not in danger."

***

It was only a few streets from Whitehall to Sophie Beardsmore's flat. Mervyn Richards did not bother going home, but grabbed a burger instead. Instantly, he regretted eating it so quickly as it had now reconstructed itself into a plug somewhere in his stomach. He could neither swallow nor burp, and the entire sesame seed output from western Turkey was stuck between his front teeth. He eventually resorted to staring closely at his reflection in an optician's shop window to see if he had removed them all.

"It says £120."

"Pardon?" Mervyn turned around.

"Let me read it for you. The new thinner lenses are from £120," the passer-by continued.

"Oh … thank you."

"I recommend them. Look what it's done for me. You'll have no trouble reading then." The Good Samaritan hobbled off down Whitcomb Street.

It had not dawned on Mervyn that there would be an armed policeman outside her apartment block. This was a temporary measure for most of the senior Cabinet members since the recent bombing. He walked nervously up the steps, thumping his chest to relieve the indigestion, but looking as if he were about to burst into something from a Puccini opera.

"I've got an appointment with Sophie Beardsmore at 7.00pm," he said in an unnaturally deep voice.

"Your name?"

"Mervyn ... Mervyn Richards."

"Mr Richards ..."

"Mervyn Richards, that's right."

"... is here." The policeman was speaking into some concealed microphone.

The very solid red door opened.

"Up here."

He followed her voice up the stairs to her flat, where the door was open. He walked in tentatively, gently tapping the frame to announce his arrival. She called him into what turned out to be her bedroom. The jibes of his friends at the Antarctic outstation rang in his head.

"Oh good, you're tall. Would you grab the other end?" she asked.

She was standing barefoot on a chair holding one end of a curtain pole. He lifted up the other end thinking that this was not what he thought meetings with ministers were like.

"How did you get on in Antarctica, being so tall?"

"There's nowhere to bang your head."

"I meant in the accommodation units."

"They're not too bad. The days of cramped quarters have long gone."

She stepped down, shook his hand and formally introduced herself, asking him to call her Sophie. "Have you eaten?"

"I grabbed something on the way here ... which I am beginning to regret." He thumped his chest again.

"Do you fancy a bowl of soup? It's homemade, with vegetables that grew in real soil."

"Yes, please."

With that, they moved into the kitchen.

"You know that this is highly irregular, don't you?" She didn't miss a beat as they sat down at her kitchen table.

For a second, he wondered what sort of vegetables she was talking about, but realised that she had moved on. "Well, it was you who called."

"I know, I know. I shouldn't make direct contact with staff and advisers from another department without going through the proper channels. It's just that I feel I am not being told the whole truth …" She paused for breath. "You see, I'm not exactly normal."

Mervyn had spent his entire life being told that he was not normal.

A few minutes later, while blowing across their spoons to cool the soup, Sophie had asked Mervyn if he had any concerns. "Did you see that photograph in the paper this morning?"

"Yes," he said, "I presumed that it was a fake. Or rather, I hope it is a fake."

She stopped sipping from her spoon.

"You see," he continued, "there was an ice sheet in the distance behind the exploration rig. Either it is well south of sixty degrees – in which case, Petronello is in big trouble and, by finding oil, has opened up the Antarctic to exploitation – or the *Adventure* rig is at fifty-nine degrees south and the ice sheet has been added. I don't understand." It all came out in a mad rush, but she grasped the gist.

"That's very odd. Apparently, at the AGM today, the chair admitted that the photograph was a fake, but then he confirmed they had found oil."

"Did he?" Mervyn had not heard this.

"So have they found oil or not? Are they south of sixty degrees or not?" she mused.

"What bothered me today," she began, listing her worries, "was the convenience of this discovery to the Petronello AGM and to the Antarctic Treaty review. Forgive me, but you are very young, and I have become even more cynical as I grow older. Is it a stunt for the shareholders? I hope they understand that they are playing with fire. We are heading, as far as I can see, for a major split between the USA, South America and Europe over this."

"Who do you think faked the photograph, if it is faked, and why?" He was finishing his bread.

"I don't know. Do you think it could be some environmental group trying to score points just as the treaty review begins?"

"I don't think so."

"Nor do I ... but it could be. After a meeting with Sir Michael this morning, I think the whole thing is political, but I could be wrong."

"I feel a lot better," Mervyn said.

"Well, I'm still confused."

"No, no. I meant that the soup has settled my stomach."

"Is Antarctica melting due to climate change?" she asked the million-dollar question.

"Well, yes, but it's not quite as simple as that. Everyone wants it to be simple; they want black and white—"

"This is the way of the world in all things. They want cold, hard facts," she interrupted.

"That's usually easy in Antarctica." He smiled at her and began to relax in her company. "They want to blame climate change, but it's not like that. It's a combination of five or six factors, exacerbated by global warming caused by humans, which might be tipping the balance."

"What are these factors?" She was now concentrating intently on Mervyn.

"Firstly, the natural cyclical changes in climate that occur without man: rising or falling temperatures, and higher or lower snowfall. Secondly, the geothermal warming of the western Antarctic waters from deep volcanic activity."

She looked at him blankly.

"You know? The Ring of Fire where the tectonic plates are moving all around the Pacific Ocean, even down in the far, far south."

She did not know about this, but kept quiet.

He continued, "Thirdly, the total area of snow versus sea; the snow, being white, reflects so much more heat than dark seawater. Fourthly, the extent and robustness of the ice sheets floating on the sea, but which are really a continuation of the ice sheets / glaciers on the land. These are important because they are a brake on the glaciers' movement; they still flow, but are buttressed and slowed by the ice shelf over the sea. There are other factors, but these are the most important when coupled with man's contribution."

She tried to digest all of these factors. "So, irrespective of man's activities to date, is Antarctica shrinking?" she persisted.

"You must be careful when you use the term 'Antarctica'. The landmass under the ice is not changing size, obviously. It is still one and a half times the size of the USA, which is a mind-blowing fact on its own. It is the ice that covers it, to an average depth of one and a quarter miles, and the ice extension over the sea that is shrinking from the combination of factors I described. The speed of the shrinking is frightening. The largest block of ice to break off back in 1956 was the size of Somerset. Currently, the ice shelf that buttresses the Pine Island Glacier is breaking up. The glacier has an area of 68,000 square miles, is made up of 180 trillion tons of ice and is now moving into the sea at a rate of thirty-six feet a year."

She wanted him to slow down, but his enthusiasm was infectious. "This will make sea level rise? And quickly?"

"Yes, but it's not that simple. If ice floating on the sea melts, sea level doesn't rise. It's the same as when an ice cube melts in your gin and tonic, and the level of water in the glass doesn't rise. It's when the ice on the land melts that sea level rises. The Pine Island Glacier melting would raise the world's sea level by twenty inches."

"That is frightening; you are right. Would you just go over the buttressing of the Pine Island Glacier again? Simply, please?"

"Imagine a really big, wide lump of ice on the sea. It is called an ice shelf. It is so big that it stops the flow of the glacier into the sea, like a great big dam. If this ice shelf melts, it lets the glacier flow into the sea, where it melts. That's as simple as I can put it."

She was taking in everything, but she would need a bit longer to digest all of the consequences.

"We haven't even got on to what happens when the land surface of Antarctica is revealed to the sun … and to man. This is why the Antarctic Treaty is so crucial," he said.

"I am speaking at the Climate Really Matters Conference in Llandudno on Tuesday. I would like to make some wider points about the environment. I am not sure why Russell Walker isn't speaking. He's your ultimate boss, isn't he?"

"I suppose so, but I've never met him."

CHAPTER NINE

"… *because she's been kidnapped!*" cried Charles.

"For why did you not tell me?" Maria sounded Mexican for the first time in years.

"Because they said they would release her … and they have! She will be all right. She's been drugged to keep her subdued, that's all."

"*That is all?*" Maria screamed.

She turned her face towards the side window in the back seat of the car. The glass between them and their chauffeur was raised and the intercom muted. Her emotions were heightened: Fear (for Angelica's safety) had used up most of her emotional energy, Guilt was having to run on her reserve tank, and even this was in danger of being requisitioned by Hate – hatred of her husband. She folded her arms and regretted not enjoying her adulterous foray more. *Although,* she thought to herself, *I couldn't have enjoyed it more.*

After just over an hour of dual carriageways and

motorways, they turned off the M4 at Junction 15 and almost immediately swept through a sea of car parks to be dropped off at the entrance to the hospital. They joined a queue that seemed to make inordinately slow progress towards the reception desks, or so it felt to distraught parents. Eventually, they made it to the front and were engaged by a friendly face.

"We've come to see our daughter … Angelica Yelland. That is 'Yelland' with a 'Y'," Charles explained.

"Do you know which ward?" asked the receptionist.

"No … they haven't told us."

"Let me check." There was much tapping on her keyboard. "No, sorry, I can't see an Angelica Yelland."

Time stood still.

"We've driven here for an hour because you phoned us!" Charles was trying so hard to restrain himself.

"Let me try to find her a different way. When was she admitted?"

"About 3.30pm this afternoon, or that's when someone from here rang me to tell me she had been admitted."

"Oh, yes, here she is. She was brought in by the police." The receptionist had lowered her voice trying to provide some privacy. "Wait a minute; there's a message."

Time went backwards.

"I'll call Charge Nurse Davenport. He will come down to get you. Please take a seat."

***

The look on the nurse's face as he walked towards them would have turned any parent's blood to ice.

"Is she dead?" Maria asked before any introductions were made. She clutched Charles's arm for support.

"Not to my knowledge. She was asleep a few minutes ago. Please follow me."

The labyrinth of stairs and corridors served only to prolong the tension. *Why so many fire doors?* Charles asked himself, *And why made of wood?*

Before entering the ward, the Charge Nurse warned them both that the police would want to speak to them and, most definitely, before Angelica could be released. "She's in here. She is comatose, so she probably won't be awake until tomorrow, but I'm sure you would like to see her?"

He pulled back the curtain around the bed for the Yellands to gain sight of a sleeping girl, intubated through her nose and with a very pale face accentuated by her jet-black hair.

Maria let out a gasp and put her hand over her mouth. There was good news and bad news.

The good news: the girl looked peaceful and superficially unharmed.

The bad news: the girl lying in the bed was Belinda not Angelica.

***

If the Yellands were shocked, so were Belinda's parents, who were not expecting their daughter back until late evening and had suspected nothing. They arrived at the hospital just as the police were finishing interviewing Charles in a small side office. It transpired that it was not the police who had found Belinda, apparently asleep on a bench in a local park, but a concerned member of the public. The police were contacted by the hospital, who were concerned that Belinda had been drugged. What had begun as a girl suffering from an overdose quickly escalated to a drugged girl carrying the wrong student union and credit cards, together with a still-missing kidnapped girl of a high profile family. A police officer was assigned the task of sitting outside the ward until Belinda woke up and could be interviewed, which would, hopefully, shed some light on events and help to find Angelica. The fact that the officer was armed had not escaped Charles's notice.

In the car, being driven back late that evening, he stared out of one window while Maria looked out of her window on the other side into the blackness beyond; her eyes were slightly protruding, and she had a mild shaking in her arms. After the weirdest roller coaster of a day, Charles had calmed down and was beginning to think things through with a little more logic. The kidnappers were clearly professionals, and whoever was behind all this wanted to cause Charles maximum pain; the promise of release after his announcement, the drugging of Belinda and the cynical use of Angelica's cards were all designed to hurt him or keep him under their control. There had also been no further contact from them, and this, too, was causing him anxiety. If they asked for money or another announcement, at least there was something he would be able to do towards her release. Silence just meant that he festered and worried.

***

When they arrived home late that night, Maria went straight to bed. Charles knew he would not sleep and became suddenly aware that he had not eaten much all day, apart from some canapés at the

AGM and some nuts mid-afternoon; he was running on empty. He poured himself a glass of red wine and hastily put together some cheese, biscuits and olives on a tray. His destination was his favourite room – a loggia now enclosed with two sides of glass, which in daylight, gave views down his garden. It was not a large room, but it felt cosy, and the walls were adorned with family photographs and mementoes from his work and foreign trips.

That night, there was only one framed picture that was the centre of his attention. He had subconsciously been thinking about that small picture most of the day. It was of Antarctica and had been cut from some book or magazine when Angelica was in her early teens. Why she had cut it out, why she had coloured something black that had always been portrayed in white, and why it had ended up framed was now a bit vague. He had looked at it many times; for example, when Petronello had won the exploration licence in the South Atlantic and when the first secret drilling samples had made it back to the lab he used in Port of Spain. It had adorned the loggia wall with as much relevance as a fridge magnet.

With his wine glass in his hand, he walked up to it and stared at it very closely. Black and white, if only? But a cold sensation skittered across the surface of his skin. He now saw it for the first time as the entrance to a dark cave. He then inexplicably saw the black splodge as a bullet exit wound, and at that moment, confronted by Antarctica in black and white, he was sure that his daughter was dead. He vaguely began watching a spider, illuminated by an outside light just beyond the window, swinging back and forth. He closed the curtains.

He decided to contact Mike Kingdom.

When you are one of the richest men in the country, how do you procure the services of a private investigator? You are unlikely to search on Google. He had emailed his best friend Colin James for the contact details, and this was passed on as if it were a Masonic secret.

Charles looked at his watch. It was 11.08pm and getting late. He started to compose an email, not expecting it to be read until tomorrow. What hours did they keep? He had no idea what a private investigator did or even looked like. Did they spend their days sitting in cars, waiting to use their telephoto lenses on unsuspecting adulterers? Or was that old hat, and they now never left the computer screen and keyboard. Were they ex-police? Ex-military? Ex-SAS? No, of course not. He was confusing private security with private investigation. How did you get into it in the first place? It is not exactly on the top of a school career adviser's list.

His mobile phone rang. The caller display read "Colin".

"Hello, Colin," Charles answered.

"Hello, Mr Yelland. It's Mike Kingdom."

He was not sure what was the most disturbing: that it was not Colin or that the speaker had a woman's voice. "I ... uh."

"Colin gave me your phone number. He said that you were very likely to call. I thought I would get in first."

"He never told me you were a woman." Charles regained some composure. "In fact, he told me nothing about you, come to think of it."

"I ask my clients not to tell anyone anything. I don't advertise."

He thought that she sounded middle-aged, and her accent was soft Canadian or similar. "I was just emailing you when you—"

"I know. That's why I called you."

"How did you know?"

"If I cannot hack your phone and computer, what sort of use am I going to be in finding your daughter?"

"How did you ...?" His voice trailed off.

"I have been following you since Colin called. That means all the way to Swindon and back, to save you wondering. Metaphorically speaking."

Charles drained the last of the wine and took a breath. "You understand the extreme sensitivity of all this? I need this to be utterly confidential."

"Of course. Would you like to know my terms and charges before I start officially?"

"No, send them over to me after this call. If they're reasonable, I'll pay them. If you are successful and find out what I want, even if they are unreasonable, I will pay them."

When Charles had used his phone to pay for the two coffees at the hospital café in Swindon, he had unwittingly allowed Mike Kingdom into his bank account. Money was not a problem, and his wealth had probably doubled since the announcement earlier in the day.

"What have the police told you?" Mike asked.

"Nothing. I only told them about the kidnapper's call at the hospital."

"Who else knows about Angelica?"

"Maria, obviously ... Tony, my brother-in-law and co-director ... the police in Swindon ... and you."

"Why do you think I might help?"

"Because I think they've killed her ... and I want you to find out who they are."

"Why do you think they have killed her? It is less than a day."

"It's just a feeling. I've done what they wanted, and she hasn't been released ..."

"She hasn't been released yet, but it's very early."

"I cannot tell you how much I want you to be right."

"How much did they want?" She was giving him no time to think.

"You mean money? They didn't want money. They wanted me to do something else."

"Such as?"

"To say something at today's AGM."

"Which you did?"

"To the letter … but they haven't released her. They released Belinda, her best friend, instead. Just to get at me more."

"Presumably, you must know who would gain from this request of theirs?"

"Yes, I have a good idea, but unfortunately, the theoretical list is very, very long, Miss Kingdom."

"Please call me Mike … and, please, you must answer everything I ask you truthfully or else there is no point."

"Of course," he said, but he could not bring himself to call her Mike.

"How well do you get on with your daughter?"

"I love her dearly … but if I am honest, we are not as close as I would like. There's no problem," he added quickly, "except that she's a bit spoilt; I have been away for much of her early years and, well, conversations don't tend to contain many words or even syllables."

"You had better tell me everything, starting from the last time you saw her."

During the quarter of an hour it took Charles Yelland to recap on the previous sixteen hours since breakfast, Mike Kingdom said virtually nothing. She wanted to hear it in his words.

"So, that's it. That's all I know," he concluded.

"No, that's all you think that you know." *And a censored version at that*, she thought to herself. "May I ask you four quick questions? And then I would like to come and see you early tomorrow morning."

He was intrigued to hear them. "Yes, go ahead."

"What is Angelica's Instagram account?"

"Surely you can find that out? I don't know exactly. It's her name, I think."

"Does she have a long-standing boyfriend?"

"No ... not that I've ever met. She may have."

"What has she got on the walls of her bedroom?"

"What? Nothing ... nothing, I think. Is it important?"

"Finally, what was she wearing on her feet?"

"What? She had on yellow hot pants and some outrageous high heels, or 'wedges' I think they are called, which every girl seems to be wearing. With her black hair and long legs, you'll have no problem spotting her."

"It wasn't for identification purposes; I just wanted to check if she had run away from home."

"Miss Kingdom, the kidnappers just wanted me to announce the discovery of oil. It has nothing to do with Angelica in that sense."

"Charles, the police are pursuing the obvious routes as we speak. They will probably do it quicker and better than me. If it is all as straightforward as you think, it will soon be resolved, and you won't need me. Except that, inside, you don't think it's that straightforward either – and that's why you've called me."

"Miss Kingdom, I hope beyond hope that the police find my daughter, but if they don't, I am employing you to find out who did it. You will be my avenging angel."

"May I come over to your house at 7.00am tomorrow?"

He was more confused than when he had started the call, and that was pretty confused. A call to Colin might reassure him that some aggressive, middle-aged woman was what he needed right now.

"How long have you been doing this work, Miss Kingdom?"

"I'm thirty-four if that's what you meant, and I'm from Portland if you're wondering about the accent … and that's not Portland, Dorset."

CHAPTER TEN

Mike Kingdom stood up and stretched. It was Saturday morning, and she had risen early after yesterday evening's conversation with Charles Yelland. Her home was up a forest track. It was a converted attic over a detached garage, with walls lined in tongue-and-groove boarding to give it a more log-cabin feel. It had a large picture window installed in the gable end, which looked out on to a glade in a coniferous woodland; there were moments when she could fool herself that she was back in Oregon. The whole place should have reeked of pine resin and damp, acidic earth, not stale cigarette smoke. There were few personal possessions, and the only concession to her earlier life was a framed panorama of Mount Hood covered in snow and smoking gently into a pale-blue sky. There was a romanticism to this, as the last eruption was in 1865. The acute observer may also have noticed the photograph of a young man on a Harley Davidson, which acted as her screen saver.

While typing instructions into her system in order to collect more background information, she mulled over what she had already discovered. Via several tried-and-tested routes, she downloaded a list of Angelica's credit card purchases, together with her school and medical records. Various financial reports on Petronello, a Department for International Trade assessment and Charles Yelland's telephone accounts soon followed. Mike Kingdom's favourite way of acquiring such information involved software she had adapted herself from a previous life in the investigative branch of the CIA. She would hack into a regional tax office computer, give herself a fictitious investigation code, and use this cover to hack into and download files from banks or government departments. After transferring them via the regional tax office on to her own system, she would delete all traces of the transactions. If anybody could be bothered, they would only find their way back to the tax office, where they would assume it was a legitimate request, or just give up.

She pulled a leather jacket around her shoulders while she downloaded some files on Maria Yelland for good measure. By the time that she had ridden off up the forest track blanketed in orange pine and larch needles, she had acquired more information than the police, who were waiting for Belinda to regain consciousness in Swindon. The motorbike kicked and bucked over the worst of the ruts before speeding off along the tarmac of a country lane. She had eliminated nothing from her enquiries, but her initial thoughts were taking shape. In the hour it would take her to get to the meeting, she reviewed it all. She could see that Charles loved his daughter in a rather dutiful and detached way, but he did not know anything about her social media profile, what was on her bedroom walls or if she had a long-term boyfriend. Mike Kingdom, herself, could see what was on her bedroom walls just from visiting her Instagram account. He had moaned about her lifestyle and the way she dressed. Unsurprisingly, he had only really appreciated his feelings for his daughter once she was not there. Strangely, to Mike Kingdom's way of thinking, he wanted her death avenged before he knew she was dead.

It was also unlikely that she had run away. Even wealthy, naïve and besotted sixteen-year-old girls do not run away from home wearing yellow hot pants and high-heeled shoes. Mike would check further, but from her school reports, bedroom walls and recent phone calls, she did not appear to be involved in any religious, political or environmental groups. It was beginning to look as if she was being used as a bargaining tool by commercial or environmental interests involved in Antarctic oil exploration. The fact that Belinda had been released, albeit in a comatose state, bothered Mike as she cranked the bike over and used centrifugal force to sweep her down the motorway slip road. If the kidnappers intended to cover their tracks completely, why not kill both girls? Why release one? Had Angelica woken up and seen them? Could she now identify them? Or was she to be used further against her father, which begged the question as to what more Charles could deliver? And why Swindon? Why take one or more of the girls to Swindon?

By the time she reached the Denham exit on the M40, she had catalogued all of the questions into some sort of order and had begun to schedule the different future scenarios. While Charles appeared to be what he claimed, she held niggling doubts about his wife. It was not what she had found out from her quick overnight search, it was what was missing.

She drove through large stone gates and down a long avenue of lime trees; there were deer in one of the fields to her left and cattle grids at intervals, across which she clattered. London could be a million miles away, although, in fact, the centre was only seventeen miles away by road. These were the benefits of owning 2,000 acres of prime Buckinghamshire-estate farmland. A large manor house came into view, and the limes gave way to a series of clipped yew hedges. She pulled up right in front of a stone portico, kicked down the stand, and walked up the steps still wearing her helmet and small rucksack. It was precisely 7.00am. She pressed an antiquated door bell and waited.

Charles Yelland answered the door himself, wearing a green jumper over a checked shirt. He wasn't sure if it was his visitor or a motorcycle delivery boy.

"Good morning, Charles."

She slipped off the rucksack and pulled up her matt-black helmet to reveal a shock of hair dyed an odd carmine red. It looked as though she had replaced one helmet with another. Two intelligent, dark eyes stared out from a pitted face, and her thin body was disguised behind the tight motorcycle leather trousers and jacket. She stuck out a gloved hand, which he shook.

"Hello. Come in." He stood aside to let her through while directing her down a long hall to a kitchen at the far end.

In his head, Charles was wondering, *What have I done telling my innermost secrets to this … person? Someone who may as well have come from another planet. She might come with the highest recommendations from Colin, but I still do not know her from Adam … or Eve.* He looked at her face beneath the red mop. She could have been eighteen as she stood there in his kitchen, in her black leathers and leaning against the units with her legs crossed at the ankles. And he had worried about the way Angelica had dressed?

Reaching into her jacket, Mike took out a cigarette – one wrapped in black paper. Charles was lost for words, but he guessed that everything she did was a challenge or a provocation – she wanted to see the response.

"I think I make you uncomfortable?" she asked.

"I think you are trying to make me uncomfortable, for some reason, or do you do this to everyone?"

"Perhaps."

"Surely, you need to … recede into the background, not stand out like a sore thumb?"

"When I want to recede, I can blend in very easily. It's a wig," she added rather unnecessarily.

The black cigarette was still twirling in her fingers. "I have a client who still takes snuff."

"I didn't know you could still get it. I thought that it went out with the Victorians."

"Charles, you can get anything and everything without leaving the comfort of your armchair, you should know that."

"I think we have what is called a generation-gap problem here. I grew up in the 1980s, and computers are something other people use for me."

"Do you still have a secretary?"

"Well, two PAs, actually."

"Amazing." She shook her head. "I think we also have a 'how the other half lives' problem."

"May I get you a drink? Tea? Coffee?" He opened a cupboard. "Or a coffee substitute supposedly made with horse chestnuts, which Angelica was drinking precisely where you are standing yesterday morning?"

"May I see?" She was standing very close to her new client, peering into the cupboard. The Turkish cigarette had not been lit and was nowhere to be seen.

"She thought it would make her hair shiny. Yes, really."

"I think Angelica is no fool. I think she has chosen to live down to your expectations. I won't have a drink, thanks."

The cigarette had reappeared, but she did not light it. In fact, she began to chew it. The sweet, burnt smell of liquorice filled the air. Charles shook his head in a way that managed to both patronise and concede defeat in one action.

"I've boiled it down to three fundamental questions," she said, revealing a tongue as black as her eyes, "For starters, how do you kidnap two girls out shopping in broad daylight in Central London? One in lemon hot pants?" She turned to look out of the window as a car approached across the gravel. "Secondly, why release one of them and why in Swindon, especially? And finally, the most important question, why ask for confirmation that oil has been discovered in Antarctica? Who gains from that?" She was back leaning against the kitchen units. "You haven't found oil, have you?"

Charles looked at her rather sheepishly.

***

With Charles at home, Tony Dewey was at head office, running the show, but perhaps 'keeping the plates spinning' would have been a more accurate description. Fortunately, Andrew, the company PR spokesman, was in fine form while dealing with the bombardment of requests from the world's press. The kidnap was still not public knowledge, but it could only be a matter of hours before someone found out via the hospital or the police. Once revealed, it could bring the complete dinner service crashing to the floor; however, until that happened, Tony was trying to keep the canes gyrating. Even worse, if that were possible, would be the revelation that the kidnappers had wanted the oil discovery confirmed in Antarctica. The media would want the company to confirm if this was true or not, and whether Charles had acted under duress at the AGM. The shares would plummet, and Petronello would become toxic, and thus unable to buy NorCarbon or to enter any other agreements.

He took a callback from a rather unpleasant Scottish drilling agent who ran a company in Norway that had won a lot of work around the world with Petronello. Tony was trying to assess, in a discreet way, whether the Norwegian government, oil companies or environmental activists might be involved. "Mac? How are you? How's Norway?"

"Wet."

"So, have you learnt anything?"

"That if ya took away the sea and the mountains, ya could fit the remaining bits of Norway onta a piece of toilet paper … where it'd not look outta place."

"Anything else?" Tony was prepared to listen to Mac's typical rant against his adopted country because he knew that Mac was very well placed to pick up what was happening.

"The young girls are beautiful until the long, dark winter of their thirtieth year, when they become ugly trolls overnight; the men miss out the first stage."

Tony winced. "So nothing useful?"

"Absolutely nothing. No rumours. Nothing. Personally, I cannae imagine the government or NorCarbon would get involved in dodgy photographs. Can ya imagine the fall out if they were to be exposed? I dinnae mean the photographs. Ha ha. The environmentalists are the most likely culprits because they're the most publicity hungry."

Tony listened to another couple of minutes of gossip and finished the call.

However, the calls were stacking up like planes over Heathrow, so he was straight on to the next.

"Have we got them off the *Antigone* yet?" he asked his head of security, who was somewhere on a rig in the Middle East.

"Yes, and without casualties," a distant voice crackled.

"Well done. Negative publicity is not what we need at the moment."

"They are on the supply ship. Six of this Sangaia group who boarded the rig, that is."

"Where is it taking them?"

"They think Port Stanley, but it is actually on its fortnightly run up to Trinidad with the core samples."

"Did they get on board willingly?"

"They did when Vernon, as rig superintendent, explained that the *Antigone* was a vessel under international maritime law and that they were pirates. He explained their options and made them an offer they couldn't refuse."

"And their ship?"

"It's a rust bucket held together by the brightly coloured paint. It is limping back to the Falklands."

"Do you think that they are involved in the kidnap?"

"I think it is unlikely. They are fanatics who saw a way to get publicity, and then got out of their depth, if you see what I mean? They didn't expect those terrible seas."

"I suppose that they and the kidnappers saw the AGM as the day to launch their separate campaigns?"

"Anything on the photograph?"

"No. That's my next call."

With that, the conversation ended, and Tony looked out over the roofs of London at the real aircraft stacking up over Heathrow.

CHAPTER ELEVEN

She was trying to rub the sticky, amber pine resin from her hands while avoiding the occasional stump or fallen branch. Mike loved coniferous forests, with the stark contrast between the dark interior and the bright edge, and between the canopy and the floor. She was not a lover of grey, of the middle or of the mediocre; she preferred no undergrowth to clutter the view. Not for her the multilayered oak woodland or, God forbid, the confusion of a tropical jungle. She liked to know the limits. The darkness and monotony minimised distraction and helped her to think through a problem. At moments like these, she did not need a million colours or infinite variety. Life was complicated enough – and in her short life, she had learnt that black comes in a hundred shades.

It was 3.00pm, and she had ridden back from the Yelland's house a few hours earlier on a blisteringly hot day, which made an hour's journey riding a motorbike in leathers a bittersweet experience. She had read all of the reports and files, and if she had thought that this kidnap was straightforward, she was now firmly disabused of the idea. Once changed out of her leathers and into loose clothing, she headed off through the trees. She stomped her way across the dull, dry, deadening forest floor, allowing her eyes to accustom themselves to the dark. She was searching for solutions, but nothing seemed to make sense. At the heart of all this, she did not trust Charles and she did not believe the Yellands were the happy family that the world of social media and glossy magazines imagined.

With Charles, it was all about business. That sheepish look he had given her when they were talking about discovering oil made her wonder if they had actually discovered oil and this was in some way a ploy to get the share price up while buying NorCarbon. Perhaps the fake photograph was just someone in the oil business or a major shareholder not wanting this acquisition to happen. All of this, she could readily believe, but kidnapping two girls was a step too far. But then again, there were hundreds of millions of petrodollars involved. She tramped further through the darkness of the coniferous stand and went on musing. If they had discovered oil, who would know? Charles had told her that only he, Jo, Tony Dewey and the rig superintendent (Vernon) would know definitively. He had always gone to extraordinary lengths to conceal any results indicating a discovery, he had said. All core samples from any Petronello drilling rig worldwide were given a code number and sent to a laboratory in Port of Spain, Trinidad, for analysis. No one on the rig would know the details except Vernon, who was loyal and another person who was incredibly well paid. Charles had explained that oil discovery deep underground did not result in a great geyser of black liquid forced up into the sky for all to see. It was not like in some Mickey Mouse cartoon; it was far subtler, involving changes invisible to the naked eye in the chemistry of the rock core samples, which required laboratory analysis. The results were sent anonymously to head office, and then only paired with their location and date by Tony.

The bright, bleached line that was the edge of the forest grew bigger; she was almost home. Why do people kidnap? It is mostly for money, sex, power or for a cause. The current demands for the announcement at the AGM rather ruled out sex. Financial gain; power, as in control of some aspect of the oil business; and a cause, such as environmental activism all remained possible. As she burst out into the sun-drenched glade, the brittle brash of pine branches crackled underfoot. She shaded her eyes while they readjusted. A large, blue-green southern hawker dragonfly quartered the grass between the forest edges, looking for a pond, always turning at right angles and always in straight lines. It ended up where it began. So did Mike Kingdom – with the kidnap.

She tried to quicken her pace, but this was really an exercise in masochism. Ahead was what she now called home – a wooden garage with an attic and rear room to the side of a forester's cottage. It was small but cosy, and she was rarely disturbed. Such a retreat was meant to rebuild her life, yet all it had achieved in thirty months was a reconfiguration of the same peripheral elements; perhaps akin to the rearranging of the deckchairs on the *Titanic*? And like Captain Smith, she was now wary of icebergs. There was also a huge void at the centre of her world. She felt like a partially deflated balloon, which you can squeeze into any shape that you like, but there is still nothing inside. At the young age of thirty-four, what had she been reduced to? A physically wrecked body that was still recovering from the 'accident', an imagination that was uncontainable, an anger that meant she was scared of nothing, and ten years' experience in the Secret Squirrel world of the CIA, five of which were in London working for the Five Eyes Intelligence Unit – an agreement between the USA, UK, Canada, Australia and New Zealand. She had left the Five Eyes two and a half years ago because she needed to heal more than her body. Private investigation was meant to keep her occupied and pay her modest bills.

Her left leg dragged slightly as she climbed the external stairs to her faux log cabin. On entering the relative cool of her attic room, she gave the bare patches and tufts of black hair on her head a good rub. Three polystyrene heads stared blankly at her from a shelf. It was easy to imagine a devil-may-care expression on the one with the red wig or the opportunity for intelligent discussion with the one wearing the black hair and glasses. The mousey brown hair on the third would not trouble the most attentive witness.

***

Tony Dewey was sitting with his arms crossed and deep in thought. On his screen, he was looking at the fifth of a series of eight photographs sent direct to him by Miguel Martinez. They were all beautiful images of the *Advantage* drilling platform off the coast of Mexico, set against a peach sky. Unsurprisingly, none of them were of the *Antigone*, and none had an ice sheet in the distance. They were old pictures, taken perhaps one year previously in the Bay of Campeche off Mexico's east coast. These were genuine photographs of oil exploration in Mexican waters, taken by a Mexican photographer. It was this fifth picture that someone had dressed up by putting a turquoise ice sheet in the distance. All eight had been purchased by a company purporting to be from London and buying on behalf of major newspapers. They had paid the bill, and Miguel had thought nothing else about it. Miraculously, the company, its addresses and website no longer existed or could not be found. The newspaper, which had done nothing wrong, believed that it was buying from Miguel, from whom they had acquired excellent photographs before. Petronello always went to enormous lengths to vent and not flare anything on its exploration rigs. While letting any methane escape unburnt into the atmosphere was more dangerous, the company did not want great flames lighting up the sky; Vernon knew what he was doing, and even with minimal amounts of gas, he had this under control. Satellite coverage would have told their competitors and enemies everything if they had not been careful. After all, Tony used similar coverage of their competitor's sites.

Why? This was the burning question in more ways than one. Why bother tampering with the photograph? Tony thought he knew the answer. This photograph was a coded warning to Charles and to him. Only Petronello would know the rigs had been switched and it should have been the *Antigone*. Only Petronello would know what the implications were of the super-imposed ice sheet – namely that if oil had been discovered 'legally' at sixty degrees south, then the new field extended very considerably into the protected waters of the Antarctic. With or without the kidnap of his niece or the publicity-seeking boarding of the *Antigone*, the fake photograph told Petronello that powerful, wealthy forces were aware of what it were doing and that they were displeased.

He lifted his glasses up onto his forehead, stretched his lips across his teeth and wiped the bristles of his beard upwards with his palm. At moments like these, he felt a great weight on his shoulders. Without him, Petronello would fall to bits. He worked the longest hours, and he was the most efficient and systematic manager of the business. It was galling to watch Charles receive all of the compliments and invitations, when most of the success had been achieved despite his involvement, not because of it. He was not the industry maverick; he was an inconsistent liability. He was a gambler who did not admit to himself that he was gambling. If you put a bet on a horse, it wins, doesn't it? Did Charles now not grasp what forces they may be up against?

And what of Angelica? Although he and his wife, Geraldine, saw their niece only every few weeks, they were probably closer to her than her parents. Maria was aloof, distant and foreign. Her impressive and immaculate mastery of all things English was learnt in Switzerland at a school where the perpetuation of the aristocratic traditions was provided without irony for the seriously nouveau riche or, perhaps, the nouveau seriously riche. This was where the daughters of trophy wives were honed and polished for the next generation of wealthy men; jewels ready to be mounted – a bright, multifaceted, international currency. And the result of this huge investment? Daughters to perpetuate the system. Except that, like gems, all systems are flawed. Angelica had proved to be a rough cut at best, and she refused to go abroad to school. Charles and Maria had sent her to a very good private school in Wiltshire that specialised in bringing out the best in unpromising stock, rather like the army or the priesthood had done in previous centuries for third sons. They could not see Angelica's hidden depths. Charles was so different from his sister Geraldine. He was asocial and introverted, behind a convivial exterior. He was not paternal and did not know what to expect from a daughter, especially an only child. She was a disappointment to him as any child would have been. After all, like all normal children, when she bet on a horse in the Grand National, it lost.

Tony had never quite worked out what made Charles tick. In the way of the new oligarch, he had acquired all of the trappings of the rich, including Maria, but he never seemed to do anything with them. How they had produced a daughter remained a mystery to him. If anything, Charles had used the money to isolate himself further and to distance himself from the world. Probably the loss of his villa in Spain would cause him the most heartbreak (and you did not need to be a billionaire to own one). Maria, by contrast, would miss the money, but as to what she did all day or what made her tick, Tony also had absolutely no idea. She had not even tried that hard to make Angelica go to Switzerland.

He came out of his reverie and typed in a few words to check if there were any responses to the bait he had dangled on the Sangaia website. There were several enquiries from press agencies and the usual blanket junk mail. Spamming had developed into an artform.

Among all of the rubbish, he saw the Sangaia response: "Thank you for your kind offer of further photographs similar to those published in the media yesterday. We are not in the business of buying faked photographs, but thank you for the additional press exposure this will give our cause."

"Bollocks!" Tony exclaimed. "Well, you can't win them all."

Unless your name is Charles Yelland, of course.

***

"What's behind your head, Miles?"

"It's a list of betting odds, Mervyn."

"Let me guess."

"We've had a little sweepstake here on how far you got with that Secretary of State."

"Sophie Beardsmore is a very pleasant lady."

"Yes! Yes!" cried the voice of a gambler who had wagered on more than an introductory handshake.

"Did you get to first base? That's a glaciologist's joke by the way, Mervyn?"

"You lot would bet on which penguin is first to crap."

"Now that's a good idea."

"Brilliant!"

"I must remember that you are stuck in the dark for another two months: 1,000 lonely souls in 5 million square miles of ice."

"That's why we miss you, Mervyn," Miles continued, "We don't have your imagination, your *savoir-faire* ... your way with the ladies."

"She's a very concerned lady," Mervyn explained in all seriousness.

"Tell her to put some yoghurt on it and it should clear up. What did she expect from sleeping with a sheep-shagger like you?"

"I didn't sleep with her!"

"Aw. Rats."

"We have a Zoom meeting later today. Just the two of us."

"I didn't think you had it in you."

"*I didn't think that you had it in her!*" a third voice bellowed off camera.

"Did you tell her about our ice sheet?" Miles asked, trying to get the conversation back on track.

"No, it didn't come up."

"Try rubbing it first!" Miles's sidekicks were in full frustrated flow.

"I will tell her in the Zoom call, I promise."

"Tell her that if she feels the earth move, it's not you, but it's the bloody Weddell Ice Sheet hitting Cornwall,"

***

Ten minutes later, Mervyn was telephoning his mother. His side of the conversation went something like this:

"Beardsmore, Mam; Sophie Beardsmore."

"Yes, she's a very nice person."

"No, she didn't go to Aberthaw Comprehensive."

"No, and that's another Sophie who's about sixty and married to the Earl of Wessex."

"This one's a minister."

"No, Mam, she's not a Baptist."

CHAPTER TWELVE

Charles was halfway down one of the two sweeping staircases that clung to the walls of the echoing atrium at the centre of his house when his phone rang. Why does an important phone call always seem to happen at some perilous spot rather than when one is sitting in a comfortable chair?

"Hello?"

"Mr Yelland? Inspector Bucknall here."

"Hello, Inspector."

"I've got some bad news, I'm afraid."

With the phone in his right hand, Charles grabbed the banister and froze. The terrified eyes of some Spanish princess, captured standing next to a greyhound in an arboretum, stared at him from an oil painting immediately above. He had never noticed the collection of foreground flowers or the turtle doves before. Why notice them now?

"What has ...?" He couldn't finish the sentence.

"Belinda Dredge died an hour ago in Swindon. She never

regained consciousness. Her parents were here with her. I'm very sorry."

"Oh my God. That's awful."

The inspector allowed a few seconds to pass and for the news to sink in. He then continued, "They are doing a post mortem today to discover which drugs were involved. As it's Saturday, I'm hoping there won't be any delay."

"But she was sleeping peacefully when we saw her?" Charles began descending the stairs again and entered the library.

"I know. I'm so sorry."

"Yes, thank you, Inspector, but is there any news of Angelica? We're going frantic here."

"No, sadly not. We are still looking at CCTV footage and following other leads. I assume that the kidnappers have not made further contact?"

"No. They haven't. I will call you the second that they do."

The phone call ended.

Charles moved a coaster around on a side table with his left hand in a distracted way. *So,* he *thought to himself, the strategy of waiting for Belinda to come round has not worked. I need to tell Maria, and then phone Mike Kingdom.*

He walked into a sitting room with pale-green walls and floor-length windows draped in shiny, delicately patterned Chinese fabrics. Maria was sitting on a plush sofa mesmerised by a Mexican soap opera – a genre that had taken self-parody to stultifying levels. Soon, an entire episode would be taken up by one frozen meaningful stare. Charles despised these unreal everyday tales of domestic disharmony punctuated by kidnap and murder.

"Belinda's died," he said.

Maria gripped a cushion and clutched it to her. "*Madre de Dios!*"

This could have been Maria or an actress on screen. Fact seamlessly merged with fiction. Everyone in the room and on the TV looked shocked, with the exception of Charles. Maria stared at him.

"The inspector has just called from Swindon."

"What did he say about Angelica?"

"Nothing. There is no news. No developments. They are checking what drugs Belinda had taken or was given."

"Charles, what next? What do they want?"

"I thought I knew, but now I have no idea."

"What do they want with Angelica?"

"I expect the next demand will make it clear."

"I cannot stand all of this waiting. This not knowing!" She was getting more distraught.

"No, but we are a lot luckier than Belinda's parents. Don't lose hope."

"Should we ring them?"

"Not now. We don't know them. What would we say? What would they say?"

"I need a drink," he said while walking across to a black lacquered cabinet where he poured two whiskies from a decanter.

His wife accepted her glass with the minimum of movement, like an invalid. He took an exaggerated mouthful and swallowed it, partly in pleasure and partly to cause himself some pain.

"Is there really nothing we can do, Charles?"

"We must leave it to the police, but I've appointed a private investigator to explore any other routes behind the scenes. One whom Colin had used a while back."

"When did you do that?" Maria suddenly became animated, as if released from some hypnotic state. She was wondering what else this investigator might find out.

"Very late last night. We had a meeting here early this morning."

"Is he any good?"

"It's a … woman," he almost said 'girl', but avoided it at the last moment.

Maria temporarily put her own indiscretions to the side. "Charles, What do you think will happen to Angelica?"

The two words "SELECT ENDING" had been staring out of the TV screen for the last few minutes, as the soap opera reached its daily climax. If only life imitated art?

***

Sophie Beardsmore had asked Mervyn if she could have a Zoom meeting with him at 6.30pm the day after his evening visit. She was well aware that it was a Saturday, but also knew that she would have a lot more questions as what was now fast becoming a crisis developed. She also did not want any eavesdroppers, although she did not know the reach of the Secret Services or, indeed, anyone else.

"What have you been eating?" she asked on seeing a large, black bowl just behind him on his table.

"Real Welsh food," he confirmed.

"In London?"

"My mam normally picks these up at low tide."

"What are they? Russian sailors looking for a good time?"

"My mam is very choosy. She prefers the older man."

"Long John Silver, then?" Sophie had picked up quickly that they both shared an odd sense of humour.

"Well, they do have one leg and a beard."

"Who?"

"The mussels."

Mervyn had packed the rye bread, seaweed extract, clams and mussels into a bowl as his mother had shown him. It was his weekend treat. He had even bought a bottle of real malt vinegar made using actual barley, not fermented in an industrial plant.

"You haven't asked me what I did today," she commented.

"I'm sorry …"

"No, it was rhetorical. It's just dawned on me that you're the first person I have met in a long time that isn't obsessed with what I do."

"I think that could just be a lack of social skills."

"Is that why you like Antarctica so much?"

"You mean because I don't need social skills there?"

"Sort of."

"It's the opposite, really. It's just that – I'm not going to lie – Antarctica's lush, but you all live on top of each other." His words sounded as incongruous as his relationship with a Secretary of State. "Living there is like being in a bad marriage but staying together for the sake of the kids."

"Are you going back?"

"Given half a chance. You may have noticed I am not a Whitehall person."

"God forbid that any of us are."

"Why did you go into politics, then?"

"Why did you go to Antarctica?"

"I can see why you went into politics: you never answer a question."

After a series of technical and legal questions on the treaty, Sophie asked Mervyn about the outstations.

"Well, at the moment, I have three friends on an outstation out on the ice above the Weddell Sea." He paused. "They are core drilling the ice to help determine how the atmosphere has changed over the last few thousand years."

"Any surprises?" Sophie queried.

"Not in the way we all expected."

She looked at him curiously, enjoying his naïve inquisitiveness and charm.

"When they checked the GPS recently, they noticed it is moving north at quite a rate. Mind you, it's hard to move south down there," he threw in as an aside, "They are monitoring a detached piece of ice bigger than any ever recorded."

"Are they safe?"

"They have to stay marooned for another six weeks, but they're OK."

"What will happen to this detached ice sheet?"

"It rather depends on whether it has completely broken off yet. It might skew around. Otherwise, it will float northwards."

"Is this big enough to flip the Gulf Stream if it melts and cools the ocean?"

"That's exactly what has been bothering me over the last few weeks."

"And I thought I should be bothered about Petronello's antics."

"Have they found out who forged that photograph yet and why?"

"It's all gone a little quiet. I am pressing for answers, which I want by Monday morning."

***

Without the large picture window at one end, Mike Kingdom's attic would have been a bit gloomy. Instead, it brought the light, green forest edge into the room. Her choice in furniture could at best be described as 'eclectic', having been bought mostly from charity shops. In such a relatively cramped space, there wasn't room for much. Through a slatted wooden door at the other end was a toilet and shower room, which looked as if it had started life on a yacht – a very small yacht. It was now 5.30pm, but it was particularly hot. She decided to take a shower as much to cool off as to wash herself. Whether it was the enclosure, the lack of visual distractions or the background patter of the water, she found it a good place to think. Something was bothering her. There was something she had missed. Was it something she hadn't followed up? She gently shampooed her very few random tufts of black hair. If any more fell out, she would just shave her head and have done with it. Her scalp would probably itch less under the wigs. The foam ran down her neck, and she used it to massage her upper body. *No,* she thought to herself, *I have not missed anything. It is something missing.* Even with her mind far away, her subconscious prevented her from rubbing the two long, deep scars that ran from her hip to past her left knee or the deep hole edged by ribbed keloid scar tissue in her left calf. She tried to concentrate on the varnished wooden boards lining the shower. Depending on her line of thinking and her mood, she frequently used the patterns of the grain and the black knotholes in the pine panels to stimulate her. Rorschach would have been proud of her as she reconfigured and reimagined the random shapes into something relevant to her thoughts. Today, she saw a sombrero.

"Maria Yelland," she said out loud, and then threw her head back, letting the jets of water rinse her body.

She pulled her towels from the roe deer antlers on the back of the door, wrapping one around her head and the other around her waist; the latter more to hide her scars than for modesty's sake. She walked out of the bathroom, slumped back into the only armchair, spread her legs and stared at the ceiling. It was Mexico that had been bugging her – not the place but the almost complete absence of it from Maria Yelland's social media. Her whole family was still in Cuernavaca; surely she must contact more than a couple of them on Zoom? Mike grabbed her laptop from the table and called up Maria's accounts again. She could find no wider family, no friends – nothing. Was she not in contact for some reason? Hiding her contacts? Using other means to communicate? Mike instinctively knew that this was important. She called up Maria's most frequently used numbers. Top of the list currently were three with Swindon codes, and none of them was the hospital. Yes! Was she connected to the kidnappers in some way, or was it even a staged kidnap?

She got up, poured herself a glass of water and sat back down, re-establishing some unspoken balance of hydration. It was at moments like these that she appreciated why she had become a private detective, if that's what she was? It was the all-absorbing preoccupation with other people's lives that completely subjugated her own. It was fun when things began to form a pattern as well. If at first you don't succeed, you have probably been looking in the wrong place. She used some energy to chastise herself, as she had been half-aware of this earlier, but she had not followed the thought process through.

Returning her hands to the keyboard, she selected the three most-called telephone numbers on the screen. The top number was to Kattaloggi (Swindon) Limited, the second was Kattaloggi (Swindon) returns department and the third was to its complaints department.

"Damn!"

Did Maria really spend her whole life shopping online?

"Damn! Damn!"

She shook off the towel on her head, rubbed her scalp against the armchair back, stood up and walked to the picture window. A grey squirrel running down a tree alternated between fast forward and freeze frame. It was the sole witness to her semi-nakedness, but it was concentrating more on not revealing the locations of its hoard of winter supplies, now almost depleted.

OK, Mike conceded to herself, *Maria is not in league with the kidnappers and spends a disproportionate part of her life shopping and returning stuff, but the fact that she is either distanced or hiding her communications with Mexico is still a key discovery.*

Turning her back on the sylvan scene, she returned to the laptop and called up the Yelland's marriage certificate. Maria's maiden name was Maria Consuela Arredondo. Using all of her CIA / Five Eyes experience, Mike searched for any internet accounts using these names in various combinations and versions, together with her date of birth. It could have been a long list, but it wasn't. There was just one account under Consuela Arredondo in the local area.

"Password," the site requested.

Mike tapped in "Angelica", and when that failed, she tried "Angelica" with her date of birth. These were the only passwords Maria used for all of her other accounts.

"You are connected."

Bingo. It was as if a starving man had been confronted by a sumptuous buffet. Where to start?

Three email addresses and WhatsApp accounts in Mexico featured prominently, but it was not these that Mike decided to explore first. Instead, a very local address caught her eye: Rod Cameron Specialist Photography. How many 'specialist' photographs could Maria want or need? Of what? Did they involve oil rigs in the southern oceans? Mike grabbed some light clothes from a wardrobe and returned yet again to the laptop. She checked which home address Maria was using, presuming that Maria/Consuela would not use her real one. It would be too high a risk to take, surely? While the computer programme was busy searching, she lifted the red wig from its polystyrene home and placed it onto her head.

"Rod Cameron Specialist Photography – Priory Court, Chalfont St James, Buckinghamshire," she read.

"Now why use that address for your secret internet account?" she said, cocking her head to the side in that familiar, inquisitive way, even though there was no audience, with one side of the red wig dangling like a curtain. "I think that I have found your co-conspirator, Maria Consuela Yelland."

She turned towards the door.

"You have been leading me a merry dance."

Which was true, and Mike Kingdom had just moved two steps forwards and one back.

***

The flashing lights had not completely disappeared, but in the blackness, they could not be avoided.

The headache had gone from being an annoying part of a background dream to the scream of a living nightmare. Her mouth was dry and her tongue was sticking to the roof of her mouth if she didn't constantly swallow. The plastic bottle of water she had been given was empty. The reality of the situation had very slowly dawned on Angelica. Coming down from a drug-fuelled high had made it all the more difficult to differentiate between her hallucinations and the awfulness of her situation. In the almost pitch black, there was little to distract her from the thoughts in her head.

When the bedroom door had opened, the light burned into her, and she could not make out who was standing in the entrance. There had been a woman who had taken her to the toilet. She had barely spoken except to warn Angelica of the consequences of trying to escape or of shouting. They would leave her one arm free if she behaved.

On the one occasion that a man had appeared, she had begged him to explain what was happening and to tell her where Belinda was, but he had been just a silhouette and had closed the door.

However hard she tried, she could not remember anything clearly after someone had made some joke about going on holiday as they had passed the Heathrow junction on the motorway.

CHAPTER THIRTEEN

John Hilton-Verey arrived later, adjusting his cufflinks in a mannered way. His two drinking partners were already at the bar, perched on chrome stools and chatting away to each other. The obese one was called Moss, and he almost engulfed his seat. One expensive shoe barely reached the foot rest, while the other pointed at the ground, dangling at the end of a short, fat leg. He looked like he was pirouetting incongruously about three feet off the floor.

"Justin," he called out to JHV, "You're 'Justin' time to buy a round!" He rotated to slap one podgy hand on the bar top to attract the attention of one of the very many oriental barmen, who appeared to greet his unfocused gaze. "Dry sherry on the rocks, and the same again for Rat Arse and me. Chop chop!"

The East Asian barman reached for the Tio Pepe bottle from a glass shelf at the same time as his thirty reflections. The bar was decorated with long, vertical strips of mirror that ran along the back wall.

"No wonder these Orientals all look the same, eh? It's all smoke and mirrors," Moss declared.

"Moss, you're a xenophobic twat," said the other man.

"Quite so, Rat Arse; I always have been,"

"I would have thought you would have avoided looking in mirrors, Moss?" JHV pulled up a stool.

"Remember, it's seven years' bad luck every time you crack one … and in this bar, that could be a lot of bad luck, Mossy Boy," said the one called Rat Arse, "Does that stool go right up your arse?"

"Don't worry, Rat Arse; it won't stop me talking crap," Moss replied.

"Absolutely no chance of that, Moss … thanks." JHV picked up the tall glass of dry sherry from the bar and reached over to sign the chit offered to him. He took a swig and allowed it to wash away a day of talking in meetings.

The Right Honourable Andrew Sedgwick Moss and Patrick Ratoath were two of JHV's sleepers. Principally, but not exclusively, this meant that they were only in positions of minor power in the Government because they had all gone to the same school and JHV had put them there. And they knew it. Moss put the 'sick' into 'sycophant' and Ratoath put the 'camp' into 'camp follower'. They had been summoned to the bar by JHV because he needed some false information disseminated. These two would be the 'sources close to the Government' quoted anonymously in the daily papers. Nothing could be attributed or even traced back to JHV.

He had chosen the bar purposely because it was noisy. At the far end of the bar, a keyboard player and a saxophonist were providing background jazz. Sounds and images were reflected around the bar in an all-encompassing sensual experience. The bar was called 'Kaleidoscope Eyes' or, more affectionately, 'KY' by its loyal clientele.

"Let's find a table nearer to the music." JHV did not need to issue instructions; anything he said was taken as agreed.

"Why? Which member of the band do you fancy?" Moss enquired.

"I would have thought that they were more your type, Moss." Rat Arse slipped rather too slickly off his stool.

"*Is that saxophonist male or female? I never can tell,*" Moss bellowed, beating the counter again. In his theatrical self-congratulatory laughter, his mouth opened wide causing his several chins to concertina over his tight shirt collar.

JHV's reply was lost in the gentle tone of the saxophone.

"Terrible business, this kidnap." Moss shook his head from side to side, staring at his drink to hide his lack of sincerity. He wasn't being insincere; he just needed someone to tell him what was important.

"Be thankful that you don't have children," Rat Arse added.

"I'm not entirely convinced she's been kidnapped yet." JHV was not going to give too many details away. "It's all a bit too convenient."

"How do you mean?" Moss queried.

They were now over the joking and into the serious reason for meeting.

"Petronello announcing the discovery of oil in a controversial part of the world and the chairman's daughter getting kidnapped?" JHV laid it out for them.

"Did you say 'controversial'?" Rat Arse asked after the saxophone had slipped in a bark among the burrs and rumbles.

"Well, who's ever heard of this Antarctic Treaty, eh?

Suddenly, it's all a big rush because it has to be re-ratified by every country that matters," JHV continued.

"All over a sheet of bloody ice?" Moss tutted and giggled. "Good photograph, don't you think?"

"A sheet of bloody ice over a bloody huge land mass, which is chock-a-block with bloody oil and minerals…" JHV paused while an outbreak of applause crackled around the bar and petered out. "A bloody sheet of ice contested by a dozen important countries including dear old Blighty."

"Bloody dangerous, sheets of ice." Rat Arse was mulling it over.

"Black ice." Moss was back playing word games in the common room.

JHV decided to put an end to the flippancy and lay down what he wanted: "Moss, will you have an indiscreet chat with everyone on your committee, especially the garrulous one who is chummy with our friend in the tabloids? Will you suggest that the US President has already been on to the PM, asking for a cut of the oil from the contested British sector. Harp on about how pissed off the Norwegians are. They contest the sector."

"No problem," Moss agreed.

"Patrick, what day is it? Saturday. Right, I shall be at a diplomatic bash tomorrow lunchtime, and the Norwegian ambassador will be there. Will you suggest to Gerald that he rings the ambassador before then to ask what he thinks about the Americans and Brits divvying up their oil?"

"This has nothing to do with Europe, then?" Patrick smiled knowingly.

"Of course not, we are talking about the South Atlantic." JHV took a final swig, allowing the melting ice cubes into his mouth. He crunched them. "Dangerous thing … ice."

Mike Kingdom was standing in Charles Yelland's loggia, or what had once been a loggia before it was glassed in, staring at a computer screen with him. It was Sunday morning, and had widely been forecast to be the hottest day of the year; the large glass windows were wide open, even at 10.30am. She was wearing a black wig and folding her arms firmly across her body to contain her frustration at Charles's computer skills (or lack thereof).

Eventually, he gave in and said, "OK, you do it," and then stood up.

A few keystrokes later, Inspector Bucknall appeared on the screen. He had a boxer's nose; curly, blond hair; and wasn't wearing a jacket. The background to the Zoom meeting was 'standard-issue office', with pale-grey furniture and the dark-green leaves of a philodendron somehow climbing up onto a noticeboard and a window frame.

"Good morning, Inspector. Any news of Angelica? And how was the autopsy?" Charles sounded like he was feeling obliged to ask about a recent holiday in Corfu.

"No news on Angelica, I'm afraid, and it's taking us some time to go through all of the CCTV footage. We are checking every vehicle that visited Coate Water Country Park or the adjacent Broome Manor Golf Course. That's also public, by the way. Oh, Coate Water is where Belinda was found. As to the autopsy, she had heavily overdosed on psilocybin and Rohypnol, having consumed a lot of alcohol. She also hadn't eaten anything for a long time. There was no evidence of anything violent or … otherwise."

Charles and Mike were considering all this, and had said nothing by the time Inspector Bucknall added, "She was not a regular user, as far as can be ascertained. There were no marks on her arms, and her nasal linings were normal."

"Do you think that the kidnappers forced her to take these … things?" Charles asked.

"We cannot tell. She may have been drunk and took them without much persuasion or deception."

"Otherwise, she had not been interfered with?" Charles could not bring himself to ask any other way.

"No."

"Inspector, my name's Mike; I am a friend of Charles, and he has asked me to listen in. As you can understand, he is a little upset. What was Belinda wearing when she was brought in?"

"Good morning, Mike." He did not miss a beat, but was seriously wondering who this friend was. "She was wearing a thin, black jacket over a long, black cotton shirt and leggings."

"Where exactly was she found in this park?" she continued.

"On a bench not far from the main entrance."

"Lying on the bench or sitting?"

"Lying with her head on her folded jacket. That's why no one immediately thought there was a problem; she looked like she was sleeping. We have found some park visitors who saw her, so we hope to get a more accurate time of when the kidnappers put her there and what vehicle they were driving."

"Did anyone see her awake or sitting up?"

"No."

"What is your best guess at the time when she was taken to the park at the moment?"

"The concerned member of the public rang the hospital at 2.31pm. She may well have been there half an hour before. Anything further I can help you with, Mr Yelland?"

The inspector was not going to allow an unknown woman to cross-examine him, whoever she was, especially on a Sunday morning. Somebody was already leaning on the chief constable, who was already leaning on him. What he would very likely be doing at that precise moment on any other Sunday was playing golf at Broome Manor, not sitting in his office talking about it.

"No, Inspector. Thank you. I will update my wife. Let us know if you identify the kidnappers,"

"One last question, Inspector. Have you found Angelica's phone, and have its various locations been tracked?" Mike wanted to use this conversation to the maximum, as the inspector was unlikely to speak to her again – his eyes were gradually losing any warmth or sympathy.

"No, her phone has not been found. Yes, we have tracked it heading away from London via Reading services. And in answer to your next two questions: yes, we are looking at CCTV footage from the motorway cameras and service station at the time she was there; and, yes, it is clear that a kidnapper had it in his pocket and, probably realising it was still traceable, took out the battery and SIM card and threw them away." Then, to make his point and end the conversation, he added, "No, we haven't dredged the lake. Goodbye to you both. We are working very hard on this."

"Thank you, Inspector. I am sure that you are. You cannot imagine what I'm going through,"

After the call, Charles began to pace up and down, which was not very successful in such a small room. "That wasn't much use, was it? I now know the names of the drugs that killed Belinda and have probably been given to Angelica, but not much else."

"Why don't you go and talk to Maria? You may not have discovered much, but I learnt a lot. Do you mind if I sit here and use your computer?" Mike asked.

"Why not? You use it when you're not here anyway, don't you? OK, I'll leave you to it and go talk to Maria."

The second he was gone, Mike took a small screwdriver from her bag and began undoing the back plate of his computer.

A few minutes later, she was looking at a map of Swindon on the screen. The first thing that struck her was that the hospital was only a few hundred yards along a dual carriageway from the entrance to the park. The hospital, lake, park and golf course were all located right on the edge of Swindon, to the east near the motorway. The second and third things that struck her were the vastness of the area covered by the golf course and the park, and the many access points and lanes that crossed the area. She had been expecting a central, urban, little Victorian park. She sat back up and stretched her aching leg. Her question about the clothing was to rule out that Belinda was wearing Angelica's hot pants, because that might have thrown up some different possibilities. It was always good to cross something off the list. There were usually millions of possibilities and suspects at the beginning, so removing anything was progress. She looked back at the map, which had now been transformed into a satellite image. She decided that there must be one or, probably, two kidnappers in order to get Belinda to that bench. How did they do that without drawing attention to themselves in broad daylight? Was she still walking at that stage, or was she carried overtly or in a bag or on something? The reservoir had an area of fifty-six acres, according to the website, and it took forty-five minutes to walk around. She abandoned this line of thought for a moment.

Mike always hated having to repeat the heavy-lifting work already being done by the police or other agencies. It almost always took her longer than them, and that was assuming she could hack into the necessary sites and could work faster than a dedicated team. The identification of the vehicle used to bring Belinda to the park was a case in point, as was the identification of the owners of any such possible vehicles, their dismissal as suspects or witnesses, and the interviewing of potential eye witnesses. An awful lot of cars would have driven along the roads and lanes, and then entered the car park in the hour before she was found. Trying to match any vehicle at Reading services with ones logged near Coate Water a little later, she would definitely leave to the police, even though this might ultimately give the best results. Was it worth trying to find some CCTV cameras in and around Coate Water or the hospital area and trying to hack into them? She decided to go on to Google Street View and 'drive' around the area. She might spot some cameras and get into the mindset of the kidnappers. Some things might look as though they were connected when, in fact, they were not. Was the park chosen because it was close to the hospital or because it was just off a major dual carriageway, which was itself off Junction 15 of the M4? It was probably both, she surmised. They clearly wanted her kept alive if possible – otherwise, they would have just killed her and disposed of the body, which would have been a much less risky proposition.

Then, there was Belinda's position on the bench. They had placed a folded jacket under her head. Was this to make her comfortable or to make it look more plausible that she was asleep and had folded the jacket herself? This might give the kidnappers a bit more time to escape down Broome Manor

Lane or to the M4 junction and off to, well, just about anywhere, including London or Bristol.

Mike went back to her virtual 'drive' around the area.

CHAPTER FOURTEEN

The PM had been woken at 7.00am, which he considered a lie-in on a Sunday morning. He had been out with his detective, jogging around the Serpentine, a lake that would be boring if it were anywhere other than the middle of London and located, as it is, spitting distance from the balcony on the front of Buckingham Palace – not that this was a regular occurrence. He had returned to Downing Street a sweaty mess. After taking a shower, he sat and ate a crumpet dripping in butter and topped with apricot jam; the run and crumpet together had probably not resulted in a net loss of weight.

After various phone calls, he needed to concentrate on his preparations for the international Climate Really Matters Conference that he was to host on Tuesday in Llandudno. The carbon footprint of each world leader and entourage flying into Liverpool John Lennon Airport and travelling west across North Wales did not bear thinking about. He had done conferences like this so many times over six years that it was no big deal. Normally, for this sort of thing, he would thank someone such as Sir David Attenborough for attending, parrot some figures about carbon emission reduction, and champion the job-creation potential of the emerging new age of green technology. Tuesday's conference had just changed out of all recognition.

***

"Holy shit!" declared the PM.

"I'm sorry," replied the Cabinet Secretary.

"I thought that it was just the US Secretary of State coming, en route to the Luxembourg NATO meeting, and then some Turkey, Kurdistan and Iraq conference in Munich?"

"It was. The President has decided to come as well. All the security planning had been done with Air Force Two, so it was not a big deal to swap it over to Air Force One. It just means that the Secretary of State sleeps in the second-best room." The Cabinet Secretary was drinking coffee in the lounge at Number Eleven, Downing Street, where this meeting was taking place.

"This is like Covid-19," the PM said, "One minute nobody has heard of it or Wuhan or bloody furlough schemes, then suddenly, there is no other subject up for discussion. On Friday morning, I knew nothing about the Antarctica Treaty or oil exploration down there, and now no one in the world appears to be talking about anything else. Do you know how many heads of state, ambassadors, you effing name it, are trying to call me?"

The Cabinet Secretary did know, actually, and was equally concerned by it all. It was Sunday morning for him as well, and he would have much preferred to be somewhere else. There were five of them – the PM, the Cabinet Secretary, Sophie

Beardsmore, Damon (who was the PM's top special adviser) and the Chair of the Intelligence Committee – all sitting drinking coffee in what had begun as a small meeting, but had grown ad hoc into a bigger affair.

"Victor, I agree, but I am struggling to work out what is driving all this?" Sophie Beardsmore was still balancing a raft of possibilities in her head. "Is it geopolitics? Is it any one of China, Russia, Norway, Argentina, the USA and whoever else is reacting now that the spell has been broken? Is this the emperor's new clothes? Are they thinking that this wonderful Antarctica Treaty was a sham and it can, after fifty-odd years, be disposed of, and consequently, that all of the earth's remaining minerals are up for grabs?"

"I am beginning to think you are right. This is about future access to minerals … a bit like the drive – or is it flight? – to get to the moon or Mars. It's more about minerals and, possibly, communications than expanding any empire."

"Everybody's scared shitless because China has sown up most of the world's rare minerals, in all the countries you've never heard of, by offering not-so-soft loans or building some airport or motorway, supposedly as a generous offer of friendship." Damon was as concerned as anyone.

"Reassure me," the PM said, "this is not about preserving the bloody planet or slowing down climate change, but this is about minerals for the next hundred years, and control of communications, power production, technology and the military?"

"And political control of the world," Sophie interjected, "Why do you think that everyone is excited? Do you think the President of the United States of America is flying here at five minutes' notice because he wants to climb Snowdon?"

"But who started all this?" Damon was going back to basics. "Didn't it start with a photograph in one of our newspapers?"

"And a kidnap," the PM added.

"Am I the only one thinking this all aligns too perfectly?" the Cabinet Secretary asked.

"The potential review of the treaty and the need to undermine it? The Petronello AGM? The oil discovery? The fake photograph? The kidnap? Come on, I can accept the occasional coincidence but not this." Sophie shook her mass of mousey hair.

"Me too," the PM agreed, "I think that someone is trying to stir up trouble and, probably, shaft us."

"Are we thinking China, Russia, the USA, someone with a grievance such as Argentina, or some malevolent force such as North Korea?" the Cabinet Secretary enquired.

"I will ask Conrad," the PM said, "I cannot believe that they or the Chinese or the Russians kidnapped the daughter of Petronello's chairman. This is all too traceable?"

"Like Novichok in Salisbury or Covid-19 in Wuhan?" Sophie offered ironically.

"Faking the photograph, I can believe, but the kidnap in addition feels a bit amateur?" The PM had finished his coffee. "May I have another coffee, Mary?" he asked his assistant, who had re-entered the room and was catering for this impromptu meeting.

"And now I understand that it's not just a kidnap, it's a murder," the PM continued, "This is probably going to hit the headlines tomorrow morning. Are we prepared? Do we have a press release yet? What does JHV think?" The questions came thick and fast. "Where is JHV?"

"On the Sunday politics show at the moment, and afterwards, he will be on his way to the Ambassador's Lunch at

Park Lane. He is happy that he can cover everything until the kidnap and murder are public knowledge. The murdered girl's parents have been very good and are saying nothing, mainly on the pretext of giving the police a chance to catch the kidnappers before they kill the Yellands' daughter," Damon explained.

"Back to today's agenda … if we had one," the Cabinet Secretary said, "What do we need to know ASAP before there are any more calls from heads of state, before the conference on Tuesday and before the one-to-ones with the President?"

"What have MI6, MI5, GCHQ and the police found out about the photograph and the kidnap? That would be a good start," the PM wondered, "And what's the general vibe from the embassies around the place?"

"I will get back to you with an update within a couple of hours," the Intelligence Committee Chair confirmed.

"By Tuesday, I need to know a lot more about this bloody treaty." The PM was thinking ahead.

"I know just the man to write you a crib sheet," Sophie offered.

"Do it, please," the PM requested.

"I will sort it."

***

JHV was unfolding one of the neatly rolled, white cotton hand towels from the pyramid before him while checking his reflection in the mirror. The gentlemen's toilets at the Royal Monachorum Hotel in Park Lane were as dimly lit as the Hall of the Mountain King, but with more dark-brown and black marble. He was quietly congratulating himself on his performance earlier on the TV, both in not overplaying the situation in the South Atlantic by leaving so many possibilities open for the media to follow up and also in pursuing his own pro-European agenda in the subtlest of ways.

"John," he heard his name called from somewhere in the back of the cave.

"Arne, how are you?" JHV replied.

The Norwegian ambassador emerged from the gloom into the light near the basins. They both waved at each other perfunctorily in the way that men do when not wishing to shake hands in a toilet.

"I am well," Arne said, and then began to wash his hands while looking in the mirror at his tanned face under his neat, blond hair. His white shirt contrasted sharply with his blue eyes, black bow tie and dinner jacket.

They appeared to be alone, but they could not know if any of the cubicles were occupied. Tacitly, they continued to make small talk until they pushed the heavy, padded door open and made their way out into the corridor, where there was no one to be seen.

"John, it appears I should have my broker buy every American oil share that I can afford, if the rumours are to be believed?"

"Remember, Arne, shares can go down as well as up. I am sure that your broker has warned you of the dangers?"

"Of course, so would you recommend I buy NorCarbon shares, instead? Or perhaps I should buy Petronello?"

"It all comes down to this Antarctic Treaty, in my opinion." JHV stopped walking to maximise their time together without fear of eavesdroppers.

"Norway claims the sector; you know this? My government will not look kindly on the Americans trying to tear up the treaty and endorsing a British claim so they get half of the oil."

"The Chileans and Argentinians might have something to say about this sector as well."

They moved to the side to let a couple walk by.

"So would the Russians and the Chinese ... I hear the Chinese are building another research station in the Australian sector," the ambassador continued.

"Antarctica is becoming a proxy for all the world's tensions ... unless the treaty is re-ratified for another fifty years?"

"There are vociferous teenage girls in Sweden and Norway who would like the treaty re-ratified."

"Balancing being an oil-producing country with leading the world on climate change is going to get more difficult."

"We have wind, solar, geothermal and tidal barrage; we won't need oil," the ambassador explained.

"You appreciate that we need to nip this in the bud, otherwise American support for British oil extraction will align with both Russian interests in being a pain in the arse and with Chinese expansionist plans? The treaty will be torn up whatever Norway thinks."

"Do you have any ideas? Remember, this is in your self-interest?"

"I think your PM needs to be very loud and prominent at the conference on Tuesday in defence of the treaty, and as a short-term measure, I would suggest that Petronello's wings need to be clipped to scupper their takeover of NorCarbon."

"I do not know the word 'scupper', but it sounds nautical, and I think it does not have anything to do with share 'flotation'?" The ambassador smiled, and they turned to join the other diners in the Grand Hall.

***

Mervyn was trying to enjoy his Sunday. He was beginning to find living in a very small and damp basement flat in London very depressing; it was barely bigger than his accommodation on Rothera and a damn sight less interesting. The flat gained little natural light and was tucked around the back of an ugly building with stone steps up to the dustbin area. He was about to attempt a few minutes tidying up and was standing by his front door, trying to open the cupboard in which he kept the hoover and cleaning materials. The two long, frosted-glass panels became dark. The doorbell rang.

Visitors? He knew no one and was in no mood to be sociable. He opened the door to a smiling couple. She had her hair covered by a headscarf and held a leaflet in her hands. He was clean shaven, with hair cut high around his ears, wearing a tired suit and holding a briefcase.

"May we leave you this leaflet? If you've got time, we would love to talk to you about it," she said.

Mervyn reached into the cupboard to his side and pulled out his brush, holding it vertically and gripping it just under the head. They both stepped back.

"May I introduce you," Mervyn began, "to my friend, Jesus?"

They looked at each other, unsure whether to continue.

While they were assessing the situation, Mervyn draped a blue J-cloth over the broom's bristles. "I'm sorry; you probably didn't recognise him without his headdress?"

They managed to maintain their fixed smiles as Mervyn animated the upturned broom.

"Perhaps, we may just leave you the leaflet?" the man in the suit replied.

"What's it about?" Mervyn asked.

"Um … the teachings of Jesus," said the man.

"Did you write this?" Mervyn turned to the broom head. The broom shook its head, causing the blue cloth to flap. Mervyn continued, "He says he didn't write it and it looks like a load of bollocks."

The woman was repeatedly licking her teeth while beginning to fidget. "Does anyone else live here?" she asked.

"Now, what do you think? In a small basement flat like this? There's hardly room for the disciples."

"Perhaps you would like to come to one of our meetings? They're very informal," the man reverted to his usual routine.

"What's the next one about?"

"Um … the Resurrection."

The broom appeared to speak into Mervyn's ear. "'Over his dead body,' he says."

The couple were silent.

"Well … anyway…" mumbled the man. The couple were preparing to go.

"Wait a minute; you don't believe this is Jesus, do you?"

"Jesus moves in mysterious ways," the man said as the woman turned to climb back up the steps.

Mervyn made the broom head move mysteriously. "He says that you're like all of the others. You don't believe he's Jesus."

"No, really."

"He says that you're like Doubting Thomas."

"Of course not."

"He wants you to feel his scars."

Mervyn leant the broom out at an angle towards them.

The man reached gingerly for the handle. "Oh yes, so it is; I'm sorry … *He* is." The man was not a good actor, but he had been taught to engage in any conversation.

Mervyn brought the broom to his ear and waggled it.

"What's he saying now?" the man asked.

"He says, 'Why don't you fuck off and stop wasting people's time?'"

The couple disappeared up the stairs, and Mervyn threw the broom back into the cupboard.

It had felt cathartic and, with his frustration vented, he decided to give Jesus and the hoover a day off. He went back into his little lounge.

***

Five minutes later, his phone rang.

"Mervyn, it's Sophie Beardsmore."

"Oh, hello."

"Mervyn, I know it's Sunday, but I need a big favour urgently." She went on to explain the crib sheet that the PM needed, and what she would like and not like included.

"OK, no problem. You've given me a reason not to clean my flat."

"If we pull this off and get the re-ratification of the treaty to the top of the agenda at the conference, it will be fantastic. I don't want to let everyone around the world get entrenched in positions that they will find it difficult to retreat from. I want everyone to fear losing out to someone else, so that re-ratification is the easy, no-lose option."

"That would be a miracle."

The broom in the cupboard fell against the door.

CHAPTER FIFTEEN

Mike had just finished a Sunday lunch that had unintentionally extended over several hours as she picked at bits and pieces from her fridge while being frequently distracted by different lines of thought. Uppermost in her mind was the complete lack of contact from the kidnappers after their initial demand on Friday morning; a demand that Charles had fulfilled to the letter, almost within the hour. The fundamental problem in any typical kidnap is the exchange or handover. How do you physically get the money without revealing your identity or get caught by the police in the process? But that wasn't a problem here; there was no money. They had got what they asked for, so why not release or kill the girls? It was as black and white as that, wasn't it? She decided that the kidnap was clearly not over; there would be future demands. Why else take Belinda to the park by the hospital, and why else keep Angelica, dead or alive?

A knock on her door made her jump. She did not get

visitors. Hardly anyone knew where she lived, and the forester's garage was at the end of a long, rough track.

She reached for her black wig and put it on her head. Approaching the locked door, she grabbed a baseball bat she kept there as insurance.

"Who is it?" she asked.

"Leonard … Leonard de Vries."

She unlocked the door to be greeted by a large man packed into a crumpled, shiny, dark-grey suit, with his tie loosened and hanging down over a bulging white shirt. Two bloodshot eyes peeked out over his puffy cheeks, and his thinning, ginger hair was smeared onto his scalp. He had a handkerchief in one hand, with one end of it wrapped around a first finger. The exhaustion of climbing the wooden steps on a hot day had taken its toll.

"Michaela, lovely place you've got here." His gentle American drawl made it almost sound genuine.

"What do you want, Leonard?"

"Michaela, are you going to invite me in? I didn't drive out here for a cup of coffee. They have that in London."

"You don't drive anywhere."

"OK, but I wasn't driven out here for the fun of it."

She stepped back, putting the bat against the wall and allowing her visitor to step into the cool of her cabin.

Leonard de Vries was the CIA's head of station at the American Embassy in London; he had been Mike's ultimate boss before she had left after the accident. His main function, however, was as the American representative within Five Eyes, which was also based in London. Mike had been one of the CIA team on Five Eyes for five years, based with her American, Canadian, Australian, New Zealand and British colleagues in a small office block near the flyover in Chiswick. That was before the accident. There was only 'before the accident' and 'after the accident'. She relived it every day and still blamed Leonard for his role in it.

"What do you want, Leonard? You're not here checking up on my health. If you are, you're two years too late." She adopted her default pose of leaning against a kitchen unit, with her arms folded and her legs crossed at the ankle. She was not smiling.

"Actually, I will have that coffee." He smiled, and the corners of his small mouth bent upwards.

"One arsenic or two?" she asked as she turned and switched on the kettle.

"Easy. I'm not here about the past. Let's have a truce for five minutes; after that, you can have a pop at me."

She pulled out two mugs and turned back to face him. "What do you want?" she asked for the third time.

"How's the private investigation line of work going? Topping up the pension?" He instantly regretted mentioning her invalidity pension.

She said nothing and waited for him to say something meaningful.

"That's why I'm here … about your current investigation." She still did not respond, so he continued, "The Yelland case is of interest to us."

"Who's 'us'? CIA or Five Eyes?"

"Both."

"I'm investigating a kidnap; that's all."

"I know. Well, a murder and a kidnap, to be precise."

"What's it got to do with Five Eyes?" As if she couldn't guess.

"Well, our President is getting twitchy about oil supply in the long term and is very interested in getting a big share of any new oil field."

"Even if it means tearing up the Antarctic Treaty?"

"Oil always trumps the environment in the USA; you know that."

"And Five Eyes?"

"Canada is worried about the environmental consequences, but it can afford that stance because it doesn't have any territorial claims in the Antarctic and has oil shales. The UK, Aussies and New Zealanders are very nervous about competing claims to their Antarctic sectors. All five are worried about Chinese territorial expansion and control of minerals. We were getting concerned about Chinese expansion in space, but suddenly, it's closer to home."

"It's just a thick sheet of ice."

"It's a landmass bigger than the USA ... That matters."

"So who has kidnapped the girls?"

"That's where you come in. We don't know. We are guessing, or hoping, that it's something commercial, by which I mean something to do with oil companies or takeovers or, perhaps, personal rivalry. Then, the President can deal with the UK on access to the oil. We are more bothered if it's a government or rogue state behind all this, for obvious reasons."

She poured the boiling water into the cafetière and got the milk from the fridge. "I thought there would've been further demands by now?" she said.

"I agree, but maybe they're just putting pressure on Charles Yelland by holding his daughter. He doesn't need another threat," her visitor suggested.

"But he's told the world that Petronello has found oil down there. What more do they want? The borehole logs?"

"You are assuming he *has* found oil down there. What if he hasn't, but they want him to maintain the lie for whatever commercial or political reason? They would need to keep the pressure on."

"Have you confirmed he has found oil down there?"

"No, but we have people in Port of Spain, Trinidad, about to check out the testing laboratory. Hopefully, that will tell us. Charles Yelland is remarkably tight-lipped in his phone calls and private conversations."

"When I asked him whether he had found oil, he sure looked sheepish."

"If he hasn't, it will be good news all round. Everyone can re-ratify this treaty and go back to interfering in each other's elections."

"Don't the Brits know what he's up to?"

"They seem to have been caught on the hop. Every minister is covering their ass or playing catch-up. The PM is mostly worried about the upcoming conference and any fall out from it."

"You haven't mentioned the environmental groups?" she asked.

"We don't think it's their style. Banners and publicity stunts, yes, but not kidnap and murder. We're monitoring a few of the groups and individuals, but there's been no mention."

"So, how can I help?"

"Actually, I think it's the other way round. What if we were to supply you with certain intel that you might like? Anything, within reason, that the Five Eyes and our friends have access to? You have the confidence of the Yellands, and they're central to all this. We'll give you the usual recompense, but I don't expect that's what motivates you?"

"Recompense? You've been in London too long, Leonard." She pushed a mug towards him. "Who should I liaise with?"

"Me and whoever answers this phone." He took out a card with some telephone numbers and codes on it, and then handed it to her. "This is sort of urgent. The President flies in tomorrow evening for this Climate Really Matters Conference in Wales on Tuesday. He wants it sorted by then, meaning he wants to know who to fire the bullets at. The other four countries are on my back constantly."

"That's your job."

"I wasn't after sympathy. What intel do you need, Michaela?"

He was just about the last person on the planet to call her by her Christian name, but now was not the moment to discuss this, and they were never going to be best buddies.

"OK, deal." There was no shaking of hands, just a pause before she continued, "I was just about to try to find out a few things. Here are three things for starters. One, what do you have on Maria Yelland? Something doesn't hang together there. I can't put my finger on it. Two, the autopsy report. I only heard it from the police inspector, but I wondered if she had been given anything else to keep her quiet? Something the professionals would use. Three, anything on Charles Yelland's chauffeur, Luis, who drove them to Knightsbridge. He was the last to see them alive … oh, and any footage of them once they got out of the car at Harrods. I want to understand how they got from London to Swindon, and why."

"I will ring it through as soon as I leave here. Shout if you need anything." He got up to signal that he was going and crossed the room. At the door, he turned. "I'm really glad it's you the Yellands picked." He sounded sincere but he had sounded sincere two years before.

***

At that moment, Luis was washing the Yelland's Mercedes Maybach S600 outside the garage block on the estate; the car was the ultimate in limousine luxury. The stables were equally top of the range and were located about 65 feet away. The heads of beautiful horses projected from every door, and at the corner of the block was an extensive tack room containing every leather, metal and fabric contrivance relevant to the words 'three-day eventing'. Returning from her dressage practice, Maria was talking to the two joiners who were fitting the new shelves and racks for riding hats and tack. Already fitted at low level were the priapic spikes to take upturned boots, positioned in front of a gentle air-drying system.

She walked outside tossing her black hair in one flowing movement.

Luis barely looked up from his cleaning activities, having finished spraying with a hosepipe. He bent down and gently sponged the side panels.

On her way to a back door, she was under the long pergola festooned in pale-pink roses at the back of the house when her phone rang.

"Hello, Rod." Her short-sleeved top and breeches were already damp, perhaps this call would help her to forget about the kidnap for another five minutes, which had been the whole purpose of the dressage lesson.

"Maria, are you alone?" Rod Cameron asked.

"I will be very soon when I have run upstairs." This was exactly what she needed to distract her. She ditched her footwear in the utility room, pushed through the door and, only wearing her white socks on her feet, she half ran, half

145

skated across the kitchen. After negotiating the hallway and then taking the stairs two at a time, she made it to the landing outside of her bedroom, dressing rooms and bathroom. She entered the bedroom, closed the bedroom door and began undressing; this took longer than desirable, as the short-sleeved top and breeches were tight against her skin even before she went riding, and she had started sweating.

"I'm in my bedroom and undressing," she heard herself say as she juggled the phone while inelegantly peeling off her clothes.

"Maria, I need £100,000," she heard Rod say or thought that she heard him say.

"Why? What's happened?" She slowed the removal of her underwear and tried to concentrate on his words. Not surprisingly, her emotions were running high, and she was low on reserves.

"I need £100,000," he repeated.

"I heard you the first time, but why?"

"Otherwise, I will release the photographs of you and me in the studio on Friday."

"What?" she sat back on her bed in her bra and thong trying to get some fix on reality, "Why?"

"Because you can afford it, that's why." He sounded icily calm and mercenary.

"But we …" She stopped herself as she realised the situation or, rather, misinterpreted the situation. "Have you got Angelica?"

"What?" It was his turn to be thrown. "No, of course not." He knew nothing of the kidnap.

"Rod, I thought …"

"Maria, Charles can afford this out of petty cash. You

146

have my bank account details from when you paid me for that photograph, don't you?"

"Yes, I do." A combination of her daughter being held for over two days, Belinda's death and, now, a blackmailing lover almost pushed her over the edge. She lay back on the bed, holding her phone close to her ear. She began to hyperventilate. Time passed very slowly.

"Rod, you really don't want to do this."

"Sadly for you, I really do."

"Rod, really, really don't do this. You don't know who I am."

"You are Charles Yelland's wife, and that's all I need to know."

She stood up, began to gather her thoughts and started to control her breathing. "If I were you, I would destroy all traces of our liaison and never contact me again. If you don't, it is not Charles you need to worry about; he wouldn't hurt a fly. I will call my family in Mexico, and trust me, they will make sure that you can never take a photograph again."

"And what are they going to do?"

"Trust me, you don't want to find out."

"Pay the money by Wednesday or the photographs get published." He rang off.

***

In a very ordinary-looking white office in a very large, circular building on the outskirts of Cheltenham, a young woman wearing headphones typed a few commands on her keyboard. Within minutes, her superior at GCHQ had listened to Maria's conversation and was transmitting it to London by encrypted link. Half an hour after this, one of the staff at Five Eyes was forwarding it to both Leonard and Mike Kingdom.

"Maria Consuela Arredondo, I have always had my doubts about you. Exactly who are you, and what do you and your family have to hide?" Mike said out loud.

At that moment, a whole raft of biographical data on Maria began to land in Mike Kingdom's inbox like sweets from a smashed papier mâché *piñata*.

CHAPTER SIXTEEN

Sophie Beardsmore had just received Mervyn's crib sheet by email. Yes, it was to her personal email address, but was that a sackable offence? Who cared? She settled down to read it with a cup of Earl Grey and half a packet of Bourbon biscuits. The chocolate overpowered the bergamot taste of the tea, but that was not going to stop her finishing them all. The heat was going out of the day, and early evening sunlight was creeping across her lounge carpet. London, outside her window, was somewhere distant; a low background murmur. She began to read the single A4 page:

Antarctica is the last wilderness on earth. Its landmass is one and a half times the size of the USA at over 5 million square miles; it makes up eleven per cent of the earth's total land surface. Its highest point, Mount Vinson reaches 16,050 feet. The average ice depth over the land is 6,000 feet, reaching a maximum of 15,670 feet. In winter, the ice over the surrounding sea increases by an area of 40,000 square miles a day until the ice over land and sea has doubled in area. The largest winter ice shelf, the Ross Ice Shelf, is the size of France. There are 6 million cubic miles of ice, which if completely melted, would raise sea level worldwide by over 200 feet. It has seventy per cent of the world's freshwater frozen as ice and snow, and ninety per cent of the world's total ice. Climatically, it is classified as a desert and has a surprisingly dry climate. It has an average wind speed of over twenty miles per hour.

The first recorded human to set foot on Antarctica was in 1821. The South Pole was reached in 1911. The population is made up of scientists, and in summer is 4,000, but only 1,000 over winter, due to not being able to leave or be rescued for almost three months.

The Antarctic Treaty began in 1961 and has protected Antarctica without any major problems for seventy years. All claims to the various sectors are suspended, and the Antarctic may only be used for science and conservation. There is to be no military activity. Any activity relating to mineral resources, other than scientific research, is prohibited.

The Madrid Protocol, the last major update, was signed in 1991. There are now fifty-four countries as signatories. The UK, USA and Russia joined in 1961, and China joined in 1983.

The treaty is run by the Secretariat of the Antarctic Treaty. The sixtieth anniversary of the treaty was celebrated in Prague.

The British Antarctic Survey, based in Cambridge, represents the UK's interests; it is part of the Natural Environment Research Council (NERC) based in Swindon, a non-governmental body sponsored by the Department of Business, Energy and Industrial Strategy (BEIS).

There are current suggestions by one or two signatories that the treaty should be reviewed. The vast majority of the signatory countries are wary of any review lest the whole framework falls apart.

Sophie swallowed the last mouthful of tea. Antarctica did not fall under her department, but the biologist in her began to feel ever less comfortable about everything that was happening. She also did not like the fact that, on behalf of the UK, Antarctica was run ultimately via the Department of BEIS. Russell Walker was not her favourite colleague in the Cabinet, and an unpleasant taste began to overpower chocolate and bergamot.

"Why have we heard absolutely nothing from Russell?" she said out loud to no one in particular, "This should be top of his agenda. What is the creep up to or not up to?"

She sent Mervyn's crib sheet to the PM, but not copied to anyone, and turned her thoughts to her own conference speech on UK environmental improvements.

**

Mike Kingdom pulled down the blinds on the picture window. She wasn't concerned that people might see her, rather that she did not like staring at blackness. She was wearing a white dressing gown and holding a Peroni in her left hand. Taking a swig, she walked over to her laptop, where her screensaver had reappeared – her beloved Dylan. She sat down and let her mind wander anywhere in her past. She was feeling strong today.

**

Michaela Anne Svobodová was born to a second generation Czech mother and father on the outskirts of Portland, Oregon, in July 1986. Her parents were musicians, and she was encouraged to be creative from an early age. Her mother, a cellist, played in an orchestra; her father was a saxophonist and played in a jazz band. Discussions over the dining table often centred on the merits of modern versus classical music. Michaela was creative, but not in music; she had an imagination and a talent with numbers and patterns. She was put through university in a CIA-sponsored programme and ended up, at the age of twenty-one, working at the CIA regional office in Seattle. As a desk officer, her reputation grew in the area of internet searching, which evolved as she was taught hacking skills and how to search people's accounts and lives. Mike, as she was now generally known, seemed to know instinctively how and where to look. In 2011, her skills in identifying bank accounts, properties and businesses used for money laundering led to the arrest of a Colombian on the Most Wanted List. Her reputation at age twenty-five was being noticed all the way east to Langley, Virginia.

In 2013, she was transferred to London to work as part of the Five Eyes collaboration under the ultimate control of Leonard de Vries. For almost five years, things went happily or *festoso* as her mother would have said while she practised the jollier pieces by Verdi. She had access to a wide range of high-level sources across the world, which made her job easier and more complicated in equal measure. She continued to track the Colombian drug barons through their networks; in particular, their attempts to launder money through the pharmaceutical industries of Switzerland and large-scale agriculture in Kenya. On one such project in Central America, she had supported a field agent called Dylan Kingdom, a Californian with a laid-back style that hid a ruthless and fearless approach to life. A year later, they were married in Las Vegas and off on honeymoon across Nevada on the back of his Harley Davidson.

***

In her elevated wooden cabin, she sat down at her computer and moved her cursor. The screen saver of Dylan and her on the motorbike was replaced with a list of incoming files from Leonard's staff. She was itching to open a file marked 'Luis Mendoza', but she needed to finish what she had started on the recorded telephone conversation between Rod Cameron and Maria. If he had produced the faked photographs and was blackmailing Maria, he was possibly capable of kidnap and ransom demands as well. Mike began accessing Cameron's files to see if she could find either the supposedly compromising pictures of Maria or the fake oil-rig image used in the newspapers. This was her specialism, and with CIA help, this should not take long. Even better, Rod Cameron was very efficient and organised. She began to hit the keys as if it were a musical keyboard; this always happened when she was on song. When she needed to press the return key, she would turn her hand upside down and run the nail of her right forefinger across the keys to the right, ending with an exaggerated tap, just as if she was playing a piano and ending a *glissando* with a high C. His work files were neatly labelled and subdivided by either subject matter, such as 'Electrical Devices', or client name. All file names included a date. Perfect. She opened 'Electrical Devices' to see how the files were organised at the micro level. She searched the file – it said that 8,000 photographs were in the sub-folders. Eight thousand? Just in 'Electrical Devices'! And there were 700 different subjects or clients.

Mike flopped back in her chair and let out a long sigh. "Right," she said to herself, "let's start with the obvious and, after that, move on to a more lateral approach."

She tapped in "Maria", "Angelica", "Consuela", "Arredondo", "Yelland", "Petronello", "*Antigone*", "*Adventure*" and several other names. Nothing. She tried key words such as "oil" and "Antarctica". Nothing. She tried typing blackmail. Nothing. It was worth a try as people still unbelievably used "password" as their password. She looked in Miscellaneous. Everything was as expected except a subfile called 'Nicéphore Niépce 1826'. Who or what was this? She opened it and bingo! There was a series of stills of three women, including Maria spreadeagled across a bed. She was obviously not the only woman he was blackmailing or had blackmailed. She quickly Googled the subfile name out of interest and discovered that Nicéphore Niépce produced the very first photograph in 1826. Mr Rod Cameron was obviously not your average high-street wedding photographer.

By finding the disgusting files, Mike had helped Maria with one problem, but had it helped to find Angelica? She spent twenty minutes searching for the faked oil-rig photograph, not just in his files but also in his emails and social media. No luck. She did find four stock images of oil rigs, but they were in a folder marked 'School Energy Projects', together with pictures of wind turbines and coal-fired power stations. Perhaps he was not involved in the fake photograph and the kidnap? In the recorded call, he had referred to "the photograph", but this could be an innocent wedding or formal picture that Maria had asked for; possibly the reason they had met in the first place.

She stood up, stretched her left leg and went in search of something to nibble. Not finding anything, she settled on a stick of liquorice; the chewing action would help her to relax and concentrate. She strolled leisurely around her cabin to give her mind a few minutes of light relief. Seventeen seconds later, she was sitting back down in front of her computer.

She checked where else the compromising photographs had been stored and saved their locations. She went into 'Videos' and, with the help of the French photographer's name and the date, found the original sequences taken of the three women. Now what to do? She had a burning desire to delete the lot. Instead, she copied them on to her system, in case they might be needed as evidence, and then deleted them all on his system, but not before replacing them with 'A Message from Nicéphore Niépce'. It said, "I have kept copies. If you ever do this again, I will send them to the police and delete absolutely everything on your hard drive."

There was no time to lose, so her thoughts transferred to Maria. At the end of the phone conversation, Maria had sounded very calm yet threatening. She hadn't cited her marriage to Charles, his connections and his wealth; she had implied that she would contact her Mexican relatives. Mike was used to what Mexican or Colombian or Nicaraguan relatives might mean. She went into Maria's private email accounts and made a note of what turned out to be her older brother's name. While she was there, Mike changed any addresses from Rod Cameron's shop to Maria's home. There was no point leaving any connection between Maria and Rod for anyone to find. They would not be sending each other Christmas cards after what had happened. She looked for Maria's brother on a CIA search engine to which she had been given access. It was no surprise that Maria's father and brother were involved in the narcotics business. Her family may have been aristocratic, stretching back to the conquistadores, but its current wealth had to be being supplemented from somewhere. Was there any connection with the kidnap? Possibly, but unlikely, as from reading a few conversations, her brother seemed to adore his younger sister. Mike stopped this line of enquiry and was preparing to take a look at Luis the chauffeur, plus the complete journey from Buckinghamshire to Knightsbridge and on to where?

***

That same evening, Luis was driving his own old VW Golf along the back lanes of Buckinghamshire. Only the occasional rabbit or suicidal moth was picked out by his headlights. He approached a small village, but he did not need to enter it as he turned off the lane onto a track and then into the driveway of a detached bungalow. Unkempt leylandii hedges surrounded the garden, which comprised nothing more than grass and some concrete imitation-stone tubs filled with last year's dead and rotted geraniums. He got out, pulled his leather driving gloves up so that they fitted his hands snugly and walked up to the front door. He rang the bell and did not have to wait long before the door was answered.

"Rod Cameron?" he asked in a heavy Spanish accent.

"Yes. How may I—"

The three bullets from the silenced gun killed him instantly, and he crumpled backwards. Luis put the gun back in his coat pocket and closed the door quickly. He walked quietly through the rooms in case there was anyone else there, but as expected, it was all clear. He unlocked the kitchen door and peered outside. A security light came on, illuminating a rear garden that looked very similar to the front, except for a large brick patio with a plastic picnic table and two chairs on it. He walked over to a manhole cover that sat at an awkward angle among the neat brick pattern. Using a screwdriver from his left pocket, he lifted the cover. After returning inside, on a small hall rug that had started to collect some blood, he pulled Rod Cameron through the kitchen and out onto the patio. Together with the carpet, he pushed the body into the manhole and replaced the cover. The evening was silent except for some distant traffic noise. He walked back inside, locked the door, turned off the lights and music player, and checked that no blood had seeped onto the hall floor. His job done, he left the house through the kitchen door and returned to his VW Golf. He got in, drove off and slowly retraced his route. Once back in his garage, he took off the false number plates and put the original ones back on. He took the coat, gloves, gun and number plates and hid them in the roof space.

A short while later, sitting in his lounge, he was sipping from a can of beer and watching the news on CNN. He sent a text to his friend in Mexico to say that Manchester United had just won. Any text that mentioned football was immediately passed on to Maria's brother. It meant 'mission accomplished'. It was not the first time that Luis had protected Maria on behalf of her brother.

CHAPTER SEVENTEEN

London on Monday, 29th June began with a glorious display of dark-red cumulus clouds that would put the fear of God into any shepherd. Although the only sheep in the capital that day were being delivered in a lorry, ready to be ceremoniously driven across London Bridge by the Freemen, or else hanging upside down in Smithfield Market. Blissfully unaware of all this, the PM was up early and reading a series of notes and briefing papers while eating two boiled eggs for his breakfast. His diary secretary walked in and pulled up a chair.

"OK, Felicity, let's run through the programme for the next two days."

"After breakfast, you have pencilled in time to check your keynote speech for the conference tomorrow – Penelope will be here soon to write any fresh bits that you require. At 9.00am this morning, a group of ministers and security advisers are coming here to prepare you on the oil discovery in Antarctica and to run through the conference and your pre-meetings. Between 10.00am and 11.00am, you are joining the Commonwealth heads of state who are guests of Her Majesty at Buckingham Palace. At noon, the US President arrives at RAF Northolt airfield in Airforce One. As it's very short notice, there is no ceremony, and he is being met by Admiral Price and immediately flying in Marine One to Chequers, where you will greet him. You will have arrived at Chequers at noon. You have one and a half hours with him over lunch, and he is staying overnight at some American software billionaire's estate and golf course in Scotland."

"What?"

"Well, it's southern Scotland." As if this made it all logical.

"Have they got any grasp of geography?" the PM said, but he was reminded that his knowledge of Antarctica a couple of days previously had left a lot to be desired.

"At 4.00pm, you fly up to the conference hotel. At 6.00pm, you host the pre-conference dinner. No speech from you. The Bishop of Bangor will say grace. JHV has found a comedian who will stick to the script while entertaining the guests."

"What time do we start on Tuesday?"

"You have breakfast with the main ecological groups at 8.30am. JHV has managed to get his mate off the BBC – the one who presents *The UK, Naturally*, I think it's called – to join you."

"You're not big on rural affairs, are you, Felicity?"

"I've only been outside the M25 six times and two of those were to Essex, which isn't rural, is it? And the other four times were to Spain. I'm a city girl."

"The conference starts at 10.00am. Sophie Beardsmore is doing the opening speech. JHV thinks that she gives off the right sort of image; well, he said smell, but you know what he means. The US President now speaks at 3.00pm, after lunch, and your keynote speech is at 4.00pm."

"Excellent. When's the fun bit?"

"Um, well, you get two helicopter rides."

The PM enjoyed the blend of innocence and confidence that a modern, urban millennial brought to his increasingly stuffy existence.

"OK, thanks, I am off upstairs to feed the cat and say hi to the kids."

***

The Zoom meeting was all set up. Charles had resisted at first, but Mike had made it clear there was only one way this would happen and Charles was not to be involved. "You will only put pressure on everyone by taking part. I want people to tell me the truth. We don't have time for fooling around."

"You'll let me know if you discover anything though, won't you?" he had asked.

"I'll let me know anything that you can't use or mess up before I have already used it to, hopefully, find Angelica."

"Thank you," and before he could stop himself, he finished with, "Mike." Trying to regain some composure and/or hide his embarrassment, he went on, "I am not used to people telling me what to do; you can understand that, I hope? I normally trust myself to get things right."

"Charles, thank you, and I also get things right; the one time I got things wrong will not be repeated, trust me." The look in her eyes brooked no further response.

***

The three-way video conference call between Mike, Maria and Luis began with the usual adjusting of seats, un-muting and unnecessary introductions.

"Hello, Maria, and this must be Luis? *Mucho gusto*," she said, using the Spanish of the Americas, not the usual European Spanish introduction.

"*Hola*, hello," Maria answered, with Luis sitting alongside the wife of his so-called 'employer', tight-lipped as if caught in a spotlight.

Mike was wearing her black wig, which was her choice when she didn't want to frighten the horses or look like she had just taken up crochet. "May I say that this call is so I can understand what happened to Angelica and Belinda from the moment they left your house until they ended up wherever. Luis, please, please tell me the truth; it will go no further. I have one aim, which is to get Angelica back safely. Maria and Charles would want you to tell me the truth, whatever it is."

"Luis will tell you the truth," Maria confirmed, blinking at Luis as if this settled any legal obligations.

"OK," Mike began, "Luis, please tell me everything that happened, including all the small details and odd things, from when you left the house with Angelica."

Maria looked sideways at Luis, and he began speaking in good English with a heavy Mexican accent. "I drove Angelica to her friend's house as, you know, I did many times. Belinda got into the car, and they were laughing in the back." He paused. "They ... asked me not to drive to Knightsbridge."

"Luis, it is fine. Just say what you did, when and what happened. Tell me where you went. Help me find her." Mike was at her most encouraging.

"They said that they did not want shopping. They want to meet friends. They ask me to drive them to Chiswick." He pronounced it 'Chis-wick'.

Chiswick? Mike wondered why the Gods were playing with her. *He is about to say that he dropped them outside of the clandestine headquarters of five international security agencies where I worked for five years, isn't he?* She held this thought for that millisecond when reality fails dismally to play ball with some parallel universe.

"It was Wellesley Road, Gunnersbury ... not far from the Tube."

"I know the area," Mike said, feeling the weight of the memories of dozens of pub lunches and picnics on the grass.

Luis was clearly struggling to balance a mixture of loyalties. "They were meeting the boyfriend of Belinda, I think."

"Luis, tell us, please." Maria had been holding back, trying not to interrupt the flow.

"I don't know; honestly, I jus' heard Belinda speak about Harvey, her boyfriend. I took them there twice before," he explained.

"Did you see or meet Harvey?" Mike asked.

"No, sorry; I never met him."

"Did you drop them at a specific house? Did you see them go into a house? Or walk off in any direction?"

"No, not a house; it's next to a bar, but they don't go in. They jus' stand there until I'm gone."

"Did you arrange a time to pick them up?"

"Yes, we agreed 4.00pm at the same place in Chiswick, but I got a text saying they would come home themselves."

"May I see it?" Mike enquired, because she wanted to know the exact words and exact time.

Luis fiddled with his phone and started scrolling. "Here," he said and read it out: "'No need for pick up today, thx A'."

"When was that sent?"

"At 9.17am."

"That's immediately after you dropped them off, isn't it?"

"I dropped them at about 8.30am."

"Is that how Angelica normally signs her texts? 'Thx A'?" Mike was keen to see if it was the kidnappers who had sent it.

"Yes."

Mike decided to change tack, like all good criminal barristers. "Maria, how long has Luis worked for you?"

"Four years, I think," Maria stated, glancing at Luis.

"Did you find Luis from an agency?" Mike was giving Maria no time to think, while watching Luis's face.

"Well, I ... he knew my brother."

"Oh, that's excellent. There is no better reference than one from close family," replied Mike, keeping it as banal as possible.

Mike had heard all that she needed to know, so she decided it was time to bring the conversation to a close. Before finishing the call, Mike wanted to let Maria know that she had removed the blackmail threat. She chose to say it cryptically to exclude Luis from understanding anything: "Maria, before we end this call, I just want to say that I have a little good news for you. I have dealt with Rod Cameron. You will not hear from him again, I think."

Luis did not miss a beat, and his face stayed impassive and neutral, even though he was the only person on earth who knew this to be unquestionably true.

***

Let's think this through slowly, Mike thought to herself after the call, *I have money coming out of my ears, and I live near London, so let me ask my older brother in Mexico to recommend a chauffeur to drive a £250,000 car.* Mike decided that Luis must be more than a chauffeur, but did Charles know that?

She checked the thin report on Luis that had become available through Leonard. Luis had been in London for nine years, and there was nothing of even mild interest – not even a speeding offence to his name. She had come across his type so many times before in her early dealings with central American drug families. He was probably paid by Maria's brother to protect his younger sister and defend the family's interests. There was probably some historic obligation that meant Luis would die rather than let Maria or, presumably, Angelica be inconvenienced in any way. Luis was paid to stick close to Maria, so now he was torn, as there was little he could do to help Angelica fifty miles away, or wherever she was.

***

Sophie was listening to Russell Walker explaining to the PM why he did not need to worry about oil exploration in the South Atlantic, because the whole world was moving away from fossil fuels and extraction down there would be prohibitively expensive. It was 9.15am, and she was counting again – this was never a good sign. She must be stressed. It had started with the number of portraits on the stairs going up in Number Ten, and now it was the number of times that Russell said the word 'carbon': reducing carbon footprints, carbon credits, carbon neutral, carbon capture, activated carbon, etc. She began to lose count. How had this happened? How had Russell Walker ended up in charge of the energy portfolio and what happens in Antarctica? Had anyone envisaged when the Department of BEIS was formed in July 2014 that oil and Antarctica would become centre stage and fall under one minister? The Department of BEIS had grown from the Department for Business, Innovation and Skills, which had merged with the Department of Energy and Climate Change. When Russell had slipped into the post, it had all gone relatively unnoticed. Sophie heard the word 'carbon' again, but she had moved on. Why wasn't Russell speaking at the conference tomorrow? Why just the PM and her? Too many questions were floating around in her mind.

"It's a presentational thing," she heard JHV say, but then his take on everything appeared to be about the package over the content. "We have set this whole conference up on the basis that climate change really matters and that the UK and Europe are leading the new Green Revolution. We must keep the speakers and delegates away from harping on about fossil fuels. We must not get derailed."

"That's all well and good, but the subject on everyone's lips is oil in Antarctica," the PM replied, "We also cannot tell the President what to say, although I'll have a good go over lunch in a couple of hours. Have we had confirmation that Petronello has found oil? If not, we can put off this issue for a while and get back to the programme JHV has just outlined."

"No, the company is sticking to its story that it has found oil," someone at the back said.

"Have they found the chairman's daughter yet?"

"No, and there's not been much progress finding her."

"If this hits the media during the conference, then we are

up Shit Creek without a canoe let alone a paddle." The PM was clearly nervous.

"The President will know about the kidnap because Five Eyes is on the case," another voice from the back joined in.

"How does Five Eyes … I mean, why do its operatives know?" the PM asked, "Are MI5 or MI6 involved?"

"Everyone's involved now: GCHQ, MI5, MI6, Special Branch, you name it. Don't forget that Leonard, who heads Five Eyes, is American and advises the President."

"Something else to discuss with Conrad," the PM made a note to himself. "Has everyone seen Sophie's crib sheet on Antarctica?" he continued absent-mindedly, "You should all read it before the conference."

Sophie blushed slightly, and the PM looked across at her, remembering too late that the crib sheet was for him only. JHV, Russell and a few others picked up on the indiscretion.

"Love to see it," Russell said, while thinking that it should have been his staff who wrote it. In fact, it was a member of his staff who had written it.

"How are we doing on security, demonstrations , terrorist threats …?" The PM moved on as quickly as possible.

"So far, so good. Four separate individuals on the Terrorist List are being interviewed at the moment, as a precaution. There have been no direct mentions. The planned demonstration will be contained along the long promenade, away from the hall entrance. There is a no-fly exclusion zone, and the bay is off limits to the public, commercial shipping, etc. for two days. Access up the Great Orme has been stopped, and Special Forces are checking it out as the only local high ground."

"Good. Anything else? I must get across to Buckingham Palace."

"Only a small political matter, now resolved. The First Minister is welcoming everyone to Wales and kicking things off. Sophie is doing the closing speech."

"Whatever." The PM was already standing and mentally preparing what he would say to the heads of state and ambassadors he was about to meet with the Queen.

CHAPTER EIGHTEEN

The screen flashed, and Mike heard a familiar voice.

"Good morning, Michaela."

"Leonard," she said in a flat voice.

"Have you made any progress, because I've got the President arriving in a couple of hours? He is expecting an update when they wake him somewhere over Ireland."

She pulled on her red wig and turned on her camera; it was definitely a red-wig day.

"That's better," he noted, referring to the fact that he could now see her, as opposed to commenting on her choice of wig.

She wondered where he was on a Sunday morning, wearing a jacket and tie just in case the US President saw him. "Is that background really your office?"

He turned it off temporarily, so she could see he was in the lounge of some London Victorian house, presumably at home. "And I'm still in my pyjama bottoms, if you're interested."

"I'm not, and you'd better hope that they don't play 'The Star-Spangled Banner' and you have to stand up and salute."

"Where have you got to, Michaela?" He had only a few seconds available for the social niceties.

She, for her part, gave him the short, sharp bullet-point version: "That photographer, Cameron, was blackmailing Maria Yelland, but not about oil, and I can't find the fake photograph on his system. We can eliminate him, I think. Maria's family is basically part of an old-time Mexican drug cartel. She was packed off to Switzerland by her father to rub the rough edges off. Her brother, Carlos, now runs the show, and he put Luis Mendoza in as her chauffeur to look after her. I don't think that Charles Yelland noticed what was happening and probably went along with having a Mexican chauffeur to keep Maria happy. I've noticed that she plays the homesick card a lot. Luis seems a bit quiet, but I think that, deep down, he is a tough cookie. He dropped Angelica and Belinda off in Chiswick at 8.30am, instead of taking them to Central London to go shopping. They had asked him to do this before. He thinks that they were meeting Belinda's boyfriend Harvey, but Luis has never seen him."

Leonard was used to Mike and her 'cut to the chase' reports. If only every other one of his directors and agents could analyse and present the situation so concisely. "Chiswick? Of all the ... I'm about five minutes away right now."

"I think that they might often meet in Chiswick; perhaps Harvey lives there or it's just handy for the motorway? Afterwards, all three may well have driven down the M4 towards Bristol."

"What do we know about this Harvey?"

"Zilch. Not even a surname. I'm guessing he must be old enough to drive, but he could be sixteen and kidnapped with the girls or a fifty -year-old pervert they met on line; anything is possible. Can your guys find his details from Belinda's phone and get back to me? While you're at it, can someone check any CCTV footage from Wellesley Road at 8.30am near a bar? From memory, I believe there is only one along there. Perhaps somebody could call in at the bar and ask? We might get lucky."

"OK, will do. Nothing on the oil in Antarctica? That's what I need to know, pronto."

"No, Charles keeps saying they have found it and were going to hold off revealing the fact for commercial reasons, but I'm not sure. Any news from the lab in Port of Spain?"

"No, but a team is paying a quiet visit about now. Yes…" He paused. "Right about now … It's 3.00am there, I think."

"Anything from the Swindon police or any police?"

"Not that I've seen. My guys tell me that the police have gotten nothing from the witnesses in the park and have not found many cars that were both at the motorway gas station and near the park … and those that they did match up are all local people."

"Shit, I thought that following the car journey was a great opportunity to find her." She paused. "Get me Harvey's details and any CCTV stuff ASAP. If we find Angelica, we solve this, I know." The latter was more to reassure herself than a considered opinion.

"Michaela, you getting the same weird vibes as me?"

She hated agreeing with him, but he was right. He had been in the business too long. "Yes," she conceded the minimum. "Leonard, does this have more to do with the conference than the Petronello AGM?"

"The same thoughts are going through my head."

"You are older than me," she added purely to feel better, "When was the last time a US President jumped on Air Force One at a day's notice and flew to the UK?"

"Never to my knowledge. Not in my time, anyway."

Mike imagined a sixteen-year-old girl – whom she had never met – in lemon-yellow hot pants, going off shopping with her girlfriend one June morning, and she was having enormous trouble equating this in any way with geopolitics, environmental activism, oil exploration, commercial takeovers, blackmail and kidnap. It brought her back to a personal level and to the difficult episodes in her own life. "Leonard, I will never forgive you."

"I know what you are thinking about and … it's OK. If I apologise, will it change anything? May we have a truce while we sort out this … problem? You and I? There is no better team on earth."

"I'm doing this for my client and … me."

"And I've forgotten why I am doing it, but it has a lot to do with a man about to eat overcooked scrambled eggs and greasy hash browns at 30,000 feet."

"Get me the information and we will sort it out." She used the word 'we' and instantly regretted it.

He knew that, despite the billions of dollars that the CIA and State Department spent, it always came down to a handful of people in the right (or wrong) place at the right time. "Until the next time," he said.

"Regrettably, yes."

The call ended. She had tried to keep her calm, but Leonard's face was enough to put her blood pressure up beyond recommended limits. However, his call had emphasised to each of them that they, and their lords and masters, needed the two of them to cooperate. She slumped back into her chair and leant backwards. The sweet smell of waffles and maple syrup was still hanging in the air from breakfast hours ago. Her senses were not just heightened but were actually engaged. She closed her eyes through some sort of sensual overload. A red admiral butterfly, embarrassed to be part of the discussion, was trying to reach the forest via the picture window. The frenzied flapping was not helping Mike to relax. She took a deep breath and opened the high-level window to let the butterfly escape.

***

The PM had left Buckingham Palace through the front gates in a cavalcade of three vehicles. This means of transport, an armoured Jaguar sandwiched between two Range Rovers, had increasingly begun to worry the PM; the first time when he had sought the sovereign's permission to form a government, the drive out of the palace had seemed like a dream, but several times thereafter, it had merely confirmed the high level of office he had reached and the level of risk he represented every time he travelled. He wasn't being driven far in convoy today, and at the end of the Mall, the cars turned into Horse Guards Parade and pulled up on the vast expanse of yellow gravel; the helicopter was already waiting where, every year, over a thousand soldiers perform the Trooping of the Colour.

He got out of the car and climbed aboard the helicopter. There were four of them on it, but even wearing headphones, it was not worth trying to discuss matters of any great importance. The flight was only just over twenty-five minutes.

***

He walked into the cool of Chequers, the red brick, sixteenth-century manor house near Wendover in Buckinghamshire, nestling at the foot of the Chiltern Hills, north-west of London. This quiet escape has been the country home of the serving PM since 1921. The airfield at RAF Northolt was thirty miles away, and the President would be landing very soon. He continued on through the house.

"I need a gin and tonic," he declared as he walked into the main drawing room.

No one else accepted his implied offer as he opened his palm and scanned the assembled faces.

"The President lands in about fifteen minutes. After that he should be here in about an hour."

"I'm starving, but had better wait 'til he gets here. Actually, if you've got any olives?" the PM asked the waiter who was just about to leave to get the drink.

The PM walked over to a tall wingback chair and sat down with a resigned thump. "Anything new?"

"The President has been pestering Five Eyes for an update on whether oil has been found or not. He was told that the company is still taking the same position that it has found oil and that the kidnap is not public knowledge and is, as yet, unresolved," began the Chair of the Security Committee, "Back in Washington, DC, the Secretary of State has been sounding out, below the radar, our friendlier allies about what they think of the Antarctic Treaty. The clamour for a serious review is growing, and I think we know where that will end up: a free-for-all down there, leading to environmental, financial, political and military carnage."

The PM turned to the small table next to him as if subconsciously looking for his drink that hadn't arrived yet. "You are right."

"The environmental protesters are beginning to gather in Llandudno," the Chair continued, "There are now thousands, and that number is being supplemented by rent-a-mob; I think it might get a bit rowdy. We are shipping more police in from Liverpool and Manchester."

"Oh, great."

"You have breakfast with some of the serious ones tomorrow morning."

"Whose bright idea was that?"

"It is much better to keep your friends close and your enemies closer," JHV offered without admitting it was his idea, "One good press release from that breakfast and a photograph of you with Astrid Jacobsen will go some way to offset the pictures of the great unwashed with their faces painted green."

"Who would have thought that it would take a couple of teenage Scandinavians to act as a lightning board for the entire environmental movement worldwide?"

"I bet that you wouldn't mind their popularity figures?"

"Right. What is he going to ask me over lunch and what do I need to say to him? "

***

"Conrad, welcome to my humble home," greeted the PM.

"I'm pleased to be here, Victor. I've never been to Chequers. Is this what they call shabby chic?" the President asked.

"If it is, then it is the original version."

"I don't use Camp David much, though it's only sixty miles from the White House. It's too quiet, and Frederick County, Maryland, is full of trees."

The PM realised that he might have an uphill struggle on the subject of the environment and climate change. They sat down together near a tall bay window. Perhaps a bucolic view of the quintessential British countryside might set the scene? But then again, maybe not.

The President was wearing a light-grey, knitted top with a zip up the front, what Victor's father used to call a 'jerkin', and black trousers. Victor was wearing a neat, dark-grey wool suit and no tie. One was in what he would call 'sneakers', and the other in brogues.

"Still no news on that kidnap? Is it public knowledge yet?" Conrad asked.

"No and no, but it will undoubtedly get out into the public domain soon. Probably just as the conference starts," responded the PM.

"I don't trust this Brit who's the oil-company boss."

"No, me either, but it's a bit hard to imagine your only daughter being kidnapped."

"True. That's nasty. Have you gotten sight of my speech yet?" He moved on at lightning pace.

"No, not yet."

"It should be with your people now. I finalised it on the plane."

"Conrad, we should agree a position on the Antarctic Treaty, don't you think? If we don't, the whole thing will disintegrate before our eyes when it will be too late to put it back together again."

"You sure it's not too late already?"

"I don't think so. If we let it go, it is the Russians and Chinese who will move in and – apart from the inevitable environmental disasters – extract the minerals, and use it for military bases and God knows what."

"That's the downside. The upside is that America gets access to those minerals too."

"What if we agreed to let you have half of any oil and any other minerals that we find north of this sixty degree line, which is outside of the treaty area?"

"We discussed this briefly; can you deliver that?"

"All oil and gas under the sea in British territorial waters belongs to us. Oil companies get licences to explore and/or produce it. We issue those licences, and the agreements say what we want them to say."

"It's shitty that we don't know for sure about this discovery. If there's no oil, we have nothing to fight over and can leave the damn treaty intact. If there is oil, then we could do some deal and leave it in place. I understand Five Eyes is working flat out on this? I'm surprised they haven't got to the bottom of it yet. I've just given Leonard, our guy, a big kick up the ass."

"I'll do the same to our people once we've had lunch."

***

"Leonard?" Mike clicked the green icon.

"You're probably getting sick of me. Don't answer that. I've got some good news and some bad news."

Mike adjusted her screen and pulled herself nearer. "Give me the good news first, and if I want, I can put my fingers in my ears before you give me the bad news."

"The team got into the lab last night and managed to copy their hard drives and the usual stuff. They also left some devices so that we can hear anything new."

There was a silence before Mike responded, "That's it? What's the good news?"

"That is the good news."

"Jeez, you haven't set a very high bar for the bad news. What is it?"

"It's all coded. Every sample is coded. It's going to take time to work out which of these core samples are from down south."

"Oh great."

"I don't suppose you could somehow get the codes from Charles or the Petronello computer system, could you? We can do it, but it might take a few days."

"Let me think about it. By the way, you short changed me on the good news, as usual."

"OK, I'll give you some more good news. I just got a bollocking from the President."

"That's better."

CHAPTER NINETEEN

Ten minutes later, Leonard was back on Mike's screen.

"Can't you just send me a text like everyone else? They're all the rage, you know?" He was disturbing her while she was trying to search through Charles's computer using the device she had installed on her second visit.

"Is this like Tinder?" he asked.

"If I could swipe left, trust me I would. What is bothering you?"

"There is no Harvey on Belinda's, Angelica's or Maria's phone history or directory."

It looked as if Mike's screen had frozen, but it was just her digesting the news. "Really? Your guys checked everywhere?"

"They're still checking, Michaela, but surely, your boyfriend is in your damn phone?" He instantly regretted mentioning 'boyfriends' and 'Michaela' in the same sentence.

"Luis wouldn't lie to me. He was sitting next to Maria, and they know the first thing we are going to do is search for

Harvey. Luis volunteered the name; I didn't ask for it. They cannot be in cahoots, can they? No, I don't believe it. She's Mexican, he's Mexican, her family is Mexican, the oil rig is in Mexico, the photographer is Mexican ... no, surely not?" She was arguing with herself.

"Let me know if you crack or discover the oil borehole core codes. I've gotta deal with the security up in Llandudno, where we may have a big demonstration and the President needs to be shielded. Bye."

Mike stood up and began her usual pacing up and down. This was not a typical investigation. After identifying the issues and suspects, one would normally expect to eliminate possibilities until, eventually, you get closer to the name of a perpetrator or perpetrators, but here, the branches of the investigation just kept bifurcating and bifurcating, without anything getting resolved. It was barely midday on the Monday seventy-two hours after the kidnap, and she was feeling further from the truth than she had felt throughout.

She took off her wig, which wasn't helping, and scratched her scalp; a few more hairs came out, and she flicked them disgustedly off her fingers. Pulling up one leg of her trousers, she pressed her thumb into the hole in her left calf. "Not everybody can do that," she said out loud to anyone who might hear – this consisted of three polystyrene heads wearing wigs of black, red and brown.

It was lunchtime, but other pressing matters prevented the preparation of food. Charles's computer was too inviting, and the need to find the borehole codes was too critical in the search for Angelica. Mike had a gut feeling that, despite her father's pessimism, Angelica was still alive. She sat down and began again to search Charles's emails and all types of written communications with Tony. There were fewer than she expected, but of course, they were often only sitting a few yards apart in their twelfth-floor offices in Victoria. She found a short email conversation between them on the results of some borehole logs in a sector of the sea off Trinidad's south-west coast, between it and Venezuela. Each ten-foot core of rock was packed in a long wooden box and given, not surprisingly, a very long code that identified – in plain language and numbers – the time, date, and depth of the top and bottom of the sample below the sea bed. Only the first two letters of the code appeared to reveal the source of the material, and these looked like random pairs of the same letters. Knowing that these samples were from Trinidad she considered the two letters 'PP' that preceded every core. She added letters, subtracted letters, worked backwards from words and phrases such as 'Trinidad', 'Port of Spain' and 'Tobago', and got absolutely nowhere. Other results for Petronello began with 'NN' and 'KK'. She guessed it was Tony who had set up this system, and he had not created one that could easily be cracked. Were they random letters, such that no amount of lateral thinking could crack the code? Even if this were true, you would need all of these random two-letter codes written down somewhere. On paper rather than on the computer system? Did Tony and Charles have a book? Vernon would need it as well because he put the codes on the boxes to be sent up to the lab every two weeks. Looking for these books was a complete waste of time.

It was at times like this that she wished she had a pet, something demanding a few seconds' attention and providing distraction. This thought itself generally only lasted a few seconds, as she remembered the last time she had something to love that had been taken away from her. She also did not need to worry about feeding and exercising the damn thing while she was off on the other side of the country on a stakeout. The thought of food reminded her that she usually failed dismally to shop for herself, without having the added pressure of providing for others. Her diet, as it was, consisted of dry goods that could be brought to life by boiling in water.

Thinking about a pet had the same effect as actually having one: it broke her line of thought, and she came back to the problem from a new perspective. Charles had told her that the core samples were sent by the supply ship on its fortnightly round trip to Port of Spain. She looked in the emails for any mention of mundane things such as the food-supply requirements for the *Antigone* or the return of empty core boxes, and she established the dates over the last two months when the ship had arrived in Trinidad. She then looked for blocks of test results following this rhythm, but a day or two later. It took her twenty minutes to hone this technique and to double- and triple-cross-check the number of samples against the dates. Everything on her list began with the two letters 'XX', and after more checking, she deduced that many hundred South Atlantic samples started with this same pair of letters. She felt a wave of exhilaration. Now she went back through all of the results from samples starting with 'XX' for two months. Under the column marked "Hydrocarbons", they all said "NEGATIVE". Petronello had not found oil in the South Atlantic. The key to this whole nightmare was as simple as 'XX'.

She walked to the tall window and stared at the dark-green foliage of the pine trees, contrasted with the flaking, rusty-red trunks, but without focusing on any of it. What did this mean? She walked to a sideboard, opened a drawer and took out a packet of cigarettes. When she was calmly inhaling the first mouthful of smoke, she weighed it all up and began listing her thoughts: *Charles is conning the City and the investors. He has probably convinced Tony to go along with it. Vernon and Jo are being paid very adequately to keep quiet. The share price will rise, and he will buy NorCarbon. Unsurprisingly in due course, the discovery in the South Atlantic will gradually prove to be uneconomical, but by then, it will be too late.*

She was reasonably certain of these conclusions, so she now moved on to speculation: *Is he involved in the faked photograph? It would hike the share price up immediately and could be conveniently denied as a forgery later. Did they purposely make the fake look amateur to give credibility to this?* Then, she moved on to the kidnap: *Surely, he is not involved? I cannot believe it, unless he is the best actor on earth. And to sanction the murder of Belinda? No, no way. In which case, this has come in from left field and completely messed up his plans. This is why he needs me her to investigate and solve this, precisely to limit the commercial damage … oh, and to find his daughter.* Mike would not like to have to estimate the relative importance Charles placed on these two elements: the percentage split between Petronello and Angelica.

She was just reaching for her phone in order to call Charles when she stopped suddenly. Her phone and, definitely, his phone were being tapped by GCHQ and probably by others. She had to respect client confidentiality and consider the welfare of Angelica. If she discussed the fact that Petronello had not found oil and this was picked up on by the PM, the President, the environmental groups, hostile countries or one of many others, then why would the kidnappers keep Angelica alive? They had already killed Belinda. Getting Charles to confirm the discovery was the *only* thing they had asked for. He would never deny finding oil if that were a death sentence for his daughter.

Leonard. Mike could not tell Leonard. This was starting to build to the perfect storm.

She stubbed out her cigarette, looking at it as if it were the most disgusting thing on earth.

***

In Llandudno, an impromptu campsite had gradually established itself on the Little Orme, which was the smaller of the two carboniferous, limestone headlands that project out into the sea either end of the very wide bay. The police, in negotiation with the local authority, had taken the view that it was better to have the demonstrators concentrated at some distance away from the pier and conference, rather than distributed throughout the town. The irony that they were trespassing on a nature reserve appeared to be wasted. The town looked beautiful in the midsummer sun; it was the epitome of a Victorian British resort, courtesy of Lord Mostyn and his vision of a tourist destination on the two-mile-long, curved bay, punctuated at either end by the rocky outcrops of the Little Orme and Great Orme. Several of the seafront hotels had been taken over by the media, and their rooftops provided elevated locations for the camera crews, with drones having been banned. The large number of people involved in making such an international event as this possible had settled in, and together with the attendees who had already arrived, were testing why the town was called 'the Queen of the Welsh Watering Places'.

Sophie Beardsmore had arrived at The Royal Snowdonia Hotel together with an entourage of Whitehall staff. She was shown up to her spacious, top-floor room in a very small lift, which was a later addition that did nothing to enhance the proportions or appearance of the original foyer. Two armed police – one man and one woman – were already in position outside the hotel's front door, trying not to look like bookends. Sir Michael had been a last-minute addition to the group when it became apparent that the US President, himself a latecomer, was also bringing a large contingent for breakout sessions.

The PM was flying in to arrive in the early evening for an evening reception at a hotel, but he was actually staying as a guest of the Lord Lieutenant of Clwyd, at his home just outside Bangor. He would be up early, ready for breakfast with the 'eco-nuts', as JHV called them. These included the leaders of most of the world's environmental and conservation bodies, as well as individuals such as Astrid Jacobsen. JHV had wanted a controlled photo opportunity early in the day to give the world's media something to chew on before the speeches started. In fact, most of the morning papers would lead with a photograph of a flock of sheep, dyed a bright, luminous green and, currently, being shepherded along the Parade near the North Pier by half a dozen protesters dressed as penguins. The headline writers in the red tops would have fun with "Flock off, Victor" and "Shear madness!"

In the morning, the President was flying from southern Scotland to RAF Valley on Anglesey, not Liverpool as originally planned. His keenness to come, with its evident risks to his popularity, worried the PM and his advisers. They had seen his speech, and it contained nothing controversial, which rather undermined his reasons for coming. He was known for wandering off message, and anything about modifying the treaty would be enough to kill it stone dead, never to be revived.

***

Mervyn Richards travelled up in a second-class carriage, having left London Euston Station about 2.00pm. It was a three-hour journey, but thankfully, did not require a change of trains. He was glad to be out of London, even if it was going to North Wales. To him, it was still Wales, but where the posh folk lived. It was all a bit genteel; no coal pits, steel plants or rugby union, but rather tea drinking, mountain railways and tourists. He had been asked to attend by Lawrence, which reflected Russell Walker's attitude to Antarctica and the environment generally. Russell and Sir John were staying in London.

Once ensconced in his tiny bedroom, with a view of the back of an Indian restaurant, he decided to call his mother.

"Mam, I thought I'd call you as I'm in the same time zone as you, for once," he began, "No, not 2021 ... no, Llandudno ... It doesn't matter ... Yes, Wales."

The conversation was back on track. "No, Mam, it's not a holiday; I'm at a conference. I'm a delegate... No, no, not 'delicate' ... my tummy's fine."

He persevered, as always, "What ice cream ...? Oh, yes, tomorrow on the pier, and I'll watch out for the seagulls. I can see one out of my window now, on the roof of an Indian." He paused, listening to her reply. "No, Mam, I think they eat anything." He kept the conversation on the subject of food, which was always a relatively safe option. "What're you cooking ...? Again? Well, be more careful when you buy stuff ... Eleven pounds is a lot of flour… Yes, good idea … call it 'Bread of Heaven' and charge them double … That's right, Mam, feed them till they want no more."

After ending the call, he went downstairs, walked around the corner – watched by a large herring gull – and ordered an Indian.

***

Two hundred miles away, a light had been turned on in a bedroom. Angelica was shielding her eyes with her free hand while they became accustomed to the brightness. She was desperate to eat the cheese sandwich that had been placed on the bed by the surly woman with the blonde hair in a tight bun. How long had she been chained to the bed? And where was Belinda? Her head was now clearing, and the reality of her situation was seriously and frighteningly dawning on her. Seeing the dirty bed and her soiled hot pants, she wondered if the dark were preferable. The sandwich was made of plastic-looking cheese between two thick slices of white bread, which squeezed to virtually nothing in her grip. It tasted wonderful.

CHAPTER TWENTY

Mike Kingdom was pulling on her leather jacket, ready to ride over to see the Yellands. She wanted to discuss face to face with Charles the deception about the oil discovery and, likewise, with Maria the removal of the compromising video and photographs from Rod Cameron's computer. Of course, she was intending to speak to them separately, although together might be fun, if unethical. She also wanted to check again what Maria and Luis knew about the mysterious Harvey. It was 6.00pm on a bright summer's evening and perfect for a blast on her Benelli Imperiale 400. However, the one hour to ride over and another hour back was a large commitment, which reduced the time she could spend on the computer catching up on everything being forwarded on to her by Leonard and his team. She locked the door, put on her matt-black helmet and made her way down the external wooden staircase.

She rode a motorbike for lots of reasons: the freedom and the ability to follow people, but mostly because she had always loved them. The fact that her husband had ridden one might have put people off bikes forever, but not Mike Kingdom. She drew some comfort from riding them. For her, they were a connection to him. She weaved her way through the rolling hills of Buckinghamshire, let off some steam down the motorway, and finally, rattled across the cattle grids and along the approach drive to the Yelland's country house. It was 7.15pm, and the shadows across the parkland pointed their way across the fields to the surrounding woodland. She had purposely not said anything specific to Charles on the phone, given that she thought others were listening in, so he was completely unsure if she was bringing hopeful or terrible news about Angelica. Both he and Maria came out under the portico on hearing Mike pull up. She took off her helmet carefully, so as not to disturb her red wig; it was definitely a red-wig day. Something about their faces brought out the compassion in her, and she immediately put them out of their misery by telling them she was not the bringer of awful news.

Mike had thought through the strategy of how to talk to them both together and separately. She had also considered where to do this, because she was not 100 per cent confident that the place was not bugged. Maria would know from the Zoom call involving Luis that Mike wanted to talk to her about Rod Cameron and his blackmail threats, and she would be eager to hear what Mike had been able to achieve. She would want this done in private, so Mike began by saying that she would like to talk to Charles on his own first about company matters and would like to ask Maria personal questions about Angelica afterwards. Maria rather quickly suggested that she would prepare some drinks and see Mike in the lounge when she had finished with Charles. A cocker spaniel, which Mike had seen at a distance before, came out wagging its tail and seeking affection.

"Who's this?" Mike asked, bending down and immediately regretting it as a pain shot up her left leg.

"Larry."

"Charles, shall we take Larry for a walk around the rose garden?" She gave him a look that didn't allow for dissension.

"What? Yes, OK."

"Maria, I may need a gin and tonic in a few minutes." Mike did not elaborate on whether it was Larry or Charles who would trigger this.

***

On walking through an old door into a walled garden, she was confronted by beautiful rose bushes, clustered and confined by clipped, low box hedges in a geometric pattern that probably made sense from the air. A wooden hothouse stretched almost the entire length of one of the four high brick walls, heated originally by some old boiler that had long ago rusted and been removed. She stopped at the first island of white roses.

"Charles, your daughter has been kidnapped, and you are choosing not to tell me the truth."

"I think I have answered everything truthfully," he said quietly, but he still managed to sound arrogant.

"That's bollocks. You have not found oil in the South Atlantic, have you?" She turned to face him.

"Well, the results have been promising and—"

She didn't let him finish. "They are not promising, and you have not found oil. You are playing a dangerous game with the City to keep the share price up while you buy NorCarbon, aren't you? Meanwhile, some not very nice people have killed Belinda and are still holding Angelica … if you are lucky."

"Well, it … the thing …" He stumbled over his words, not forming any meaningful sentence. "You see … I didn't …"

"Charles, while I am wasting my time checking whether you are lying to me or not, Angelica is tied up in some basement. You do understand that, don't you?"

"Yes."

" I don't care who you are or how rich you are, and I don't care if you like me – most people don't – but I'm not wasting my time; do you understand?"

"I do."

"Good, so now it's straight-answer time, got it?"

"Yes."

"And the reason we are standing in the garden watching Larry run around the rose beds is because I expect your phones and the house are bugged. I'm not sure you have grasped that half the spy agencies worth talking about are very interested in finding out what's going on."

"Really? How do you …?" he began, but her look stopped him asking the question.

"You have not found oil; period?"

"No."

"You and Tony know this, but who else?"

"Jo and Vernon."

"Tell me about them and not that they are nice people." She saw a bench in an alcove, but decided it was better to stand.

"Jo has been my PA since I started. She really is a nice person – sorry. She would not hurt me or Angelica, I know. Vernon is a Trinidadian whom I inherited from a previous company; he is the best rig superintendent I have ever met. He has a lovely family on Tobago, living a very nice existence. I pay him more than you can imagine. He is loyal."

"The lab you use is in Port of Spain; did he choose it?"

"No, I see your line of thought, but, no … Trinidad is an oil-and-gas producer; we have interests there. Our licence is for part of the Venezuela–southern Caribbean undersea oil field. The lab in Port of Spain is well established and perfect for Mexico and … the South Atlantic. It's run by Americans, in case you're wondering, and we use codes so that the lab has no idea where the cores come from."

"What such as 'PP' for Trinidad, 'NN' for Mexico, 'KK' for Nigeria and 'XX' for the South Atlantic?"

"What …? How?"

"Who's behind this?"

Larry ran up to them both, bored with following the scent of foxes on the gravel paths.

"If I knew, I would have dealt with it by now, believe me," he said, speaking with passion for the first time in the conversation.

"Top of the list? NorCarbon?"

"Yes … or someone connected to or interested in them."

"They don't want to be taken over?"

"No, and there are a couple of people involved who don't like me."

"Business or personal?"

"A bit of both."

"Do you know anyone called Harvey, or have ever heard the name?" She was doing her oft-used sudden changing of tack.

"No, no … I can't think of anyone. Is it important?"

"Very."

Larry beat them back to the kitchen door. On the walk from the rose garden, Charles had pleaded with Mike not to reveal that oil had not been discovered, for Angelica's sake. He assured her that there were no other lies and he would do anything she asked of him. She told him not to talk about the lack of oil on the phone or in his house, car or office.

"You wouldn't believe who's been listening to your conversations, Charles." With that, she walked through the kitchen, down the hall and into the lounge.

Maria was waiting nervously, already clutching an empty glass. Mike put a finger to her mouth and pointed to the French doors. "I think I'm ready for that drink, now."

Maria poured them both a stiff gin, dropped in some ice from the bucket and opened two cans of tonic.

"Shall we drink them on the terrace?" Mike asked, walking across the vast area of carpet broken up by groups of large sofas and low coffee tables.

"It's a lovely evening, so why not?" Maria slid open the doors and stepped outside.

They walked a short distance to a set of garden furniture comprising a faded teak table and chairs and sat down.

"Any news of Angelica?" Maria asked, cradling her glass.

"No, I'm sorry, but I told you that I have sorted out the other problem, I think? I hacked into Rod Cameron's computer."

Maria put down her glass and began rubbing her neck.

"I know he was blackmailing you … and at least two other women as well," Mike continued.

"How? I … don't understand." Maria was staring blankly at Mike. "I was … God, I was so stupid."

"I destroyed the video and the pictures. I left a message for him saying that if he did it again, I would wipe his hard drive and ruin him."

"Oh, thank you so much."

"Have you heard from him again? He wanted the money quickly, I am guessing?"

"No. Nothing."

"You need to know that your phone is being hacked and your house is bugged. Things are getting even more serious than you thought. The email and phone accounts you set up with Rod's address to talk to your brother are being hacked as well."

"My God. How do you know all this?"

"It's my job." She took a sip before launching into a series of important questions. "Maria, I know about your brother, your family and their source of income. Don't worry, I'm not interested in any of that unless it leads to Angelica."

"I've tried to hide it from Charles for all these years."

"I guess Luis is part of the 'family', is he?"

"My brother helped me get him appointed as our chauffeur. He's a good friend of the family. Carlos wanted someone to watch out for me."

"You trust him?"

"Of course." Maria was almost affronted.

"Tell me about Harvey, this boyfriend of Belinda's that Luis mentioned," Mike asked, and she became aware that she was only sipping and the ice was melting fast.

"I have never met him, and Angelica never mentioned him to me. It was Luis who heard them talking about him, and like he said, he dropped them off in Chiswick instead of Knightsbridge."

"There's no Harvey or anyone with a first name beginning with 'H' in either of Belinda's or Angelica's phones. There's nothing more at all that Luis has said or that you know?"

"No, nothing. I have asked Luis. He would tell me."

"I must get back home. Ring me if Rod Cameron calls again and ring me if you learn anything about this Harvey … but use the phones as little as possible. Just assume that lots of people are listening, OK?"

"Thank you. Thank you for what you did with the video and pictures; I don't know how to thank you."

"Charles will be paying me a lot, don't worry. Now, I am off to find your daughter."

***

Someone else was busy looking for her daughter that evening, as he sat in his office on Shrivenham Road in East Swindon. Inspector Christopher Bucknall had been allocated twelve officers solely to find out how Belinda got from Reading services to the park bench at Coate Water and whether Angelica and an accomplice or other kidnappers had carried her there. The overall team had grown exponentially, and there were now sub-teams out of Wiltshire Police HQ in Devizes and others from London, together with a bunch of people that Inspector Bucknall had never come across before from the Secret Services, although their role was a bit hazy. The chief constable was normally not involved in quite such a hands-on way as on this case, and he never missed an opportunity to tell anyone that he was under great pressure from the Home Office and others. Officers and resources had miraculously been found and reallocated.

The inspector looked up at the large whiteboard and read the long list of unknowns scribbled down the right-hand side. He had personally interviewed Luis Mendoza by phone and had established that the two girls had been dropped off in Chiswick at 8.30am. Even if they had jumped into a car within fifteen minutes, they could not realistically have got to the motorway services at Reading until 9.45am, allowing for heavy traffic. It is forty-five-minute driving time to Coate Water, and Belinda was on the bench by 2.30pm, probably much earlier. Unless they spent a very long time at the services, where did they go? His colleagues had checked all vehicles entering the services between 9.30am and 10.30am against any that were recorded near Coate Water from 10.30am to 2.30pm; this totalled nineteen cars, five vans and three lorries, all identified by matching CCTV from Reading services and the various traffic cameras that led to the entrance of Coate Water car park. These vehicles had all stopped at the services, left the motorway at Junction 15 and then turned off down the dual carriageway towards central Swindon. He was relieved at the relatively small number, but this was not surprising, as drivers heading for Swindon from London don't usually stop at Reading services unless they are very low on fuel or need the toilets. They are almost at their destination.

When Luis had also told the inspector about Harvey, he could not believe his luck. He was used to witnesses saying that the car was black or the registration number began with the letter 'N' or, perhaps, 'M' or 'W'. His team only had twenty-seven vehicles to check against the one name: Harvey. He would now make major progress on the case. Breathing a sigh of relief, he began imagining the next stages of the investigation. As expected, it had not taken his team long to check these vehicles, unfortunately none were registered to a Harvey or to a Chiswick address. Even worse, all the vans and lorries were making deliveries and were tracked to the minute by their operators. One car, an Audi estate, was owned by a Swindon family, the Sylvesters, who were well known to the police. The family was ostensibly run by the grandfather, Waldo, who had an innate ability to slip through any net. Their skip-hire business, Swindon Sylver Tip, was an ongoing problem for the local authority, the Environment Agency, the Health and Safety Executive, and just about anybody involved in regulation and control.

Christopher, who used to be Chris before his two promotions, stared at the whiteboard. Another question took his eye. Did Harvey, and implicitly anyone else, drop the girls at the motorway services to be picked up by others? This would complicate things exponentially, but not as badly as if there were a pedestrian footbridge between the two carriageways, which would mean that Harvey, Angelica or anyone else could get into a car and drive back towards London. He checked and there wasn't a foot or road bridge across the motorway, which was a relief all round.

So, what next? Check out the Sylvesters? Look at all of the CCTV footage to see if the girls changed vehicles? He would get off duty soon and enjoy the last few hours of a beautiful evening.

CHAPTER TWENTY-ONE

Mike Kingdom was on her knees, making a lot of noise. This didn't matter as no one could hear her. She was removing cooking equipment from a cupboard, looking for a large colander, when the phone rang. She cursed, stood up awkwardly, and put the metal pots and dishes on the work surface. It was someone called Tom from Leonard's office.

"Miss K-Kingdom," he began, revealing a slight stammer, "L-Leonard asked me to call you urgently."

"OK, fire away," Mike guessed it must be urgent, but she was aware of the irony that it was Tom delivering the message.

"We have just received a report from the police," he continued, and she shuddered, fearing the worse. "They've found a body."

Awful images crept into her head and her thoughts went back to her own accident. "Oh ..." She was at a loss for words.

"It's Rod Cameron, the photographer," he continued.

Oddly, Mike felt relief that it was not Angelica. "What happened to him?" she asked, regaining her composure.

"H-He was murdered."

"How? Where?"

"Shot three times, they think, and thrown down a m-manhole at his house. A neighbour, who cleans his place, went in this m-morning and found blood, and the hall rug was missing."

"Right, thank you. I expect that's all the police know at this stage until they get the forensic report?"

"Yes, that's it. I will send over everything as I get it."

"Thanks, Tom. Oh, Tom" – she had a sudden thought – "would you get all of the mobile phone records for Angelica and Belinda and ping them over to me urgently? I know that Leonard has had them checked, but I want to look myself. Thanks."

Mike had left a plastic strainer hanging in her hand. *Has his blackmailing caught up with him?* she thought. *Could it have been Maria or one of the other two women whose pictures I found on his computer? Perhaps Rod Cameron has been doing this for a while?* She tried to replace all of the culinary equipment, but the cupboard had clearly shrunk in the last few minutes. In her chat with Maria, she had seemed as normal as you could be, considering her daughter was being held by kidnappers and her lover was blackmailing her. Could she have stayed so cool and acted the part in front of Mike? It didn't feel that way, which left Mike with the problem of who had eliminated Rod and what the connection with the kidnap was, if any.

She pulled up onto the screen Maria's hidden telephone account, and then spent fifteen minutes looking at the log of the times, destinations and locations of all recent calls.

Unsurprisingly, they were all to Mexico. Mike swapped over to Maria's main mobile and checked the time of Rod Cameron's call in which he had demanded the money; this was at 2.30pm. Less than half an hour later, Maria had phoned her brother for 40 minutes. Had she asked for £100,000 or had she asked for Rod to be eliminated? Surely, she had access to that amount of money, but perhaps not at short notice or she didn't want to risk Charles spotting the transaction. Whether Maria had asked or not, had her brother given instructions to Luis to shoot Rod Cameron? For Maria, this would have been a dangerous strategy, knowing that her video and pictures were on his computer and that this would be the first place the police would look after checking his mobile phone.

Of course, it could be one of the other two families or something to do with the fake photograph. Mike decided to leave this line of questioning and return to the kidnap. She kept reminding herself that she was not being paid to solve Rod Cameron's murder.

After making a strong coffee, she saw that Tom had given her the access to the two girls' phone records she had requested. With a biscuit in one hand, Mike started with Angelica's log, knowing that searching through phone records was a tedious and inefficient way forward, albeit one that was necessary. Straight away, she searched in Angelica's contacts for a Harvey or any first name with the initial H; there was just Harvey Nichols, which appeared handily next to Harrods. There was somebody called Harriet and a company called Hargreaves, but nothing that looked promising. Checking the call log, Mike saw that the last short call received was from Charles at 11.16am, presumably as he rang back after the kidnapper's first contact. The last text before these was to Luis at 9.17am, and there was a phone call at 8.36am to a nail bar in Marlow. It was very short; perhaps she was leaving a message? Mike searched through her social media and found the message to Belinda confirming she would be at her house around 8.30am, ready for their day's shopping.

Belinda's phone could potentially take longer to search, as she was much more active on Instagram and several other apps, but her boyfriend must be one of her favourites and most-frequent calls – and what girl doesn't take a selfie with her boyfriend? There was no Harvey or any similar name. Mike changed tack and went through the calls going back in time. Most of the calls and messages were to the same five people, about some upcoming beach party in Brighton. Mike reached for the packet of biscuits only to discover that she had eaten the last one. *If you went to a beach party, you would go with your boyfriend, surely?* Two of the five individuals in the conversation were male, or ostensibly so; there was a Cyril Lansdowne and a Robert Valberg. Who calls their son Cyril? It must be a nickname, unless he was in his seventies? She swapped over to Belinda's Instagram account and looked for either Cyril or Robert and found a whole series of messages. It struck her like a thunderbolt. Cyril Lansdowne was 'CyrilSquirrel1' and Robert Valberg was 'RV674534'.

Mike scrunched up the biscuit wrapper and threw it in the bin.

Robert Valberg was her boyfriend. Luis had overheard the girls talking about RV, presumably his nickname, and with his Mexican ears, he had thought he had heard 'Harvey'. Mike needed to keep calm and to concentrate. She did not have time to waste on any self-congratulation. The sun was just beginning to cast geometric shapes onto the side wall of her lounge, turning the varnished pine a deep golden colour.

Valberg? What nationality was the name Valberg? A quick check threw up Swedish and Norwegian, where Robert was also common as a first name. Mike searched for any Robert Valbergs in the Chiswick area, assuming he lived nearby, but she drew a blank. She had his mobile number, but did not want to ring it immediately, in case he had been kidnapped as well. She moved on to his car. He must have a car, or did another friend such as Cyril Lansdowne drive them? Robert and any other car owner must live in London. Why else would the girls be driven south-east to Chiswick if Robert lived west of there? *Damn!* She thought to herself, *London is so big. Why didn't they meet in a village?* It would have made her life so much easier.

She suddenly remembered the short list of vehicles that Inspector Bucknall had compiled. Did either of the names appear? She checked the list. Life was a roller coaster at the moment, and not finding either name was a low point.

If this had been some commercial espionage dispute, Mike would have done all of the searching of car databases, DVLA, car insurance companies, AA/RAC, credit cards, etc. herself. Time would have been of secondary importance. With a kidnap and murder, she did not have this luxury, and even if she had to swallow some pride and bitterness, she knew she had to call Leonard. The Five Eyes had almost unlimited resources, and if its operatives couldn't find it, possibly it was beyond her, anyway. She put on her red wig and made the call.

"Michaela? You've cracked it? Because the President flies down from Scotland real soon." Leonard didn't take a breath. This was a man under pressure from all sides, but mostly from very high up.

"Leonard, I need your help. I think I have identified the boyfriend – Belinda's boyfriend," she explained.

"Who is he?"

"Robert Valberg. I cannot find him in Chiswick. I cannot find his car. I just have his cell phone number, which I haven't called in case he is a victim or a perpetrator."

"OK, I'll have him checked out, and we'll let the police know, so that they can run the official checks."

She gave Robert Valberg's phone number to Leonard. "There's a friend, but I don't know if he's connected, Cyril Lansdowne; he features in a lot of the chatter. Will you check him out, too?"

"Anything else?"

"I think Luis Mendoza may have been involved in the Rod Cameron killing, but can we leave that off the record for a few days?"

"Sure. So nothing more on the oil? That's all the President wants to know."

Mike took a deep breath, but she knew deep down that she could not tell Leonard the truth. The President could not stand up this afternoon and say that oil had not been discovered. Angelica, and perhaps Robert, might still be alive, but they would be killed instantly if that came out.

"I'm making progress on the Port of Spain analyses you sent me."

"Michaela, you wouldn't hold out on me just to get revenge, would you?"

There was an uncomfortable silence.

"I am better than that."

There was a second silence.

"Nice rose garden the Yellands have. Just the right distance

202

from their house, wouldn't you say?" he asked.

She imagined that there was a smirk across Leonard's face
– probably.

"Poor phone coverage, out there, I find."

***

The PM was staring at the food that had been placed before
him. He had been up since 6.00am. It looked like a full English
breakfast, but to the side of the bacon and sausages was a cockle
and laver bread cake that appeared to be winking at him. He
looked across at his guests', many of which looked seriously
healthy – the breakfasts, that is, not the guests, who generally
were very pale, were on the thin side, and were wearing clothes
that had not been troubled by the irons or trouser presses
handily placed in most of the hotels' bedrooms. He was
worried about the huge consequences of the events of the day
ahead, which appeared to him to be outside his control. He
would have described himself as a 'centrist', which is political
speak for going with the majority. He would also have said,
slightly more profoundly, that he cared for the environment
– although this probably went as far as the fact that he would
prefer the Amazon rainforest to be left in place and not turned
into face cream, which he did not use. If his annual holiday in
the Maldives – provided discreetly by an investment fund via
his sister – could continue during his lifetime, that would be
great. In this, he was talking about both the Maldives and his
holidays lasting his lifetime.

He couldn't remember when he had been approached by
so many people at all levels from all parts of the world on one
matter. He had still not grasped why the US President had

flown in to speak. Was he missing something? He was distracted by the loud voice of the person to his left – a skull wearing a straggly, black beard – who was head of the Environment Agency, the Worldwide Fund for Nature or some other greenish organisation. Whichever his position, at breakfast, he had managed to consume more calories than anyone else and still look like he had been embalmed in some Nosferatu film. To the PM's right, he had a fourteen-year-old Norwegian advocate of sustainability based on the dangers of climate change. This girl was incredibly pale and had never seen the sun around which her world predictably rotated. Her name was Astrid, and she didn't have a clue about protocol or hierarchy or, indeed, anything apart from this one issue. The PM envied her one-issue politics, but not the fact that she had sailed over on a replica of Thor Heyerdahl's Viking reed boat, *Kon-tiki*, from Sweden to some pebbly shore of a constituency in the north-east, which the PM hoped would be redefined by the Boundaries Commission to include more than the handful of people who had voted for him last time. The fact that it was the health-and-safety boat from the construction company building offshore wind farms that had rescued her had not been lost on him.

"Prime Minister, the devastation of the rainforests is well established, but what about the destruction of Antarctica? Are you going to confirm the Antarctic Treaty for another fifty years?" the bearded man asked.

"Well," the PM said, debating internally whether laver bread could be considered a crime against humanity, "The treaty has been fantastic, utterly fantastic. We should not give any part of it up lightly. Just because one company finds oil does not automatically mean a sixty- or seventy-year-old agreement should be tossed in the rubbish bin."

"You didn't say yes." The Norwegian teenager seemed to have no qualms about challenging world leaders. "And the UK's reputation on dealing with rubbish bins is terrible."

He had instantly regretted using the metaphor. Pausing to think, an increasingly unusual practice, he defended the UK's position on recycling. These were some of the figures and soundbites given to him by JHV: "Do you know that we now recycle – that is, do not need to quarry – twenty-nine per cent of our building aggregates ... that's 58 million tonnes? Splendid."

"Impressive," said the bearded skull, "but what about household waste? Why does our plastic end up in Indian rubbish tips?"

"That must stop. We have a major consultation ongoing at the moment. That must stop," the PM confirmed.

"Norway recycles ninety-seven per cent of its waste. The UK recycles sixty per cent," the young environmentalist said, promoting her home country.

"That's great, and we are well on our way ... yes, thank you..." He paused, leaning to the side to let the waiter take his empty plate. "I hope you sing the praises of your government loud and clear."

The PM's head was full of numbers given to him by JHV, who always seemed to have at his fingertips the EU's and Norway's comparatives with the UK. However, the PM was wily enough to know that it is always better to talk about another country rather than your own. So he asked around the table what made everyone proud of their country.

"That Norway will reconfirm the Antarctic Treaty and not allow the extraction of minerals from the sectors it claims with Chile, Argentina and the UK, Prime Minister."

Damn, the PM thought to himself.

CHAPTER TWENTY-TWO

Inspector Christopher Bucknall was someone who took things personally. With a soft, round face under blondish curly hair, he probably did not look like a policeman. He had broken his nose in his teens, and this further softened his appearance. His blue eyes, with their naturally small pupils, deceived most people into thinking that his was a gentle spirit. Most of the time, this would be true, but on distressing cases like this one, he became, well, passionate. He had a fourteen-year-old daughter, and the idea that someone might kidnap her or worse tested him to the extreme. Not being able to identify the vehicle from such a short list had frustrated him. OK, he wouldn't buy a used car from Waldo Sylvester, but he and his family were not kidnappers and killers. If anything, they were the opposite. They had a bunch of lucrative businesses and a tight family; you do not jeopardise that lightly, especially using your own traceable vehicle. From his first days in uniform, Chris Bucknall had been cynical and sceptical about every response he had ever received, but not one of the twenty-seven vehicles and their owners gave him any real cause for concern.

He looked out of the window, across the roundabout towards Sainsbury's, and squashed his nose flat against his face – not an option open to most people. He had quite a large team, all of whom were addressing the singular problem of answering the question 'How did three, possibly four, people get from Reading services to Coate Water, down the M4 in a three-hour timeframe?' It was not the most testing problem he had ever been set. He knew everything about the two girls and with one of the probable drivers named as Harvey, how hard could this be?

Irritatingly, the phone rang on his desk, breaking his train of thought.

"Bucknall."

"Inspector? Brian Smith here. I wanted to give you the latest intelligence we have. Belinda's boyfriend may not be called Harvey; it is likely to be someone called Robert Valberg. We are checking him out now. It was him that the girls met in Chiswick."

Why did MI5 always use either Smith or Jones? Could he not be trusted to know someone's surname? Someone he would probably never meet again.

"Hello, yes, thank you. That's really useful."

"We will send you any update when we have it."

"Thank you, Brian," he put added emphasis on Brian.

He sat down, pressed the button to speak to Sylvie asking her to get his senior support into his room ASAP. He opened the search facilities and tapped in "Robert Valberg". Nothing came up in Swindon, nothing came up in Wiltshire and there was not much nationwide; he found a speeding offence and two cautions, both in Scotland eight years previously. Some Austrian actor who died in 1955 dominated the public search results.

Two officers tapped on the door, opened it and entered.

"Progress?" asked the female officer with the brown hair and distinctive pixie ears.

"Robert Valberg; V-A-L-B-E-R-G." He spelt it out unnecessarily, as he needed to maximise the new information even though it didn't look wholly promising.

"Who's he?" a sergeant with a pair of black eyebrows asked.

"Belinda's boyfriend. Probable driver. They met him at Chiswick. One minute's searching has produced … zilch." Bucknall milked it, but it was basically schadenfreude.

"Nothing?"

"Well, you know that a distinctive name like that should throw something up near Chiswick or Swindon. There are only twelve in the whole of the UK."

"I'll check them out." The black eyebrows were knitted together.

"Determining where he lives would be great, but can we at least find the bloody car? Sarah, please ring every letting and estate agent in Swindon and just ask. Teddy, will you do the car? Ownership, insurance, MOT, fines, rental, anything."

Sarah wrote the name on her pad in such a way that her hair bobbed up and down.

"That's it. One step forwards, two back." Chris Bucknall could not remember another case with a straightforward task that had hit brick wall after brick wall. In his eighteen years in the police, he had noticed that, when investigations hit brick walls, it was always for one of two reasons at either end of the spectrum. It was either down to the crass, unpredictable action of an idiot that beggared belief or someone very clever was hiding the evidence or actively disguising it. There was actually a third reason, which was that the team was making mistakes, but it just did not feel like it in this case.

"We don't even know if this Robert Valberg is an innocent party, and has been kidnapped with the girls; he just drove them and is now back in London; or is the kidnapper." The inspector tried to frame the problem.

"If Belinda is … was… seventeen, how old is her boyfriend likely to be?" Teddy asked.

"Twenty-ish?"

"I will check driving tests and licences, as he may not have been driving long."

"Sarah, check colleges, apprenticeships, Chamber of Commerce … the usual. He or they must have a reason for coming to Swindon."

"Perhaps the car developed a problem? They might've come off looking for a garage?" Teddy suggested.

"Check that too. There are a couple in that area."

***

"… one and a half times the size of the USA." Sophie Beardsmore was being interviewed on breakfast TV by a male interviewer who looked as though he had a puff pastry crust on his head, but this actually resolved itself – on closer inspection – as a dense, blond wig. She was quoting one of her favourite statistics about Antarctica from those provided by Mervyn in his crib sheet. Sophie was sitting in a beautiful chair, upholstered in a green and grey Welsh tapestry, in the lounge of her hotel. She was wearing a flowing, large, brown kaftan, which JHV, who was watching in London, described to Mossy and Rat Arse as the second largest brown and flowing thing in Wales after the River Taff downstream of the old tannery.

"I was imagining the amount of oil, coal and minerals in the USA. Just think how much there is in Antarctica under the shrinking ice cap. The pressure to extract them is enormous and will only increase, won't it?" the interviewer asked earnestly.

"True, but this has been known about for many, many decades, and not one shovel of mineral has been extracted. The Madrid Protocol of 1991 has seen to that," Sophie explained.

"But oil has just been discovered at sixty degrees south. All hell is about to break loose, isn't it?" he persisted.

"Firstly, it is north of sixty degrees, which is outside Antarctica and the treaty area, and it's a big leap from finding oil to producing it. Let's wait and see."

"An oil spill at sixty degrees would be devastating, wouldn't it?"

"Oil spills are deeply regrettable anywhere, but standards improve all the time." She wanted to get off of Antarctica and on to the wider subject of climate change.

"Norway, Chile, Argentina and the UK all contest this sector or sectors, don't they?"

Sophie began to think that her interviewer was remarkably well informed. This was not surprising, because one of Mossy's friends had given him a copy of Mervyn's note. "They do. The whole point of the treaty is the multilateral suspension of claims. This is a clever idea that could be widened to include outer space, the moon and planets, and to many other terrestrial areas that are the subject of this conference here in Llandudno." She tried to move the conversation on.

"So you will support a re-ratification of the treaty for another fifty years?"

"Well, I am not the minister in charge of Antarctica." In London, JHV and his chums suddenly stopped talking.

"You are the Secretary of State for the Environment, Food and Rural Affairs?"

"Yes, but Antarctica falls under the BEIS, not my department."

"Business? Energy? Industrial Strategy? Why is Antarctica under BEIS? And where is Russell Walker in that case? He should be here."

"You have the PM and the Secretary of State for the Environment, Food and Rural Affairs attending, with a large entourage, to discuss climate change. Antarctica is one, albeit important, part. We cannot have the whole of the Government up here."

"I am truly shocked." The interviewer threw his head back, and not a single hair moved out of place.

"The BEIS has kept us all informed via the PM. They have an excellent special adviser in Mervyn Richards, who knows Antarctica intimately."

JHV was on the phone to Russell only seconds before Russell was about to call him. This had not gone according to plan.

***

Mike Kingdom had become increasingly interested in the interview on her small TV. It was attached to the wooden wall by a weakened hinged arm, which made it slant; this made watching programmes with horizons, especially sea horizons, disconcerting. She was busy searching for Robert Valbergs and Cyril Lansdownes, but had got distracted. The whole idea of geopolitics and Antarctica had not really entered her thinking, and she pondered the powerful forces hiding in the shadows. The whole contested sector arrangement had also escaped her. Would Argentina use the treaty breakdown to gain access to a sector? What would Norway do? It was ostensibly a very eco-conscious country, but would commercial forces override this?

She was thinking about Norway when she turned off the TV and resumed her searches. Valberg was a Norwegian name. Coincidence, surely? She didn't like coincidences. Why had she (and presumably no one else) not yet found anything about Robert Valberg? The ones she had found were over sixty, lived in Aberdeen or were wheelchair-bound. There was no Robert Valberg that could be boyfriend age to Belinda.

A single hornet flew across her picture window, in search of wasps attacking the wooden exterior. She never saw two, just the one, and she had never found a hornet's nest anywhere in the forest. Another mystery. While thinking about how far the hornet was away from its nest, her mind wandered on to the total lack of any connection between Robert Valberg and the vehicles Swindon police had logged and checked thoroughly. Why was that? A potential answer came to her from nowhere. The vehicle, after leaving Reading services, drove west down the M4 – this was unavoidable, but it didn't have to come off at Junction 15. It could have come off before and been driven down country lanes, or it could have come off later, at the second Swindon junction, and doubled back through the town. She temporarily shelved the first idea as this route would probably still bring you to the same roundabout near the hospital – it was possible, but unlikely. The second idea meant that the car could approach Broome Manor Lane or Coate Water from the west, and would not have been picked up by the police. But why do that? Why take that route? Who would know that route? Probably not some twenty-year-old from Chiswick.

She let her mind wander without constraint. *The kidnapper, or most likely kidnappers, were clearly being devious, so what else might they do? Use a vehicle they didn't own. Did they steal one in advance? That involves work and introduces an unnecessary element of risk; the police may be alerted and be looking for the vehicle even before the kidnap took place. They could borrow one, but it would probably be traced back to them eventually. They could use false plates on their own car, but this has the risk that the motorway cameras or traffic police might pick up any discrepancy.* She paused, reached for her pack of cigarettes and lit one. *They could hire a car. They could hire it away from Chiswick and use a false driving licence.* She drew in a lungful of smoke and blew it upwards towards her open Velux skylight. She liked the hire-car idea because it would ostensibly be legal in the highly unlikely chance that they were stopped. Coupled with the circuitous route through central Swindon, it would make it difficult to trace. She tapped the ash into an upturned scallop shell, which was now sporting brown stains and burn marks. *The Reading services stop must have been unplanned unless … unless someone else was joining them or changing cars?*

She had hit the buffers, but still felt that she had made enough progress to have justified the cigarette. She never just smoked. She had to have done something to deserve it. Checking all of the options she had just devised would take the very large teams working on this case months. If they had used a false driving licence, it might never be possible to find them using the car journey as a basis. The sooner she rang Leonard, the better. She reached for her phone and dialled.

"Hello, M-Mike."

"Tom? Hi Tom. Would you action a few things and tell Leonard ASAP?"

"Sure."

"I don't think that Robert Valberg is his real name. I think that he was the lure to trap Belinda and Angelica. Cyril Lansdowne, the other name in some conversations with the girls, also looks as though it's a false name. Neither appears to own a car."

"OK."

"Can you influence whoever, including the police, to concentrate on the car? I think it went past Junction 15, came off at 16 and doubled back through Swindon. I think it may be a hire car, so that should reduce the number of vehicles that left Reading services and followed this route in that possible three-hour time frame."

"OK," he repeated, "I'll tell L-Leonard and pass on your ideas."

"Anything new coming my way, Tom?"

"M-MI5 have found some CCTV footage in Wellesley Road in Chiswick. They are running face recognition at the m-moment. L-Leonard says it will be here soon."

"That would be great. Hopefully, that will give us Robert Valberg's and Cyril Lansdowne's real names, or remove them from the investigation and give us other, more useful leads. We are running out of time." The last sentence was Mike talking to herself.

CHAPTER TWENTY-THREE

Maria Yelland was sitting in a comfortable chair. She was so heavily sedated that she could not join in a conversation without losing her train of thought. Her breakdown had resulted in a visit by paramedics in the early hours, and they had come close to taking her away, there and then, to hospital. The combination of Rod Cameron's blackmail, his murder and Angelica's kidnap for three days had proved too much for her. Everyone connected to the Yelland household had been deeply affected, and the start of the new week had an ominous, heavy feel to it. Even Stanley, the delivery driver, had asked Luis about Maria in the courtyard before driving out slowly down the avenue towards the stone gates and the main road.

At 10.00am, a dark-green Range Rover drove up to near the front door. Tony and Charles's sister, Geraldine, stepped out from the back doors and down onto the gravel. Wearing jeans; a loose, pink blouse; and a cardigan around her shoulders, Geraldine jogged up the steps to the front door. Tony spoke briefly to his chauffeur and joined her as the front door opened. His glasses only partially hid the dark bags beneath his eyes, and his normally neat beard looked scruffy. Geraldine hugged her brother, not letting go until Tony entered the hall and shook his brother-in-law's outstretched hand. Charles put a finger to his lips.

"Oh, sorry ... how is she?" Geraldine whispered, but the warning to be quiet was meant for Tony, who had received the message from the long stare that had fixed his gaze from the moment he came through the door.

"She's in the lounge, but pretty zonked out." Charles walked down the hall and pushed open one of the double doors.

Maria turned her head and her eyes followed a millisecond after.

"Maria, my darling." Geraldine leant to hug her sister-in-law, keeping the cardigan on her shoulders with her left hand. Geraldine's long, dark-brown hair brushed either side of Maria's face, on which there was only a slight reaction that, eventually, evolved into a smile.

Tony stepped forwards to help move a chair closer to Maria, into which Geraldine flopped and then bent forwards.

"How are you, darling? What have they given you?" she asked.

"What's happened?" Maria asked in her mild confusion.

"Nothing, Tony and I have come over to see you."

"I'll sort out some tea," Charles said, and then ushered Tony out of the room. As they walked down the hall, he whispered, "Let's talk outside. Walls have ears."

***

Five minutes later, they were walking together under the dark shade of the long pergola heavily laden with pink roses and a tangle of wisteria leaves and branches.

"Tony, thank God they sedated her. I can barely cope myself. She was losing it. Completely."

"Hardly surprising ... and what's with the paranoia?"

"What? Oh, Mike Kingdom believes the house, car, office and I don't know where else are bugged."

"Really? By whom?"

"No idea, but she seems convinced. By the way, she knows that the *Antigone* has not discovered oil."

"How did she find that out? Only four of us know."

"She hacked into the Port of Spain lab and found the results. She even cracked our code system and knew XX was the South Atlantic. Unbelievable."

"She's not going to say anything, is she?"

"Of course not, she is looking for Angelica and knows that if people find out there's no oil, the kidnappers will ..." He didn't finish the sentence.

"We must absolutely keep this quiet until the police find her."

They had reached a large oak Lutyens bench, bleached a pale grey.

Tony sat down. "Charles, I don't want to place you under more pressure, but I have been up all night dealing with NorCarbon." He rubbed his hand up over his beard and nose pushing his glasses onto his forehead.

"What do they want? More money?"

"No, to buy us."

"What?" Charles gazed out across the lawn to a majestic cedar of Lebanon, which was casting an almost black shade on the bare ground beneath it.

"They seem to know that we have found nothing down south and, having heard us say that we have, want to take advantage of our weakness. You know how much they don't want to be taken over."

"They have grasped that we are not for sale, haven't they? Who do they think they are?"

"They have American money behind them. I have been talking to the bloody USA half the night. The hedge funds over there love all of this."

Charles turned to look directly at Tony. "They're behind that ... sodding photograph, aren't they?"

"I cannot think of anyone else who would benefit more. If they let on that we have not found oil, our bankers will all run for the nearest exit, where they will trample over the shareholders already running out the door. We will not be taking over NorCarbon. They have stuffed us good and proper."

Charles was looking at an old blackbird's nest half hanging out of the wisteria. "Tony, they couldn't be holding Angelica, could they? That's too ridiculous, isn't it?"

"Somebody is holding her, and that's ridiculous, whoever they are. They must be connected to our business or why ask for that announcement? And the only thing that announcement does is shaft us."

"But this isn't a bit of industrial espionage or a bit of disinformation; this is kidnap and murder. The directors will go to jail for the rest of their lives. They wouldn't do it."

"Somebody is."

Charles turned his head, not quite following.

"Somebody is doing it," Tony explained the point.

"What are we going to do?" the boss asked his co-director.

Tony 's face was sallow and drawn; the bags under his eyes were two dark smudges. His glasses were dirty, but he didn't seem to notice. He stretched his lips back and forth across his oversized teeth and laughed. "We're going to find Angelica. You and me, we're going to shout about our oil find from the rooftops and worry about the consequences in six months' time. This will stuff NorCarbon and their American backers, who are expecting us to roll over, but my guess is that they will lose interest in Petronello in five minutes."

"Tony, thank you."

"We have a plan. No backing down. OK?"

Charles smiled for the first time in days. "Deal," he said.

At the far end of the pergola, a blackbird was busy rebuilding its nest, having made a bad decision a few weeks earlier.

***

JHV was watching four wall-mounted TV screens; they were showing the BBC, ITV, Sky and CNN coverage of the Llandudno conference, building up to the arrival of the President and the PM's keynote speech. The first three were on mute. He was in his spacious office in Portcullis House next to the Houses of Parliament. Despite the building resembling a dark, satanic mill from Lancashire, it was actually quite new and preferable to the poky office he had been offered in the old building. His windows also overlooked the Thames and it was handily located at the corner of Bridge Street and Victoria Embankment. He had two computer screens on his desk. Patrick Ratoath was on one of them, sitting on a wooden chair with a leather back that looked like it was part of a dining set.

Today's newspapers were piled next to him. Andrew Sedgwick Moss appeared on the other, slumped on a swivel chair, which was sinking under his weight. JHV was sitting at his desk, holding a master control. He muted the final TV channel.

"I thought that you had it all pretty well under control, Mossy," JHV said reasonably quietly even with the door to the corridor shut, "We appear to have gone off message."

"I was walking a thin line," Mossy offered in defence.

"Mossy, you couldn't even walk a fat line let alone a thin one," Rat Arse said.

"We're trying to get the treaty reviewed or at least the mineral extraction part." JHV was not happy. "The President is meant to be gently pressing for a partial review, and the PM is meant to blather on about the need for caution, but not close any doors on a review."

"That's what we've been promoting," Mossy stated, "but remember that this is a bloody climate change conference. Not everyone, to say the least, is on board."

"Sophie was meant to take the flak. That's why Russell isn't up here," Rat Arse explained, "He can subsequently disclaim what he doesn't like and build on the good bits."

"Where did that fact sheet come from? I can't work out if that is helping or hindering. Which of you bright pair thought of that?"

"Not me," they said in unison.

"The PM circulated it. Apparently, it came from a Mervyn Richards, a special adviser to Russell," Mossy told them.

"I've never heard of him. He can't be very senior. Why did Russell ask for it?" JHV asked.

"Probably so he knows something about it, given it's the topic of the moment," Mossy speculated.

"The pictures and quotes from the breakfast are good." Rat Arse was looking for positives.

"True, but I'm getting an uneasy feeling about the green mob building up in Llandudno." JHV didn't want a groundswell of pro-environment sentiment sweeping the country, having got the President and PM on board for a review.

The phone rang on JHV's desk.

"Hi Yes, come over ... Yes, I'm here for a while," he paused, "That's Russell. He wants to come over for a chat. Remember, it's all going pretty well. We don't want him going wobbly. I want to make sure that he doesn't do any interviews today or tonight."

"I've got a holding statement prepared in case of emergencies, which we can release on his behalf," Mossy interjected.

"Great. Let's see what state he's in."

***

Five minutes later, there was a tap on the door, which was opened without the tapper waiting for a response. In walked Russell Walker, holding a small bottle of water. "Good morning. I wasn't sure if I'd missed the tea trolley," he said, indicating the bottle.

"Good morning," echoed the two voices on the Zoom call.

"I hope that bottle's recyclable? Don't want a picture of you with it today. You know, plastic in the oceans and all that. It'll ruin everything." JHV never seemed able to shut off.

"Are you talking about the oceans or our campaign?" Russell queried.

"Both probably."

"I hear that Sophie's said that the treaty is sacrosanct."

"Not exactly, and the President will do the dirty work for us, neatly packaged by the PM in his keynote speech. So, tomorrow, you can start discreet discussions with the Norwegians, if you wish." ("If you wish" was as deferential as JHV ever got.)

"What about the Americans?" Russell asked.

"They will get their side deal from the PM and back what we and the Norwegians agree. The Argentinians can shout into the wind, which I understand blows frequently down there."

"Thanks for the Antarctic crib sheet. I passed it on to relevant people," Mossy said.

"I didn't ask for it." Russell glared at Mossy.

"It came from Mervyn Richards, one of your special advisers," JHV probed.

"I thought the PM asked for it?" Russell wondered.

"Odd," was all JHV said.

"I presume I had better keep my head down today?"

"Exactly," JHV was quick to jump in, "We have a press release ready to go if you or BEIS are pressed. Otherwise, let's prepare for tomorrow when this damn conference is out of the way."

"Antarctica? Who'd have thought it?" The Secretary of State for BEIS mused on an issue that had appeared out of nowhere exactly three days earlier.

"That's why we're here for you." JHV offered his most angelic smile.

"I'll have a chat with this Mervyn Richards. I had better get up to speed on Antarctica if I'm meant to negotiate with the Norwegians. I don't even know what the capital is."

"Oslo," Mossy chipped in, but this was not what Russell meant.

"Good idea," JHV said, but he was thinking what a complete idiot he had to deal with. Thankfully, JHV had discussed and agreed the main heads of terms with the Norwegians already.

***

At the Yellands', Charles and Tony were walking back along the covered walkway, talking about ride-on mowers versus tractors. The lawns at the front of the house were immaculate and drew the eye over the ha-ha, a ditch with a hidden wall, to the fields beyond, which were full of Highland cattle. It brought the landscape right up to the house. The seamless transition, with no need for visible fencing, would have had Capability Brown smiling from on high.

"We've had eight calves this year," Charles was saying as his phone rang. He answered it: "Yelland."

"Mr Yelland, we have one more request before we release Angelica; do you understand?" enquired a male voice, speaking very precisely and in a monotone, as if trying to disguise an accent or, perhaps, sound threatening.

"What? What request?" Charles put his free hand against an oak pergola support and looked at Tony.

"We want you to issue a press release immediately that says the oil discovery is much bigger than you first thought and it extends much further south than sixty degrees." The man sounded as if he were reading from a script.

"Why don't you ask for money? Why this?" Charles was exasperated and clutching at straws.

"We do not need money, Mr Yelland. Do you understand our request?"

"Yes, but what about Angelica? Let me speak to her."

"She is sleeping right now."

"You killed Belinda … How do I know that Angelica is alive?"

"That was an accident. There is no time to talk. Goodbye." He rang off.

"Shit!"

"What did he ask for?"

"To issue a press release that the find is bigger than announced and extends south of sixty degrees."

"We can do that, Charles. Who cares? We will backtrack in six months. Were they using Angelica's phone?"

"No. Caller ID was withheld."

"OK. Ring the police, then ring Mike Kingdom. I will prepare the release."

CHAPTER TWENTY-FOUR

Mike Kingdom was standing in front of her window, looking at the Oxfordshire countryside – although the edge of the forest could have been almost anywhere. She was wearing no wig and no shirt, but was lounging in loose denim dungarees. In the warm, yellow light of mid-morning, she resembled a prototype model for a Minion. The stub hanging from her lip didn't help the look. The cigarette was not the usual reward, but the result of her frustration at not being able to make any progress. She watched the wildlife. Young rabbits had come out to the edge of the woodland and were hopping through the wiry grass, flicking their white scuts in the air. The ringing phone broke her train of thought, and she walked over to pick it up expecting it to be Tom or Leonard.

"It's Charles," he began, once she had answered. "The kidnappers have just phoned. They have made another demand."

She waited.

"They want me to say that the oil discovery is more extensive than originally thought and that it extends south of sixty degrees," he continued.

"They used those exact words?"

"What? No. No, not exactly, but they were brief."

"Did they ring on Angelica's phone?"

"No. The number was withheld."

She looked back out to the forest edge where the rabbits had spooked each other and disappeared into the scrub.

"Was it the same man?"

"I think so. He speaks very slowly and in a monotone."

"Did he say anything else?" she asked. The cigarette stub was now in the scallop shell.

"No … well, I asked why I should trust them, as they had killed Belinda, and he said that was an accident and rang off."

"How old do you think he is?"

"Difficult to say. He doesn't say much. Between thirty and forty; I don't know."

"And no accent?"

"Could be eastern European, but it sounds like he is reading a script … slowly."

"Have you phoned Inspector Bucknall?"

"Yes, just before calling you. They will try to trace the call."

"Are you going to do what they say?"

"Of course. Tony was with me when they phoned. He is drafting a press release now. I don't care about the consequences. We'll just do what it takes until you or the police find her."

"Anything else?"

"No. Well, I rang the doctor this morning, and they came out and sedated Maria. She was having some sort of nervous breakdown. Geraldine, my sister, is with her now."

"OK, thanks, Charles; I need to make some calls."

After the call had ended, she sat at her desk to gather her thoughts. Her first thought was that Angelica was probably still alive. They might need her, and they were still issuing demands; this was good news. Secondly, this confirmed to her that they were dealing with professionals who were following a plan and, possibly, a script. This was not a bunch of criminals grabbing a rich man's daughter and demanding cash in used notes. Thirdly, as she had suspected, the kidnap was down to one of three reasons: commercial gain, geopolitical manoeuvring or environmental activism. She couldn't think of another reason why anyone would go to so much trouble to kidnap and make such specific demands.

The mugs and dishes were stacked on the draining board. She opened the cupboards nearby and put them away, wiping those that were not quite dry. Whether this was displacement theory in action or domestic tidiness didn't matter – it helped her.

She tried to rank the three reasons. Commercial gain and, in particular, financial gain had always been top of her list. Companies like NorCarbon did not want to be taken over, nor did it want Petronello to expand its operations. Some of its shareholders, investors, bankers or market speculators stood to gain fortunes by the failure or success of the company. However, internationally listed companies could not go around kidnapping the daughters of other CEOs. NorCarbon was in the public eye and subject to scrutiny. It would have to be a rogue operator.

Geopolitics had risen up her list since watching the coverage of the Climate Really Matters Conference a couple of hours earlier. There were undoubtedly authoritarian regimes that would like to tear up the treaty, and also democratic ones that were in an internal debate between environmental objectives and the need for minerals. The US President's spokesman had as good as said as much this morning, in advance of his speech later. Sophie Beardsmore, on the other hand, had stressed the need to re-ratify the treaty. Mike walked back to her desk, imagining how much oil, gas and iron ore (and rare minerals used in computers and batteries) might lie beneath the ice in an area that big. She had put environmental activism at the bottom of her list because there was a patent conflict in her mind between having a caring attitude towards the environment and violence, kidnap and murder. However, Extinction Rebellion was now pushing at boundaries previously held as sacrosanct. Had the wider movement come to the conclusion that they had been too slow and too weak in defending the rainforests? Antarctica was pure and white – the last pristine wilderness on earth. Mike shook her head. Kidnap and murder were a dangerous ploy. The double bluff, if that was what it was, of demanding what you don't want to raise awareness and galvanise world opinion was an all or nothing gamble.

She decided to phone Leonard or, if he wasn't free, to ask Tom to get him to call her. She had a few questions and wanted to make sure he knew about the fresh demand as soon as possible.

***

Mike's gentle environmental activists were, at that precise moment, standing with their legs akimbo to form a human chain across the seafront in Llandudno. Each demonstrator had handcuffed themselves to their neighbour, beginning at the sea-wall balustrade and extending across the main road to the heavy metal railings of a hotel. Others were walking down the line and applying superglue to each pair of hands, so that even if the handcuffs were cut, solvent would be necessary to break the chain. The TV networks were in the perfect places to film all of this, which was precisely what the organisers wanted, because this blocking of the seafront was a diversionary tactic. Protesters in full scuba diving gear had swum underwater across the bay to the pier and were climbing up it. They unfurled huge banners that proclaimed "LEAVE ANTARCTICA ALONE" and "RE-RATIFY THE TREATY". Then, they either chained themselves to the stanchions or created swings that hung down beneath the Victorian pier, making it difficult for them to be raised, reached or dislodged.

Press photographers were having a field day. Everywhere they looked, there was a front page picture: the human chain against the backdrop of the offshore windfarm was a lead writer's dream; the father in a polar bear outfit, holding his two young children; and two men dressed as penguins, shuffling an egg along the road.

Mervyn had been told by the police that he ought to stay in the conference hall, which curtailed his plans for a fifteen-minute walk along the seafront. In a state of heightened anxiety, he was standing holding a cup of coffee in one hand and a piece of cake in the other. The conference programme was tucked in his armpit, causing him to sweat even more. At that moment, his phone rang. He managed to keep his left arm steady and balancing the cup of coffee, and with his right, he stuffed the last bit of cake into his mouth, causing the programme to drop to the floor.

He pulled out the phone and garbled, "Mervyn Richards".

"Mervyn, it's Lawrence. I wasn't sure if it was the coffee break yet?"

"Yes; yes, it is."

"How's the conference?"

Mervyn was wondering why his immediate boss was ringing him from London. "Very good so far. Everyone's waiting for the President at 3.00pm and the PM at 4.00pm."

"You remember that crib sheet on Antarctica you recently produced? It is now being widely quoted, and I wondered who asked you to produce it?"

Mervyn reached across another delegate and put the coffee cup on a table. He moved away out of earshot, contemplating his answer. "I believe it was requested by the PM at the Cabinet meeting on Friday, after he had seen the photograph of the oil rig in the papers."

"Sure, but how did you get briefed? I didn't do it and Sir John didn't."

The sweat broke out even more on Mervyn's forehead. A hot summer's day, an airless room and the coffee all contributed to his uncomfortableness. *I could do without all of this,* he thought, and he began to feel as he had done when the evangelists had called at his flat, but without the handy broom cupboard. He took a couple of deep breaths and looked out to sea. "The Secretary of State for the Environment, Food and Rural Affairs asked me to produce it for the PM."

"Really? Was it Sir Michael or one of his team?"

Oh, what the … Mervyn could not be bothered any more. "The Secretary of State rang me direct."

"Really? You didn't discuss this with me."

"I presumed she had discussed it with whoever secretaries of state need to discuss these things with."

"Well, really! We need to talk about this some more."

Mervyn was now an interesting shade of red and could feel the blood throbbing in his left temple. "Actually, I can see Sophie across the room. Stay on the phone, and I'll get her for you; then, she can tell you to eff off and save me the trouble."

A waitress was sweeping up some broken glass, but luckily, her broom was out of reach.

***

Sophie Beardsmore was also in meltdown, but unlike Mervyn, only through the heat and the inadequate air conditioning. The grey, spotted kaftan that she had changed into for the conference was loose, but still she felt hot. The last thing she wanted to do was talk to some European energy minister about global warming, and so she decided to increase the flow of air around her gills by circulating. Spotting Mervyn, she glided across the room, like an oversized dalek.

"Mervyn." She surprised him.

"Secretary of State," he replied, not having any real idea about protocol in a public forum.

"How are you enjoying it so far?"

Inside, he was fuming, but seeing Sophie forced him to breathe in and calm down a little. "I think I may have just resigned unintentionally," he said, not addressing her question at all.

"How?"

"My boss, Lawrence, just rang to ask who had instructed me to produce that crib sheet on Antarctica. I told him to … Well, I may be in some trouble."

"Did you tell him it was me?"

"Yes, I had to. I'm so sorry; I'm not cut out for all of this. Sorry."

"Don't be silly. You did an excellent job. I will be talking to Russell tomorrow about the whole Antarctica Treaty, and I will sort this out." She could see that Mervyn was hyperventilating, possibly because he was tall enough to occupy a higher layer of even hotter air.

"Something's going on," she continued, "and I am going to get to the bottom of it. I am seeing the PM and the President in a couple of hours, so I will raise a few issues then."

"Will the President know where Antarctica is?" Mervyn was not cut out for diplomatic life.

"Most politicians can't spot their reflections in a mirror, so you have high expectations. What matters is that his many thousands of support staff will know all about it, as will a wide selection of his donors, who will have vested interests." Possibly, the Secretary of State was not entirely cut out for diplomacy either.

"I think that I will save Lawrence the trouble and resign. I will go back to glaciology and get on the first flight south."

"I don't advise that. You would lose out. Hang on in there for a few days. I want to talk to the PM about reassigning Antarctica to my department, so that it would come under the environment. That would be a bold statement of support for the treaty and..." She paused. "I would like you to come across to my department as well."

"Well ... thank you." Mervyn was flattered.

"Stick with it. We need people like you." With that, she turned and cut a swathe through the thinning crowd making their way back into the main hall.

"Michaela?"

"Leonard."

"We must stop meeting like this."

"Nothing would give me greater pleasure." She was already feeling unclean just talking to him.

"Tell me what's new. I've got the President arriving in one hour on Anglesey, wherever that is, and half the long-haired hippies of Europe are finding clever ways to attach themselves to every lamppost."

"Really?"

"I hear that they're called 'the great unwashed'," he continued, "I can't believe shampoo has been a best seller in Llandudno this week."

"You're not exactly 'woke' are you, Leonard?"

"I'm as 'woke' as the next bigot."

Unfortunately, she needed the almost unprecedented access to all of the privileged sources that this man could provide to her or she might have told him to shove off back to Texas or Alabama or wherever he had come from. "Has Tom updated you?"

"Yes."

"The latest blackmail demand may be commercial, political or environmental but, whichever, it could embarrass the President. This is not personal or to get a few dollars."

"I agree."

She still couldn't tell him that oil had not been discovered. "If this Robert Valberg – or whatever he's really called – is the bait to catch the girls, there must be an older person involved. Will you check out this Cyril Lansdowne and a couple of the others in those conversations with Belinda and Angelica?"

"We are checking already."

"Have the police found anything about the vehicle or route?"

"Nothing. They're very good at excluding things, but not so hot at finding new stuff," he said.

"I'm going to Swindon now. They didn't go down the M4 for the fun of it. There's a reason, and there's nothing more I can do while sitting here."

"I always said that you would make a great field agent."

He'd touched a raw nerve. "Never could tell the difference between a desk agent and a field agent, could you?"

"They're the same. They've both got bottle, but one occasionally uses it to piss in."

"Still can't say sorry and that you were wrong, can you?"

"Not today, Michaela. My job's on the line. You get me the information, and I'll apologise."

"It won't bring Dylan back, though."

"None of my dead agents are coming back to life. I live with it."

"Let me know anything you find out about the people, the vehicle or the route."

Neither she nor Leonard had time for this today. Mike had forty-five minutes of bike ride ahead of her to fume at Leonard in her head.

CHAPTER TWENTY-FIVE

The route was easy down the A420, if you knew where the speed cameras were. Mike roared past Kingston Bagpuize, wondering how it was pronounced, and recognised the Defence Academy at Shrivenham where she had stayed for a few days on a Five Eyes course. The day was hot, and the cloud was in two distinct layers: milky cirrus was forming at a high level and a handful of small florets of cumulus were trying to form a bank on the edge of the chalk downs. Passing obliquely under the London Paddington to Bristol railway bridge, she approached the first few scattered buildings on the fringe of Swindon. A rough plan had formed in her head, but it would need to be very flexible and heavily influenced by what happened at her first port of call. Before reaching the A419 peripheral road on the edge of the town, she approached the roundabout at Gablecross, but then veered off to the right and into the Swindon Police HQ car park.

Outside a red brick building with rows of square windows, she took off her black helmet and locked it in the rear top box on the bike. You never knew who was hanging around a police car park. She had put everything she needed in her rucksack, including her powerful laptop and a selection of not-off-the-shelf equipment. She phoned Inspector Bucknall's direct number.

"Inspector Bucknall."

"Hello, Inspector; it's Mike Kingdom here. I understand that Brian Smith may have contacted you about my visit?"

"Yes, he did, and I was separately contacted from the chief constable's office. You are very well-connected, Miss Kingdom?"

She didn't answer his question. "May I see you for a few minutes and pick your brains?"

"When would suit you?" he said unenthusiastically, yet remaining on the courteous side of the line.

"I'm outside your office now. May I come up?" She looked at her watch. It was midday.

***

Mike Kingdom had reached two conclusions earlier, namely that Angelica had about three hours to live and that she was being held in the Swindon area. Once the President and PM had spoken later in the afternoon, Angelica would be of no further use and would be a liability. She could identify 'Robert Valberg' and, probably, anyone else involved; this meant she could not be released. She may well be dumped in the countryside just off the M4 on the kidnappers' route back to London. She was in the Swindon area because, in Mike's opinion, the whole kidnap had been seriously pre-planned and this is where it had been decided the girls were to be held. She did not buy into the idea that Swindon was the place where the kidnappers' car broke down or that some other unexpected event had occurred, causing them to turn off the M4.

She was escorted to the inspector's door by a woman in uniform, who tapped on the door and waited.

Rather than call out like a headmaster, Bucknall came to the door and opened it himself. "Miss Kingdom. Thank you, Lesley."

"Mike," she said, and shook his hand.

He was much softer-looking than she had imagined, and she quickly appraised the small, framed photographs on his desk, which were of his family and of him posing in a rugby team picture. He could not avoid looking at her black wig, remembering the bright-red one she had been wearing on the Zoom call. She took off her rucksack and placed it on the floor as she sat down.

"I'm Christopher, by the way." He seemed to have resolved not to waste time with any frustration and hostility.

"Christopher, I can imagine that the last thing you want at this moment is someone like me taking up your time ... which we really do not have very much of."

"I thought that you were a friend of Charles Yelland?" He was still confused and was now registering her soft American accent.

"I have been employed by him to find Angelica, but I am also linked to the intelligence community ... if we may leave it at that?"

He shrugged his shoulders and opened his hands, placing them palm upwards on his desk. "I don't remember a case with so much interest from ... above." He let the last word hang.

"Have you found out anything new in the last hour?" she asked as she got out her laptop.

"We've identified every vehicle that stopped at the services at the right time and also came off at Junction 16. Another twenty-four vehicles came off there in addition to the twenty-seven we had already identified from Junction 15. Of the twenty-four, we have traced all but two, although that may now be sorted. I will check in a second. We checked Junction 17 as well, for that matter – although, unsurprisingly, only one delivery vehicle went that far west before coming that far back east to Swindon."

"May I see the list?" she asked, sliding a finger along her brow just under the fringe.

"Here, look on my screen," he said as he tapped the keyboard.

She stood up and walked around the desk to his shoulder. He smelt of something sweet, such as violets or roses; it was very feminine. She scanned the list of vehicles, registration numbers, registered owners, their addresses and several more columns.

"There's no Robert Valberg or anything like that," he said trying to help.

"Anyone known to you?"

"Two, but only because of very minor crimes or convictions."

"Nine are Swindon postcodes. Are they near Coate Water or the hospital?"

"What do you mean by close? None is nearer than a mile, I think. We are only four miles from Coate Water down the A419 from here." Though what that added to the conversation wasn't clear.

"Will you send that list to me?" She walked back to her rucksack and took out a memory stick the size of a credit card, but much fatter, and handed it to him. "And the list from Junction 15 that you had previously?"

"Sure," he said.

"May I grab a cup of tea as well?" She smiled at him in the closest approximation to flirting that she could manage. "One sugar, no milk."

He stood up and walked to a connecting door. He asked someone out of sight to bring two teas. That was all the time needed for her to insert a small device into a spare port on his computer.

He resumed his seat, ejected her memory stick and gave it to her.

"May I sit quietly in the corner and use my laptop on that desk for a few minutes? Then I'll leave you in peace," she requested.

"Fine. Push those three files to the side."

***

Five minutes later, she was sipping a cup of tea and scrolling through the lists on her laptop, carefully angled away from the inspector's eyes. She was working as fast as she could. Somewhere not far away, Angelica was probably terrified after four days of being held in some basement or garage. She would, perhaps, have been even more frightened not knowing what had happened to her best friend Belinda, who would have disappeared never to return. The kidnappers may have drugged her so she would not know what was happening. These thoughts brought back the moments of terror from her own past when she had watched Dylan dying in front of her eyes in Amsterdam, while she was lying in a ditch trying to stay conscious after losing so much blood.

Tony was in his twelfth-floor office, sitting with Jo. The doors were closed.

"Jo, you're probably wondering what's going on. I need to tell you, or you'll think Charles and I are nuts," he declared.

She was wearing an aubergine-coloured suit and a white blouse. She was playing with the gold and enamel Hermes bracelets on her wrist, which were making a dull clunking sound as she fiddled.

"Angelica's been kidnapped," he continued in a matter-of-fact way.

She stopped fiddling and let out a small gasp.

"She was taken before the AGM, at which they demanded that Charles announce a major oil discovery even though, as you know, we have not had any success worth talking about. The police are busy searching, and there is a press embargo that has not been breached so far."

Jo's hand was now covering her mouth and fear had entered her hazel eyes.

"Belinda, her friend, was dumped in a park in Swindon and was found on Friday afternoon, but has died in hospital."

"No." Jo's hand stayed on her mouth and the fear now gave way to disbelief.

"The kidnappers have just made a second demand that we issue and promote a press release saying that the Antarctic Treaty must be reviewed and mineral extraction allowed. They want it promoted before the President and PM speak in Wales later this afternoon."

"They haven't asked for money?" She was ever pragmatic.

"No, this is not about money. It is either NorCarbon in some shape or form, or even larger global forces."

"Who are we talking about?"

"Vested interests in Antarctica ... the Russians, the Chinese ... who knows? So, can you and I put together the press release and get it out there as loudly as we can. Don't worry about the repercussions; we'll deal with them afterwards when Angelica is safe. Petronello will be badly damaged, but we'll survive ... just."

"How is Charles ... and Maria?"

"Maria is sedated, and they have just taken her to hospital. She has suffered a sort of nervous breakdown. Charles is... well, Charles. He is devastated, angry and frustrated. You know more than anyone that he has never been good at losing."

She stood up in a robotic way, shook off her dark thoughts and sat at a keyboard. "Shall we get Andrew in? Or is it just you and me?"

"You and me. Andrew will understand."

"OK, fire away," she said.

***

Mervyn had left the conference in disgust. This was not how he wanted his life to be. He liked order. He hated people. His attention deficit hyperactivity disorder (ADHD) had never been diagnosed at school, meaning he had grown up angry and unable to understand why he felt as he did. He had made it through university by concentrating on his geology and his glaciology. Geomorphology was structure, crystallography was maths, and palaeontology was long lists of Latin names. He buried himself in these fact-based disciplines and ignored anyone around him. The social side of student life passed him by completely. He remained awkward in other people's presence, unless he knew them well. When he eventually ended up in Antarctica, he knew he had found a second home. Yes, he was virtually trapped with a handful of individuals, but the numbers were so small that he could cope, and some were not bad company. They learnt when to leave him alone. He revelled in the repetition of tasks and the lack of the overwhelming cacophony of urban life.

It was the lunchtime recess, and he could not face eating a buffet lunch at round tables talking to random strangers. That was his idea of a nightmare, having to ask people if a seat was taken and if he was able to join them. Social interaction was not on his agenda. His delegate badge was hanging around his neck, but it was swivelled so as not to reveal his name; it dissuaded people from talking to him. He took it off, together with his tie, and put them in his pocket. There was a good chance he would not go back to the conference and – who knows? – not work in London again. A phone call to his mother would sort him out later, but first, he needed a pie and a pint while standing at a bar.

Most of the demonstrations and activities were happening on the seafront, so he headed into the town, using any quiet-looking side road to lose the crowds. He walked along, unaware of the attractive semi-detached villas with yuccas growing in pots on the gravel of their token front gardens. A Victorian pub next to an old, white coach house on the corner of a street took his eye, and he stepped into the cool and relative dark. It was half-empty and did not seem to be full of conference-goers. He could hear Welsh being spoken at a table in the bay window. There was a slight stickiness to the carpet, and the smell of greasy pastry filled the air. At the bar, which was made from large pieces of dark-purple slate from Penrhyn, four of the stools were occupied, but the three nearest to the meat-pie cabinet were vacant. Feeling hungry, he migrated to the bright lights and hypnotic rotation of the shelves displaying foil trays filled with pies of all descriptions. He chose an oggie, a sort of miner's pasty, and a pint of beer.

Perched on his stool, he stared at a framed poster of the Royal Navy's worst ever submarine disaster off Llandudno in 1939. He was reading about the HMS *Thetis* when the conversation at the other end of the bar caught his attention.

"You wouldn't last five minutes down there, although your fat might keep you warm," declared one of the men.

The butt of the abuse had his broad back to Mervyn, blocking most of the view. His podgy fingers were permanently gripping a half-drunk pint resting on the bar. "I have no intention of working on an oil rig there or anywhere else, thank you, Rat Arse."

"A ready supply of butch young men doesn't tempt you, Mossy?"

"Yes, but I am allergic to hard, physical work."

"Why limit it to 'hard, physical' work? You haven't done a day's work of any sort in your life, you lazy git."

"I use my brains."

The other three laughed and pointed at him.

"JHV finds me very useful, you tossers. Who else could have thought up that picture and had it produced? That all takes brains," the man called Mossy defended his character.

"I don't give a shoot who came up with the idea as long as the Vikings are happy. Let's have another round of drinks. The President isn't on until 3.00pm, and by the time our wonderful

PM speaks, it will be game, set and match," the man called Rat Arse suggested.

"By the way, Mossy, game, set and match is a sporting term … which involves exercise. You may like to look the expression up?"

***

Later, back in his hotel room, Mervyn was regretting the meat pie and beer. The smell of the Indian takeaway that was coming from the ventilation shaft outside his half-opened window was not making it any better. The overheard conversation was troubling him. He recognised the name JHV, but he had never met the man. As he became more tense, the recent meal sat ever less comfortably in his stomach. He reached for an indigestion tablet to chew and dialled his mother's number.

CHAPTER TWENTY-SIX

Mike Kingdom had long finished her cup of tea. She had gradually emptied her rucksack and spread its contents across the desk, slowly making it her own. The inspector had spent his time either on the phone, scrolling using his computer mouse or clattering his keyboard using a two-fingered technique that was effective if unorthodox. They had not spoken.

"Do you have an armed-response team ready?" she asked suddenly.

"Yes, of course. For the last three days, we have had one waiting here in the east and another in the district centre … that's west Swindon. We also have the traffic boys on extra patrols up and down the M4 between Junctions 15 and 17. There are apparently two Special Forces units from Hereford in a camp nearby. Throw in some Special Branch and the helicopter on notice, and we have it covered. I'm not coordinating any of this, by the way."

"Impressive."

"I have never known a job like this where resources are not a problem," he continued, "and where they probably won't be needed."

"You don't think she's in Swindon or nearby?"

"No, I don't, but I'm pretty much alone in this view. I think they were driving the girls, drugged or otherwise, from London to a destination down the M4. They stopped at the services either to fill up or to swap vehicles. Then, they had some problem with Belinda, who reacted badly to the drugs she had taken or been given, and they needed to get rid of her. I don't think they wanted her dead. They pulled off the motorway at Junction 16 and made their way back east to the hospital. They pulled into Coate Water car park, a few hundred yards before the hospital feeder road. They walked her the few yards to a bench and dumped her. She was bound to be found soon, and even if she recovered, she could only give us some false names of people who will be out of the country by the time we find out who they really are. Next, they drove Angelica on down the M4 or A419 to end up in Bristol, Wales or the Cotswolds." He obviously needed to get this theory off his chest, as if no one would listen to him.

"Hmmm." She was staring blankly over her screen and evaluating his theory.

"What's wrong with that scenario?" He raised his arms and put his hands behind his head.

"Nothing, if you are prepared to accept that Belinda reacted adversely to the drugs in the car, shortly after they left Chiswick around 9.00am."

"What's wrong with that?"

"Nothing." Mike began to admit to herself that she was letting emotion interfere with her analysis.

"You don't want that to be right?" he asked while lowering his arms and gently folding back the cuffs of his white shirt's sleeves.

"True," she conceded, "because if you are right, she could be anywhere in a fifty-mile radius, and we won't find her before they kill her in a few hours' time."

"We may find her, but we would need intelligence help. My team can track vehicles all day long, but if the names and addresses are false, we will get nowhere."

She was warming to him. He gave off a confident but gentle air.

"You do have intelligence help ... me."

His face betrayed a wry smile. "You know that, if I'm right or mostly right, we need the kidnappers' real names, nationalities, mobile phones, GPS coordinates and so much more, or sadly, Angelica is very likely going to be killed. I say that as the father of three kids."

She turned her head towards him in a way that made the two sides of her Cleopatra wig flick back and forth before settling down. "What if your theory is wrong?"

He brushed a very small speck of fluff from the top of his desk onto the floor. In all probability, this was to allow him time to think. "If I am wrong, she is within a few miles of this office. That is where the kidnappers were aiming for when they left London. They went past Swindon, avoiding the obvious exit and cut back through the town to a house. At some point soon after that, Belinda had a bad reaction to some drugs and the major problem arose. They dumped her in the park."

"Did you knock on the door of every house that adjoins the park, golf course and lane?"

He looked at her as a father would to a ten-year-old. "Yes, it was one of the first things we did. We were checking for people who may have seen something."

"What about the twenty-four vehicles that drove through Swindon? How's it going?"

"A bit of a nightmare, but we're getting there. If your objective is to avoid major roads, buildings and places with CCTV, there are thousands of routes; I know the town well. Maybe the kidnappers do too? The M4 was very slow that day, and I think they got behind schedule"

She had been pressing him, and he seized the moment to challenge her. "What's your pet theory?"

She stretched her left leg and played with her mouse to keep the screen alive. "I think she's nearby and not just because I want that to be true. I think they got to the pre-planned location, and then it started to go wrong. They dumped Belinda, but they're still there for another few hours, and then they will disappear from our screens."

"And who are 'they'?"

"Well, this kidnap is different. We are not talking about money, and by that, I am not excluding commerce and power. We are talking international gangs, conglomerates or governments."

"And what are the Secret Services doing at this precise moment?" He was transfixed by her dark-brown eyes as she weighed up her answer.

"Well, let's just say that, whatever they are all doing, it will come to me via this gizmo about half an hour before it comes down to your computer over there." This was said without any one-upmanship.

"And what does that second gizmo do?"

"This other one? Oh, that explodes and destroys everything near it if anyone tampers with the first gizmo."

"Oh great," he said, "Try not to burn the desk; it's public property."

***

Tony had changed his plans. In the immediate aftermath of the second ransom demand, he had thought that not involving Andrew, their PR man, was a good idea. In talking to Jo, he had come to the conclusion that it was not. It would be Andrew whom every editor and researcher would contact once the dam broke. He was trained in these matters and could give interviews. Tony would be inarticulate and easily riled. He also had a face made for radio, as Andrew had once said. Charles was not up to it; he was finally showing the strain, what with having Maria in hospital as well. He needed to be free to answer his phone to the kidnappers and the police – hopefully, with the good news that Angelica had been released. Tony, unfortunately, had a horrible feeling deep inside that she would not be released alive. Given the options open to him, Tony thought it was easier for Andrew to take the flak as the messenger and not the source.

"Happy?" Tony asked.

Jo and Andrew nodded.

"Then press send."

Andrew looked at the great list of TV and radio stations, news agencies and newspapers to which the five line press release was being sent. He reckoned it would be three minutes before his phone would ring non-stop for the rest of the day; it was 12.45pm, and everyone at the conference would be at lunch. The press release was also being sent to the relevant Government departments and, as implied by the kidnappers' demand, to the conference managers in Llandudno.

"I will put on my tin hat and man the ramparts," Andrew said as he beat a hasty retreat to his office.

Tony and Jo watched him leave, wearing his blazer with its silver buttons and not a hair out of place on his head. 'Trim' was the word most used to describe Andrew or, perhaps, 'dapper'.

Tony sat down, ready for his own barrage of calls, which would surely follow a few minutes later. His would be from bankers, investors and shareholders, who would all want to know that their money was safe.

***

In Llandudno, the news swept through the dining hall, the hotels and bars like a hurricane; nowhere was unaffected by the storm of social media indignation and outrage. Expletives could be heard everywhere, and the Twittersphere was awash with emojis and GIFs. Sophie Beardsmore, who was meant to be closing the conference after the PM, was in the middle of a slice of carrot cake on a paper plate with, annoyingly, "Made from recycled paper plates" as the motif. She had not yet seen what was written on the toilet paper. She put down her fork and sat back as her phone went into overdrive with its continuous vibrating and flashing. The press release had managed to hijack the Climate Really Matters Conference completely and turn it into a debate about the review of the Antarctic Treaty. Her speech would have to address this in some way. She needed to speak to the PM, who was having lunch at some hotel with a dozen environment ministers from around the globe; a version of the Last Supper, perhaps? She also needed her speech writer to start thinking of some platitudes and vapid statements. This was not Sophie's style, but Government policy had yet to be fixed on the issue. It had only came up four days previously and needed serious internal debate within Cabinet, not decided on the hoof in North Wales reacting to a President, a load of demonstrators and an oil executive calling for the treaty to be reviewed and, effectively, abandoned.

Turning around, the first person she caught sight of was Mervyn, who was walking towards her with his tie loose around his neck and hanging over his delegate's badge. He looked flustered and was making odd eye movements. Obviously, he had heard the news as well. As much as she had enjoyed his enthusiasm, he was not what she needed at the moment. She made polite excuses to her neighbours at the table, who were already asking if the treaty was doomed, and stood up. She decided to walk to the room designated for the chair and the speakers, and then text her speechwriter.

Before she had gone twenty paces, Mervyn was at her shoulder. "Sophie," he said before he realised that he should have called her 'Secretary of State'.

She looked at him askance. "I have heard, Mervyn; thank you. I am on my way to deal with it." She was a little stressed herself and was counting the numbers of waiters as she walked.

"No, sorry, it's not about that. Well, it might be about that; I need to tell you something." He was rambling.

"You've got about fifty yards, then I'm in my room."

He looked around as they walked and picked his moment to bend down to her ear and say, "JHV was involved in the fake photograph." He stood back up to his full height and kept in step with her.

"What?" She kept waddling, and the other delegates had no choice but to move out of her way.

"Give me two minutes in your room. Please." His mother would have been proud, as when he was ten, she had given up telling him to say please. His social awareness was so bad that forgetting a 'please' was the least of his problems.

"OK." She turned down a short corridor and opened a door marked "Speakers".

Inside were three people, tapping at phones and laptops.

"Sophie, have you heard?" asked a tall, distinguished man with rheumy eyes.

"Yes, I have Eric. Will you give me two minutes, and then I will join you."

She directed Mervyn to the other end of the room, and they sat down at a desk.

"Quietly and calmly," she said, having noticed that he was about to explode.

"I have just had lunch in a bar a long way over there." He pointed vaguely inland. "Someone called Mossy was saying that JHV finds him very useful and that this Mossy had thought up that picture in the newspapers and had it produced. There were four of them at the bar. I only caught the name of one other guy – Rat Arse or something like that. They sounded a bit public school."

"How do you know they were talking about the fake photograph?" Sophie asked under her breath.

"Because they were talking about Mossy not wanting to work on an oil rig down there."

She moved a lock of mousey hair from her eyes and took stock. "OK, Mervyn, I will deal with this. Please don't tell anyone else. I will deal with it. I suggest you get a glass of water and sit quietly at the back of the hall. Now, I must speak to the PM and adjust my speech, given the press release from Petronello. And, Mervyn, don't worry."

"Thank you ... I'll go and call my mam first."

"Good idea."

***

In Portcullis House, another person was occupied by the Petronello open letter on the Antarctic Treaty. JHV could not keep the smile from his face as he watched the TV stations and read all of the texts and messages. He opened the bottom drawer of his desk and lifted out a half bottle of vodka from next to his stack of mints. He topped up his glass. His phone rang, displaying the caller's name as the PM, so he thought he should answer it.

"John, have you seen the press release?"

"Yes. I am watching the main news channel coverage as we speak," JHV said, taking a sip.

"All hell is breaking loose up here. I have just finished the environment ministers' lunch, and they didn't talk about anything else. The demonstrators outside are going crazy, and I've got to meet the President in an hour. What shall I say in my speech?"

"Whatever you do, don't shut the door on a review of the treaty. Leave it ajar. Bang on about ecological protection and ever-increasing environmental standards. Say that Antarctica is a top priority for the Government, and steer the conversation back to the bigger and broader objectives of the conference. Keep saying, 'Climate really matters'."

"Will you send Penelope some notes and get her to change my speech?"

"I'll get right on it."

"Thanks, bye."

JHV opened a buff-coloured folder on his desk and pulled out two sheets of paper. He had written them earlier and would get them sent over to the PM in a short while. The treaty was now well and truly dead, and he would reap untold benefits. He did not need to hammer any more nails into its coffin. Petronello, the President and so many others were doing that for him. He would sit back and encourage caution on the review, knowing that genies were notoriously difficult to put back into bottles.

All of this over a few million square miles of ice. *Really?* He swallowed the rest of his warm vodka. It needed ice. He must get a fridge in his office.

CHAPTER TWENTY-SEVEN

It was almost 1.00pm, and Mike Kingdom needed a cigarette, but she couldn't spare the time. She took out a liquorice stick and began to chew it.

Inspector Bucknall wasn't fazed at all and even smiled. "Are you hungry?" he asked.

"Starving, I didn't have time before I left this morning to think about food."

"I am going to get a sandwich from down the corridor in a minute. What would you like?"

"Anything that once had a pulse. But to be honest, I could eat anything, really. Thank you."

He stood up, took his wallet from the pocket of his jacket, which was hanging on the back of his chair, and walked out of the office. Something about the way he walked reminded her of a quarterback. She took the liquorice stick from her mouth and put it back in the packet. Turning back to her laptop with its two attached gizmos, she checked her entries and pressed the return key.

Mike's skill was in the collation and cross-referencing of databases; this is what had made her name and attracted the attention of the powers that be in Washington state and in DC. Her software evolutions were added to the standard selection of CIA search options and became legendary. She was not just a geek but seemed to have the mentality of both a field and an investigating officer. She understood what was likely to be needed, but also what was not available. Her amendments allowed for gaps and for spelling mistakes. They ranked results and permitted refinements based on flawed data-set input. In short, they were realistic, pragmatic and usable.

She had spent the last twenty-five minutes checking one hundred and sixty-seven houses that were on three roads and a lane that backed on to or adjoined Coate Water. Unlike Christopher Bucknall, she thought it was not all about the vehicles and distant unknown destinations; she thought it was about carrying Belinda's body to the bench. The hundred-plus houses she had identified had direct or very close access to the park via back-garden gates, alleyways or nearby cul de sacs.

The boring but clever technique she had developed was based on what was missing from a collection of databases, not what was included. Most search systems look for everyone called Jack and match them with everyone who owns a BMW. This is great if you know the suspect is called Jack and/or owns a BMW. Her system looked for common things a BMW driver called Jack might do or not do. If that doesn't sound earth-shattering, it is because it is not. In the last half an hour, she had – with a small amount of help from the Wiltshire police's computer system and the CIA's second-level mainframe network, whirring away deep underground in caves in Virginia, Iceland and New Zealand – set in motion an examination of a number of properties near Coate Water. Many houses used by organised crime (and used as safe houses by spying agencies) share certain negative characteristics; that is to say, things that don't happen there. Their occupants, for instance, may not have applied for postal votes, they have not enrolled into the local schools, they have not made planning applications, they were not late paying their council tax, they do not have criminal convictions, etc., encompassing another fifty or so categories. If you search which houses have the fewest of these criteria, you will eliminate the vast majority of them. In this case all bar two.

She didn't know what the suspects had; she knew what they were likely *not* to have.

Christopher Bucknall came back in with packets of sandwiches, a tube of Pringles and two cans of Pepsi. "Sorry, not a great choice. Hope you like Chinese pork and piccalilli? Apparently, it's part of a new fusion range. Confusion, if you ask me."

She reached for her purse. "How much do I owe you?"

"One liquorice stick. I haven't had one since I was kid."

She smiled and thanked him.

A short time later, while crunching Pringles and swigging Pepsi from the can, she called up Google Street View and looked at the two houses. One large detached house backed directly on to the park and the other, a much-extended house, was on a large plot at the end of a side road. They both had a brick-built ground floor with white clapperboard above. They both had dormer windows and either walls or mature hedges. One was next to a short track that possibly led through to somewhere near the Coate Water car park, the other presumably had direct access to the golf course via a rear-garden gate. Unfortunately, she couldn't see enough of the properties to gauge if there were secure places in which Angelica might be held or windows that could be blocked in. Mike stared at the properties, imagining what Angelica might be going through inside. Which one?

She came out of her reverie and reminded herself that this was just a theory. Angelica could be in South Wales or back in London – or worse.

Mike was now searching the details of the two properties on the council database. The detached house was called Harlech and belonged to a Mrs Harmston. Two other people were living at the address: Roy and Luke. Given their ages, Mike surmised that this was a divorced or widowed mother and her son with a partner. The other house belonged to a Mr Biddlecombe, who was forty-three years old with a wife and two youngish children. Neither property looked promising as hideouts for kidnappers.

She went back to the photographs from the street.

Christopher walked over carrying his empty can and collected hers to put in the recycling bin. He caught a glimpse of the two houses on her split screen. "Thinking of buying locally?"

"Out of my league, I think. I'm just familiarising myself with the area."

"It's one of the wealthier parts of Swindon," he said, and then sat back down.

"I'm going to ride over there and have a look. Call me if anything happens."

It took a couple of minutes for her to pack everything back into her rucksack. She stood up and walked towards him.

"Thanks for everything," she said as she put the rest of the liquorice sticks on his desk, at the back of his computer. Effortlessly, she pulled out the small device.

"No heroics?" He had a feeling that she was not revealing everything to him. "Mike, you have my number."

She left his office, exited the building and stepped outside under a cloudless, pure, blue sky. In tight, black motorcycle leathers, she was going to be hot, but hopefully, the rush of air on the bike would cool her down. It was only ten minutes to Coate Water. When she reached her motorbike, she unlocked the box and removed her helmet; in putting it on over the black wig, it took a little time to get it comfortable. She started the engine and rode slowly out of the car park.

A few hundred yards away, a screen lit up and bleeped. The driver sat up and immediately started his engine. He drove out of the supermarket car park and saw the bike leave the town-centre exit of the large roundabout.

***

"I need to speak to you urgently and privately. I am in the room reserved for the speakers. When are you coming across?" Sophie messaged the PM.

He was, at that moment, just saying goodbye to the last ministers to leave before going up to a hotel room to freshen up. He was fifteen minutes away from the conference centre, unless his cavalcade of three vehicles was diverted to avoid the increasingly angry mob that now numbered in the thousands. He would have words with JHV and Russell when he got back to London. It was them who had suggested the conference so many months ago, yet they were noticeably not present now that the proverbial was hitting the fan.

"I'm not coming across until 2.00pm, when I am greeting the President. If urgent, please come here," he messaged back.

"I'll come straight over," she replied.

"I'll let Melissa at reception know."

She rang the car pool coordinator and took the first available car. They insisted that she had armed security, and this took another ten minutes to organise.

***

The gulls were mewing from the rooftops. They were both disturbed by the increased human activity and excited by the opportunities to feast on dropped food and carelessly waved ice creams. Their white breasts were highlighted by the summer sun as they padded up and down the ridge tiles and balconies opposite the conference centre. Sophie stepped out into the bright light to be met by a police officer who escorted her to the Discovery that whisked her towards the hotel the PM had used for his working lunch. They passed a long line of police in riot gear, who were now forming a line to match that of the shouting, placard-waving demonstrators further down the Parade. There was a frisson in the air that had not been there earlier in the morning.

***

Melissa met Sophie at reception and took her, via the lift, to a long corridor with strange, bold wallpaper in black and white, which resembled the world's longest barcode. Halfway along, they were greeted by two armed policemen, who moved to the side to let them pass.

Sophie was as down to earth as was possible and wasted no time on horoscopes and superstitions, but every minute that had gone by since she had been in Llandudno, she could not escape the mounting feeling that things were about to go very wrong.

Melissa knocked, opened the door and let Sophie walk into the large suite. The PM had taken off his jacket and was standing there in a clean white shirt and suit trousers. His tie was in his right hand and his hair needed a comb.

"You're probably bringing me some wonderful news," he said ironically on seeing Sophie's serious face.

She slumped into a wide armchair upholstered in pale-green crushed velvet and blew out a breath upwards to move a lock of hair that had fallen across her eyes. "Sadly not. Something's going on, and I think that you and I are being shafted good and proper."

He abandoned his tie on a side table and sat on another large, green chair. "How?"

"I have a very strong suspicion that the faked photograph was set up by JHV, aided by those creeps Andrew Sedgwick Moss and Patrick Ratoath."

"What makes you suspect them?"

"They have been talking too loudly in a local hostelry."

"Sounds more than likely … drinking and talking loudly, I mean."

"Don't you think that it's odd that Russell and JHV aren't here?"

"I have been wondering about that myself." He leant back and tried to relax his aching back.

"In four days, we've gone from never talking about Antarctica to it dominating the entire political agenda. Good heavens, we have the damn President flying in to speak at short notice."

"True, and the crowd up here seem well-organised and vocal."

"I don't think this is about one oil discovery by a company that would benefit from a scrapping of the treaty. I understand why they might press for that, but I think this is bigger. This is about geopolitical expansion."

"I'm tending to think along the same lines."

"This is about Russian or Chinese expansion in space and in the Black Sea ... and in the South China Sea. Yes, it's about Antarctica, but it's about tearing up the international order."

"It could be in American interests as well."

"This is about somebody very powerful getting control of land, minerals, communications, etc., by a multipronged attack. This is soft loans, building a free airport, land first on the back of the moon, extend a coral island, disseminate fake news, provide the chips for 5G technology ... and I don't know what else."

"So why are JHV and, maybe, Russell involved?" the PM asked.

"Victor, they don't have a backbone between them. They will bend whichever way the wind is blowing or based on whoever pays them the most."

"Sophie, you know the daughter of Petronello's chair has been kidnapped for four days. They have not demanded money; they wanted him to announce the oil discovery at the AGM and, in the last few hours, to send a press release to this conference."

She grabbed one of her chins between a thumb and forefinger, and a forlorn look entered her eyes. "Victor, I don't like JHV, Russell or their schoolboy chums, but I hope that they are not caught up in kidnap."

"The kidnap is only known about by a handful of people because we needed to keep it quiet. When she is no longer a valuable bargaining chip … I think she will be killed."

"That's terrible. What are you going to do? The President speaks in just over an hour."

"Yes," he said, picking up his tie and wrapping it around the collar of his shirt, "I must go and meet him. As to the others, I will get Serena at Homeland Security to look into it discreetly. We cannot risk it getting out from MI5 and MI6 via Five Eyes to the USA, and certainly not this afternoon."

"So do you and I change our speeches?"

"No, keep it all as anodyne as possible. Personally, I'd like to re-ratify the treaty without change for another fifty years and leave some other poor sod to worry about it then."

"It is ironic, really, that you cannot say that. That is exactly what the demonstrators and most people probably want to hear."

***

Angelica was sobbing. She could not understand why her mother and father would not pay the ransom. She had asked the woman how much they had asked for, and the woman had laughed and said that some things were worth more than money. What did that mean? Angelica tried to move, but her back ached from the awkward position of lying on a bed with one arm manacled above her head and her ankles locked together. When she did move, her skin was sore where she had lain on wet bedclothes for four days. The pieces of tape she had torn off Belinda's and her own faces were still next to her, acting as a constant reminder that her best friend was no longer there. Had Belinda's parents paid the ransom? It just didn't make sense.

Trying to cry quietly made it worse. She resorted to biting the blankets or pulling them partly over her face. What were the police doing? They must be looking for her. But where was she? She realised she had no idea, but she was sure it was a long way down the M4 from London. In a moment of clarity, she tried to think of anything she could do to help. The possibilities were limited, and her wrist and ankles were red raw from trying to escape. Looking up at the blind, she wondered who could see it. She could move the blind a little, but all that did was let in some daylight. She had waggled it for a while, hoping that someone might notice it, but this clearly hadn't worked – perhaps it was not visible to anyone.

Her eyes fell back on to the short pieces of tape. Could she stick them on the outside of the blind? A sort of 'X marks the spot'? Using her mouth and fingers, she straightened out the short lengths of dark-grey tape. She only had one hand free, so she couldn't hold the fabric away from the window while reaching up to stick on the tape. It took ten minutes of stretching and failed attempts before both pieces were attached in a crude cross pattern. Laughter was coming up from the kitchen below, as was the bass rhythm from music being played on a radio.

It was twenty minutes later when Cyril came into the room, lifted the blind and removed the tape. He belted her across the face with the back of his hand, and she hit her head on the metal bedframe.

CHAPTER TWENTY-EIGHT

Mike rode into the car park at Coate Water and drew up next to another bigger motorbike. Why this should give her comfort was hard to say. She repeated her routine and put her helmet in the box on the back, as well as her small rucksack. She unzipped her leather jacket and straightened her wig. Apart from two women walking a Yorkshire terrier, there was no one else in sight. A very few white clouds were just beginning to form in the sky, and there was a smell of cut grass in the air. From the heat of the car park, she set off up a small track between trees, which should lead to the first large detached house. The immediate shade provided a little relief from the day's heat, and her eyes began to adjust to the reduced light. She approached a high brick wall that aimed to give the house some protection from intruders, who would perhaps be using the park at night, and looked up to the open bedroom windows. The sound of children splashing in a paddling pool and laughing loudly made her think that this perhaps was not where Angelica was being held.

Further along, the track narrowed where the trees and bushes overhung more. She had an uneasy claustrophobic feeling, but pressed on until she suddenly gasped. Ahead, she saw an abandoned bike without a front wheel, which had been thrown into the hedgerow. The bike brought back vivid memories of that crazy day on the outskirts of Amsterdam.

***

She had been tracking the Colombian individuals for months from her desk in Chiswick. The drugs shipment was to be concealed in four specially designed refrigerated containers, ostensibly full of green bananas. The fact that the fruit gave off a strong smell of ethylene as they self-ripened provided some disguise against inspection. However, it was the false metal plate, which ran the entire length of the underside of the shipping container, that concealed the packets. If you walked inside, you would just see the usual ribbed-steel floor. You could x-ray the container, and there would be no telltale black patches where drugs were packed in among the forty-pound boxes of bananas. The new void, created by the plate, was only three inches deep, but when multiplied by the floor area of the four containers, this added up to a major drugs shipment.

Leonard had thought it would be more credible if Dylan, as the on-site liaison officer with the Dutch narcotics police, had a wife with him in the house that had been rented near where the Colombians were living in a suburb of Amsterdam. Mike would be there primarily to provide the very latest intelligence in real time, particularly if there were last-minute changes of plan by the drug traffickers. She was a desk officer, untrained in field work, and would not take part in the raid with the police.

It seemed fairly straightforward, and she got to be with Dylan for a week or more. Unfortunately, it didn't work out like that.

Four days before the predicted arrival of the container ship, it was passing to the north of the Azores, making good progress across the Atlantic Ocean. Dylan and Mike were taking a few hours off and driving along a quiet, tree-lined road next to a canal, on the way to have a picnic. They had just overtaken a lady on a bicycle when the occupants of an oncoming car opened fire. The windscreen shattered, and their car swerved off the road, down the grass slope and hit a poplar tree. Mike was thrown halfway out of the passenger door, badly cutting her left leg. She had dragged herself onto the grass as the car burst into flames. The only witness to her screams was the lady who had also crashed; the bike had lost its front wheel and was lying on its side.

***

In Swindon, she stared at the abandoned bike and tried to banish the memories that continued to flood back. She walked on up the track and approached the rear access lane at the back of the second property she had identified. It had another brick wall surrounding it, built in a strange bond with a large diamond pattern of protruding dark-blue bricks. There was broken glass stuck into the mortar coping to deter intruders – one of the disadvantages of living next to an unlit, wooded track by a park. It was at the end of a row of houses on a side road and was not overlooked. The curtains and blinds on the upstairs windows were closed, and there was no sound coming from the garden. There was a solid wooden door in the perimeter wall, and opposite this, there were piles of grass clippings, decomposing from green nearer the top to brown at the bottom. She crept up to the door and tried to peer through the crack. On seeing nothing, she wondered what to do next, but this decision was taken out of her hands as a blow hit the back of her head, slamming her face into the door. Her wig fell backwards, and she crumpled to the ground.

The door opened, and she was bundled, semiconscious, into the back garden. The door shut, and the bolts slid back.

***

It wasn't exactly the White House. The PM and the President stood grinning and shaking hands for the world's press in a conference-hall foyer with the flags of the two countries leaning in a perfect V-shape behind them. Afterwards, they took the short walk down a corridor to the room reserved for the speakers and honoured guests, but the amount of armed protection for the President turned it into something resembling the rush for the 6.00pm train out of Paddington on a Friday evening.

Once in the relative quiet of the room, the PM could finally start to talk with some freedom to the President. "Conrad, sorry you had to put up with the demonstration." The PM was patting down his hair, as if he had just finished a ride on a funfair.

"Victor, if that's the worst I have to put with, I am very happy."

They made their way to the end, where a door was opened allowing them into a small ante room devoid of people. There was a table covered in a white cloth and about ten chairs, all sprayed a matt gold, of the type used at weddings. A framed print of the seabirds of Wales was the only concession to decoration.

"Apologies for the room and the need to improvise, but things are moving apace," stated the PM.

"I have spent more time in rooms like this than I care to remember, trying to raise funds in every one-horse town from Arizona to Iowa."

"Conrad, I am wondering if we should backtrack today on the treaty review. I am worried that you and I are being railroaded by forces unknown into tearing this thing up. We've got the Chinese satellites knocking ours out of orbit, their new missions to Mars and beyond; their buying of bits of Jamaica, the Maldives and Sri Lanka; Russian submarines patrolling under the Arctic; the Ukraine War; and all of the rest. I just feel that this Antarctic Treaty is a protection not a threat."

"Great, but what about the oil discovery? The vultures have seen the carcass and are flying in from miles around."

The PM resisted the temptation to explain the geographical distribution of vultures around the world. He needed Conrad on his side. "True," he said, "but the stuff in the ground isn't going anywhere. Why not leave it there for another fifty years?"

"We need this stuff now to power our automobiles and for computer screens and communication systems. Victor, you know that everything we use is either grown or comes out the ground. What will a few mines matter in millions of square miles? We are not going to use Antarctica to grow wheat."

"And what about the dozen military bases that will be built there in minutes?"

"Three-quarters of Antarctica is claimed by you Brits, the Norwegians, or the Aussies and New Zealanders ... and you're a friendly bunch." He laughed.

"Yes, but fifteen per cent is unclaimed, and there are new

Chinese, Russian and – dare I say it – American claims. Do we want to open this can of worms?"

"I would. Now we know for sure that there is the last great oilfield on earth in sectors claimed by you Brits, the Argies, the Chileans and the Norwegians."

"We haven't even mentioned the environmental damage." The PM suddenly remembered the conference and his speech in a couple of hours. He had already removed some flowery references to a virgin, pure as the driven snow, being courted by a raft of suitors. The chances of her being deflowered soon were looking increasingly likely.

***

Patrick Ratoath and Andrew Sedgwick Moss were about to walk in to take their seats at the conference, together with some of the other members of the committees and sub-committees that they sat on as advisers. At that moment, their computers and phones in London were being checked for any evidence that they were involved in the fake photograph and its distribution. JHV was also part of the investigation organised by the Metropolitan Police Force. Serena at Homeland Security had coordinated the whole activity, following the PM's call. With Parliament in summer recess, and the Speaker of the House of Commons not contactable, it fell upon the Serjeant at Arms and the Clerk of the House of Commons to agree to any search of the 'precincts', as the buildings – including Portcullis House – are known. Since the Damian Green case in 2008, new guidelines, protocols and precedents had been established. It looked as if the whole process may take weeks to resolve before the police could enter the buildings, and it also looked as though JHV, unbelievably, would have to be contacted first, which would rather defeat the process.

In the end, it was resolved very quickly and efficiently by applying for a search warrant for Ratoath and Moss, who were unlikely to be covered by such parliamentary privilege and certainly not at their home addresses.

The specialist officers, together with those from MI5 and GCHQ, took less than an hour to read Moss's emails and access his files. The man was as slack in his computer security and filing as he was in the rest of his life. The oil-rig photograph from Miguel Hernandez, communications with the intermediary company, and damning mentions of JHV and Russell Walker were all easily retrieved.

In Portcullis House, while JHV and Russell Walker were watching the news channel coverage and awaiting the President's speech, the police investigations continued.

***

It was 2.00pm, and Christopher Bucknall had been reflecting on Mike Kingdom's visit earlier. He had never met anyone like her, and he still couldn't really deduce the reason she had come to the police HQ. Deep down, he felt a slight unease of the sort that can only come from years of experience of cases and investigations. Why had she gone to all the trouble of coming into his office when she could have worked on her laptop at home? The only thing he had given her was the list of visited properties, and she could have guessed they were the ones adjoining the park, golf course and adjoining sideroads. She was no fool. Her dark-brown eyes had betrayed an intelligence and stubbornness. They also displayed a cunning and deviousness that now bothered him. He had been told she was security cleared and part of the Secret Services network, but an odd, young American woman in a black wig on a motorbike did not stack up.

He was chewing on his second stick of liquorice – which he might come to regret later, having forgotten its laxative qualities. He didn't know how, but he felt that she had combined his list with other information available to her from the Secret Services; information that he had not been given, for whatever reason. This was not a normal case, and major interests in London were in play. He was going around in circles, but then came back to the thought that she probably had more information than him. If this were the case, she had obviously come to the conclusion that Angelica was being held in east Swindon, not far from where Belinda was found. Mike Kingdom had not spent fifty minutes riding down at such a critical time unless she thought it would lead to Angelica being found safely.

When he had walked over to her at the desk, he had seen the two houses on her screen, and despite the jokes about buying expensive properties, they were of interest to her. *In fact,* he reflected, *she had packed up her bags and left almost immediately. To wander around the area?* He didn't believe it. Moving his mouse, he selected Google Street View. Knowing that area well, he clicked on the arrows and drove 'virtually' down the three or four roads and lanes that were near the Coate Water car park and the bench where Belinda was found. It took him less than three minutes to identify both houses. He read the officers' short report on what they found from knocking on all of the doors in the area, and he found nothing to worry him. On finding the names of the occupiers and their families, they also looked extremely normal.

It was only a ten-minute journey by car, and curiosity got the better of him. He collected his jacket and walked down to a car, accompanied by a constable whom he had asked to be his driver for half an hour. As he was throwing his jacket onto the backseat, his phone rang. The chief constable was convening a meeting immediately. Christopher Bucknall was needed on Zoom in twenty minutes, along with all of the other key investigating officers. He reopened the back door, retrieved his jacket and retraced his steps to his office.

CHAPTER TWENTY-NINE

Around a breakfast bar of black faux granite, which glinted with what appeared to be embedded soap flakes, two men and a woman were speaking in Russian. They were sitting on wire-framed stools and drinking coffee. The grey venetian blinds on the kitchen windows were partially tilted to give a clear view of the back garden, which had been put down to grass; a climbing frame and trampoline were the only other features visible. About twenty downlights provided a dazzling brightness, which reflected off every conceivable chrome appliance, from the coffee maker to the six-slice toaster. A large painting of sea, beach and blue sky – broken only by a small, red sailing boat – dominated the end wall.

The older of the two men was called Kiril. He had a Slavic face with a wide forehead topped by a flat crewcut. His eyes were deceptively friendly, but they betrayed little; they helped to make him look younger than his twenty-eight years. He was wearing jeans and a white polo shirt sporting the Ralph Lauren logo.

"She is American," he said.

"So what?" his younger brother Ruslan replied.

"I couldn't take the chance. She was looking through the gate into the garden."

"She was just being nosy."

"In four hours, we are done here. Up to then, we take zero risk, OK?" Kiril's eyes went from warm to chilling in a flash.

"She wasn't wearing a wig as a disguise. She has virtually no hair ... you saw that, didn't you?" Ruslan pressed his brother.

"Who cares? We do not take any risks." Kiril made it quite clear.

Ruslan leant back and folded his arms. He was an impetuous twenty-two-year-old with soft, brown skin and long eyelashes. He shared his brother's genes, which meant that he looked eighteen. He had been chosen for that very reason and had trained since he was in his mid-teens. The Foreign Intelligence Service of the Russian Federation (or SVR-RF) had given him the name Robert Valberg and the task of befriending the daughter of the chair of Petronello. Initially, it had not gone well, because it was Belinda and not Angelica who had fallen for him. The plan did not take much tweaking. His brother had experience of several covert missions in the UK and had lived under cover as Cyril Lansdowne for three years. At a superficial level, the British are so accepting of people who look or talk 'funny'. You just have to say that your mother is Polish or Japanese or Nigerian, and no further questions are asked. Robert Valberg was, to all intents and purposes, Norwegian, and Cyril Lansdowne was British with a Latvian mother; this was all that was necessary, together with immaculate forgeries of passports and driving licences.

The brothers were not being 'run' from the Russian embassy in London; instead, they were controlled out of Moscow via Germany by expat Russians whose families had left twenty-seven years before as *Aussiedler*. Kiril and Ruslan were part of a team whose job it was to destabilise the West to the advantage of Russia. Their task was to disrupt the Llandudno conference by kidnapping Angelica and making specific demands about the Antarctic Treaty. In addition, others' infiltration of the green movement provided cover from which to foment dissatisfaction at the conference. Yet more were undertaking a fake-news war on social media. While there were tacit agreements between Russia and China on some subversive activities, on manipulation of the internet, Russia was supreme. Like an unlikely alliance of the unloved children at school, China was the rich kid who could buy influence without getting its hands dirty, and Russia was the poor bully who punched at easy targets and ran away smirking if challenged; both strategies were successful. China had long seen Antarctica as an opportunity. China had twenty per cent of the world's population and was in desperate need of minerals and, separately, food. A thawing Antarctica would give China the chance to extend its global network of commercial and 'defensive' ports; it already either owned or had major influence in Zeebrugge, Valencia, Piraeus in Europe and dozens of others, from Kenya to Sri Lanka. The untold mineral resources of Antarctica were at the top of the Chinese and Russian lists. A moratorium on extraction for fifty years was not in their interests.

The third member of the kidnap team was a woman in her mid-forties, called Elena. Her blonde hair was scraped back into a bun, and with her sallow skin, she could be mistaken for the men's mother. Due to speaking good English from living in the USA and UK for over twenty years, she provided the cover for the operation. The house in Swindon was rented on a long-term let in her false name, and it was she who had legitimately answered the door to the two police constables.

The two girls had been targeted by the brothers. This meant the girls knew their faces and could describe them and the small flat in Chiswick where they met and supplied the girls with party drugs. Ruslan and Kiril, using the false names of Robert Valberg and Cyril Lansdowne, were not traceable, however hard the authorities tried. Absolutely nothing was registered in their name except a rental car that would never be used again. They would travel back to London in a newly hired car. A clean-up team would move into the Swindon house and dispose of the rented Vauxhall. The girls were expendable once the objective had been achieved, and Kiril would dispose of Angelica's body on the return journey to London. A route avoiding town centres had been devised, and a small wood identified where she could be dumped.

Unfortunately, the meticulously devised plan had started to go wrong immediately when they had discovered that the motorway was very slow after an earlier accident. It had become worse when the car's low-fuel warning light came on not long after they had passed Slough, heading west. Kiril knew he had filled the tank fully in preparation for the journey, but he did not know if someone had siphoned petrol off overnight or if the sensor was faulty. They had pulled into Reading services to fill up, irrespective of the actual reason. In fact, he had discovered that it was the sensor malfunctioning, as he could only put in a very small amount of fuel. It was also at the motorway services that Kiril had read the 'turn off mobile phones' sticker on the petrol pump. They had forgotten to deal with the girl's phones by taking out the batteries and SIM cards and throwing them away. At this point, both girls were laughing but drowsy, having been given drugged chocolate. To them, it was all a big game, and they were drifting in and out of consciousness.

Kiril had then faced a dilemma. His instructions were clear: take the girls to the large house in Swindon, where they could be easily hidden, and at 11.00am, telephone Charles and read the demand to him. The timing of the ransom call was critical as it had to be before Charles entered the AGM. Kiril was now not going to get to the house in time to make the call. Helpfully, the girls were almost comatose in the back of the Vauxhall. He had driven over to the furthest point in the car park, away from the coffee shops and restaurants, and had got out.

"Give me their phones," he had barked at his brother.

He had dialled the number for Charles on his burner phone while Ruslan had got out of the car with the girls' phones. He had read out the message slowly as instructed and was preparing to get back in the car when Angelica's phone rang.

"I told you not to contact anyone. You will not be told again," he had improvised. He had then given both of the girls' phones to Ruslan. "Take out the SIMs and clean these. Then, get rid of them."

Ruslan had taken out the SIM cards and wiped the phones to remove any fingerprints. He had walked a few yards to a bin and dropped them inside.

The girls did not know where they were going, but a designer outlet village had been mentioned earlier, as if it were a secret destination for them all; clothes shopping always got their attention. It had been two weeks earlier that the two brothers had driven the prepared route to Coate Water as a rehearsal. It had always been part of the plan not to come off at Junction 15, because it was only two miles to the house and there were CCTV cameras. Instead, they drove past and filtered back through Swindon – ironically, passing the designer outlet village. Belinda had passed out not long after they had driven by Slough, but only then did she begin to be physically sick. Angelica was unconscious and breathing strangely. Kiril had explicit instructions that the girls must be kept alive in case they were needed for showing in videos to put pressure on Charles. He decided to change their circuitous route and make directly for the house.

Ruslan was getting rattled and had shouted at his brother, but a stare from Kiril had silenced him. They were maintaining radio silence and were not able to phone Elena to prepare her.

"Belinda is disposable," Ruslan had hissed under his breath, although this was unnecessary as neither girl was conscious or spoke Russian, in which he was now speaking, "She doesn't know where we are."

"Easy, easy." Kiril needed to think, as Belinda was now leaning back with her eyes rolled up into her head. She was beginning to spasm.

"*What did they put in that chocolate?* It's killing them, and we'll be blamed."

"We have to keep Angelica until Tuesday evening, that's the instruction … She might be needed." Kiril was talking to himself while listening to the satnav in the car, which was taking them on the quickest route through Swindon. "Nobody is going to find us in that house. Everything is squeaky clean, it is not overlooked, and Elena will answer the door to any callers," he continued.

"What if she dies before we get to the house?" Ruslan was turning around and staring at Belinda, who was now twitching and gurgling.

"It will save me killing her on Tuesday."

"Let's get rid of her. She knows nothing about us except our faces. Even if she wakes up, what will she tell anyone? On Wednesday, we are flying to Germany."

"We will ask Elena." Kiril needed to discuss this with someone other than his impetuous brother.

Ten minutes later, they had driven off of the tarmac onto a large area of red paviours. They had pulled up outside a double garage connected to the main house. The wide electric door had been opened remotely by Elena, who had been sitting discreetly in the lounge window. She had become a little worried as they were now more than an hour late. Kiril had driven into the large, dark void, and the door had closed slowly behind him. With her footsteps echoing, Elena had walked down the corridor next to the utility room and had opened the connecting door to the garage.

***

Now, upstairs, Mike Kingdom was regaining consciousness and trying to find her bearings. She was in a very dark room that reeked of public toilets or, possibly, worse. Her feet were tied in some way, as were her hands, but these could be moved a little. She had tape across her mouth, which was stuck to hairs that she didn't think she had. Under her head was a pillow that, now she came to think of it, was the source of the smell of vomit. She was still wearing her clothes, but her wig had fallen off. It took all of her effort to turn onto her side, and she grunted, although it came out as a strange muted sound.

"Ssshh," a voice next to her whispered.

"Angelica?" Mike mumbled, but it only sounded like four very similar syllables.

Someone reached across and tore the tape from her mouth.

"Shit! Angelica," Mike said, well aware that people paid hundreds of dollars to have that done.

"Oh my God, how do you know my name?"

"I was trying to save you. Are your hands free?"

"Yes, one is … because I promised not to shout or try to free my legs."

"Can you reach the blind?"

"A little." She reached up to grab the bottom of the fabric, letting in some light.

Mike tried to look around the room while her eyes readjusted to the light.

Angelica suppressed a scream as she looked at Mike's bleeding nose and the purplish surrounds to her dark eyes. Together with the strange tufts of hair and white pallor, she resembled a voodoo doll.

"Why haven't Mum and Dad paid the ransom? Harvey and Elena won't tell me anything."

"It's not about money. Who's Elena?"

"I don't know. Harvey's mum?"

Mike tried to process this information. "What time is it?"

"I don't have a watch. Cyril took it."

"Look at mine."

After some physical contortions involving the lifting of the blind and the twisting of Mike's right arm, Angelica said, "It's 2.15pm."

"Shit."

"You're left handed, like me."

They could have been chatting over a coffee in a Costa.

"What day is it?" Angelica continued.

"Tuesday, and you are in Swindon."

"Where's Belinda?"

"She's fine. She went to hospital. She's fine." Mike did her best, but it would not win an Oscar.

"She was sick everywhere."

"I can smell it."

"They just rolled up the duvet and put it in the corner over there."

"You don't see that on TripAdvisor every day."

Mike tried to free her hands or feet by wriggling, but to no effect. "Can you see if there is a button on these handcuffs? Some have a button."

Angelica let go of the blind and was feeling in the dark. She could not reach Mike's feet, however much she stretched. The handcuffs on her wrists revealed no button. "Sorry."

"Worth a try."

Just then, the bedroom door opened to reveal Elena in silhouette with Ruslan standing behind her.

"Who do you work for, Miss Kingdom?" Elena asked with a slight American accent.

Mike was thinking fast, *How do they know my name?*

"Nice bike," Ruslan said from behind her.

Damn, she thought to herself, and she realised that her keys were not in her pocket. It would not have taken Ruslan five minutes to find the bike – or her rucksack and computer.

"I'm a reporter," Mike said, hoping that explained the laptop and the snooping.

"*When are you going to let us go?*" Angelica screamed.

"Well, it will all be over in a couple of hours," Elena said quietly, which only added to the finality of the statement.

CHAPTER THIRTY

Russell Walker was about to leave Portcullis House for the long summer break; he had stayed to tidy up a few matters. His constituency was only just outside London, which meant that – unlike MPs with constituencies hundreds of miles away – he saw his family most nights. He was walking down the corridor to say goodbye to his best friend JHV when he was stopped in his tracks. Entering JHV's office were Serena, the Minister for Homeland Security, the Serjeant at Arms, the Clerk of the House of Commons and what looked like several police officers. He turned down a side corridor and found another way out of the building. Wishing everyone near the front door a happy holiday proved a test of his acting skills. His normally red face meant that no one could see that his blood pressure was off the scale. He left the building, never to return.

When JHV had shouted, "*Come in,*" he had not expected to be confronted by a party of five people.

It was the Serjeant at Arms who spoke first. "Mr Hilton-Verey," he began, "these gentlemen here are police officers. They want to speak to you about some serious issues. Rather than take you to a police station, I have agreed to let them interview you here. Are you OK with that?" He was trying to walk the tightrope of defending parliamentary tradition while not inconveniencing the police in their everyday duties.

"What?" JHV stood up to face them all. "Yes, of course; come in. So, who are you?" He pressed the remote to turn off the news channels, only flicking his eyes away from his visitors for a second.

"I am Chief Inspector Workman, and this is Detective Sergeant Warboys," the dark-featured man with rather sunken cheeks introduced himself.

"I will be down the corridor in my room," Serena said to no one in particular, and then vanished from view.

"We will wait outside," said the Clerk of the House of Commons, and he and the Serjeant at Arms left, closing the door behind them.

"What may I do for you, Chief Inspector? This is all a bit of a surprise." JHV was a master at self-control. He indicated for them to sit in the chairs opposite his desk.

The policeman read out some formal warnings and gave JHV the option of going to a police station with them.

JHV was frantically trying to think which of his long list of nefarious activities had been drawn to the attention of the police.

"We'd like to ask you what you know about the whereabouts of Angelica Yelland," the Chief Inspector clarified.

"Who?" JHV asked.

"You've never heard of Angelica Yelland, her father Charles or her mother Maria?"

"No … wait, isn't he the chairman of that oil company?"

"Yes." The chief inspector waited.

"I've never met him or his family," JHV said indignantly.

"But you know Angelica has been kidnapped, don't you?"

"Yes, it was announced confidentially by the PM to a few of us, but I don't know her. Everything's been kept out of the press," he replied. "And that has held watertight," he added as an afterthought.

"You categorically deny that you are involved in any way with her kidnap?"

"Yes, of course. My God, what makes you think I would be involved in anything like that?"

"What do you know about the faking of a photograph of an oil rig that appeared recently in the newspapers?" The chief inspector changed tack, but his slightly hooded eyes remained lazily trained on his suspect.

"What? Nothing. Well, again, only what's been discussed in Cabinet and with the PM."

"How well do you know Patrick Ratoath and Andrew Sedgwick Moss?"

At this, the detective sergeant looked up from his notepad.

"I went to school with them both, and they're both involved in the Government; so, quite well." There was no point denying the obvious, but JHV did not like the way this was going.

"We have seen email exchanges, and Andrew Sedgwick Moss is being interviewed as we speak," confirmed the chief inspector.

"What email exchanges?" He knew that he had sent no emails on such an incriminating subject, but Mossy was a potential liability. What had he written down?

"He seems to think that you and Mr Ratoath are set to benefit handsomely from the photograph and the disruption it has caused."

"I'm sorry, I don't know what you are talking about, but if there are any more wild accusations, I had better get my solicitor involved."

"Of course, we can continue this down at the station, but we thought that you might like to speak to us here in the privacy of your lovely office." There was just a hint of aggression in the chief inspector's voice.

"I don't know anything about kidnaps and fake photographs, other than what I've been told here via the PM. There are some matters that I probably shouldn't discuss with you or anyone else."

"It's the PM via his Minister for Homeland Security who has asked us to investigate." The chief inspector let this sink in.

The bottom fell out of JHV's world. His mind was clicking through the possibilities, and he hadn't appreciated that he had been silent for so long.

"Mr Hilton-Verey, Mr Moss has kept a detailed record of the payments from the company NorCarbon and the percentage split with you and Mr Ratoath" The chief inspector was speaking very slowly.

JHV sank back in his chair. His career was over, thanks to that idiot Mossy.

"Now, I think that you really should tell us where Angelica Yelland is being held before anything even worse happens to her.".

***

In North Wales, the police were interviewing Rat Arse and Mossy separately. Mervyn had decided he could no longer listen to politicians and had ordered, and then cancelled, a taxi to take him to the station. The police wanted him to stay in Llandudno so they could take a formal statement from him on the conversation with JHV's friends he had overheard. Mervyn was always on a short fuse, but today had been the worst day of his life. He had decided he hated politicians, with the exception of Sophie, who was genuinely interested in facts and new ideas and discussions. Everyone else he had met had closed minds if it did not lead to some personal gain. As to special advisers? Politicians had no interest in their advice, special or otherwise. He had tried to stay calm and be objective, but they all made his blood boil. Even the so-called 'green movement' had resorted to violence. Was it really that difficult? Leave the treaty alone – any idiot should be able to grasp that. If he could keep it together, he would get back to London and apply to go down to Antarctica and cool off. He guessed there would be no difficulty; there was not a long queue of people wanting to spend months on the ice, especially over winter. He found a quiet corner and called his mother on Zoom.

"Hello, Mam."

"Mervyn, I'm glad you phoned."

"What's wrong, Mam?"

"You look nice in a suit and tie," she said, in a rare maternal display of affection.

"I'm at the conference, remember? In Llandudno."

"Uncle Cledwyn and I went to Bangor to watch the bowls."

"When was that, Mam?"

Mervyn drew his head back quickly, as Uncle Cledwyn's bulbous nose and puffy face came into view from stage left, filling the screen. He looked like a close up of Falstaff.

"Hello, Mervyn."

"Hello, Uncle Cledwyn … How are you?" Mervyn's blood pressure was unlikely to drop any time soon if people kept photobombing his Zoom calls.

"I'm very well, Mervyn."

"Why is Mam glad I phoned?"

Uncle Cledwyn turned around and moved out of shot.

"I tried to buy you a new jumper for Antarctica," his mother said.

"Good, because I'm leaving London and going back as soon as possible."

"I went in the Army and Navy Stores in Harbour Road."

"Mam, that's the Army recruitment office."

"Well, they didn't have any jumpers. They knew about the Arctic. They gave me a leaflet."

"Bye, Mervyn." Uncle Cledwyn was leaving in the background.

"Why's Uncle Cledwyn carrying a cardboard box, Mam?"

"He always carries a cardboard box in case the neighbours ask what he's doing visiting me."

"Mam, you've been dating for fifteen years. The neighbours will have noticed."

"He's not stupid, Mervyn; he doesn't bring the same box every time."

***

Inspector Bucknall was sitting in his office, doodling on a pad. He had already arranged the remaining liquorice sticks into every combination of triangle and square he could think of. Although the chief constable had convened the meeting and spoken for about two minutes, it was a policeman of the up-and-coming new breed who was now chairing it (or giving everyone a kick up the backside, as it could be more accurately described). Chris Bucknall hated this man whom he imagined having a degree in psychology, a Duke of Edinburgh's Award and ten minutes' real experience walking around Glastonbury Festival in his shirt sleeves. How was delaying key officers for half an hour going to speed up the hunt for Angelica?

Some other officer, probably from the traffic division, was updating everyone on the black Vauxhall Insignia that was now the only unaccounted-for vehicle that came off the motorway at Junction 16. It was a hire car and the name and address in London didn't check out. A man using a false name had provided a driving licence and paid in cash; this was not a mainstream car hire company and had been chosen precisely because it took cash. The fuzzy scan of the false driving licence showed a young man, possibly twenty-five to thirty-five, with a broad forehead and, perhaps, olive skin. Whether this man just hired the car or was one of the kidnappers, no one yet knew. Several officers from Chris Bucknall's team were trawling through CCTV footage, tracking the car's erratic route through Swindon. Coverage stopped or ran out at the roundabout at the end of Queens Drive. Unfortunately, there were five other exits to this roundabout, and it was now confirmed that, whichever of these the Vauxhall took, it stopped before it passed another camera. They were still checking some domestic and commercial CCTV footage. It was estimated that it could have stopped at or near accesses to any of about 720 houses.

Chris Bucknall sat up and began searching through his files and emails. He was looking for anything with the false name, Cyril Lansdowne. He found nothing new.

Mike Kingdom had mentioned the name to him when she had originally talked about the mysterious 'Harvey', now known to be Robert Valberg. He had not heard from Mike Kingdom since she left his office, and he now had a slight gnawing feeling in his stomach, which came from experience, not gained from having selfies taken at Glastonbury. He tried her mobile, but there was no response. She could be riding her motorbike, he supposed, but he was still not reassured. There was something about her that was odd and not just the wig, limp and black tongue from eating liquorice. She was clever – very clever – and connected to the Secret Services in a way he would never be allowed to know. She was looking at those two properties for a reason. He left his computer running and muted the microphone. He tilted the screen upwards so it showed a view of his office above his head. Grabbing his phone, he ran downstairs.

***

His driver raced down the A419 and Marlborough Road with the car's blue lights flashing and siren blaring, but then turned them off as they neared the hospital entrance. At the Coate Water roundabout, he hesitated and instructed the driver to go round again and make for the car park. It was the obvious place to leave her bike and then cut through to the houses. Driving past cars and camper vans, he could not see it anywhere. He asked the driver to stop and come with him. They were unarmed, but two bodies are better than one. Together, they got out of the car and ran through the trees until the first walled garden came into view. They crept up to the gate and, like Mike Kingdom earlier, saw the opened bedroom windows and heard the voices of people having a barbecue or kid's party in the back garden. They moved on up the track, past a broken bicycle.

***

Kiril had just left the bedroom, having warned both of them that if they made one more sound, he would shoot them. It was the only time Mike had seen his face, and she did not like the dead look behind his pale eyes.

"Let Angelica go and keep me as a hostage," Mike offered, trying to engage him in conversation.

"Why?"

"She has done nothing to harm you. Surely you have some humanity?" Mike was trying to gauge his accent and how much English he understood. He sounded Russian and that gave Mike a horrible feeling that it was only a matter of time.

"When does the conference end?" she asked, trying to provoke him into some interaction.

He smiled with his mouth, but not his eyes. "Conference ends when I come back here. Very soon and for last time."

"Cyril! Robert! *Please!*" Angelica screamed, but he turned and closed the door, and the room returned to blackness.

"Is he going to shoot us?"

"No, he's just frightening us. You stay calm." Mike was calming Angelica, as if the girl were the daughter she would now never have.

***

Ten minutes later, they heard a door slam and the noise of some argument in the kitchen.

"Are they leaving?" Angelica asked.

"I doubt that." Mike sincerely hoped that Angelica was right, otherwise they had minutes to live.

The bedroom door opened slowly, and the first thing they saw was a barrel of a gun. Angelica screamed and screamed.

CHAPTER THIRTY-ONE

There was a lot of blood, but it was surprisingly confined. Professionals shoot to kill, not to leave the possibility of some paramedic having the option of revival. One body had been shot in the chest, near the heart, while the one lying next to it had been shot in the centre of the forehead. Inspector Bucknall had been very wary of entering the house and had waited for the arrival of one of the armed teams. The front door was wide open, and this was somehow worrying the armed officer in charge more than if it had been closed. He feared a trap and especially a booby trap in the form of a bomb. It was a tough call, as Angelica could be dying inside. With the arrival of the second team, the decision to approach the front door was taken, and one officer, wearing heavy protection, began to crawl across the lawn, keeping as close to the front of the building as possible. More police vehicles were arriving and the cul de sac entrance was already blocked by a traffic officer on a motorbike. Two ambulances had come the short distance from their station on Queens Drive and were parked out of danger's way beyond the 'Police – Do Not Cross' tape that was being strung across the road.

It was a strange apparition that appeared at the front door; a sight for sore eyes or, perhaps, of sore eyes. A thin woman who was almost bald, with just tufts of hair, and a face with two emerging black eyes. She was in a blood-soaked white tee shirt and black leather trousers. She resembled a Madagascan lemur on its hind legs. Next to her, was a girl with matted, black hair, who was sobbing and wrapped in a blanket, a glimpse of her yellow hot pants visible through the gap in the blanket.

"*Mike!*" Chris Bucknall shouted, "*Are the kidnappers gone?*"

"They're dead … in the kitchen. It's all safe,"

Every policeman with a weapon drawn relaxed before re-tensing again as Angelica collapsed into Mike's arms. The nearest officer, quickly followed by a colleague, entered the hall as if they were still about to be confronted by armed kidnappers. Three others ran across and grabbed Angelica, moving her away from any danger zone.

Inspector Bucknall put a reassuring arm around Mike Kingdom. "Is your nose broken?" he asked.

"Is yours?"

"Yes." He was getting used to her oblique take on life. "Do you need a hospital? There is one nearby, as I am sure you are aware. Or can we sit in my car and talk?"

"Let's talk," she said, looking across nervously at Angelica as an ambulance edged forwards beyond the cordon.

***

Shutting a car door somehow provides the illusion of its occupants being protected from the ills of the world. The noise level dropped by half, and all movement was reduced to snapshots through the windows.

"Where's your bike?" It didn't sound like the most important question, but it broke the ice.

"In the back garden. They found my keys and brought it from the car park,"

"What happened to your face?"

"It got pressed against the back gate while I was trying to work out which house Angelica was in."

"Is she OK?"

"She's been tied up for five days and threatened with a gun, and her best friend's been killed, but apart from that, she'll get over it."

"Do her parents know she's safe?" he asked.

"Yes, I spoke to them."

"They left you your phone?" He put an arm on the steering wheel and managed not to sound too cynical.

"No, from my laptop. It was in the kitchen."

"Who were they?" He hadn't bothered to ask how she got the Wi-Fi router password.

"Russians. Three of them: Kiril, Ruslan and Elena."

He paused as a large, white van bringing the Incident Support Unit drove past, temporarily blocking the view.

"Who killed them?"

"You mean, did I kill them? I was chained to the bed alongside Angelica."

"So, who killed them?"

"Someone came in downstairs and shot them in the kitchen."

He ran his hands around the wheel as if wiping away grease. "And came upstairs and freed the two of you?"

"Yes." She was not being overly forthcoming.

"Was it some of your 'colleagues'?"

"No, but some of my 'colleagues'" – she paused after that word – "would like to speak to some of your 'colleagues'."

"I think that man over there is Mr Jones. I expect he is one of your colleagues?"

"No idea. I have a very small social circle."

***

Half an hour earlier, the silenced barrel of a gun had been put through the bedroom door.

Mike had thought this was the end.

A hand flicked on the light, and the bulky figure of Luis Mendoza filled most of the doorframe.

"*Luis!*" Angelica had screamed, her mind completely confused by drugs and events.

He had turned around and run downstairs, only to reappear with a set of keys. Carefully, he had undone the cuffs on Angelica's wrist and ankles. "Angelica, go into the next bedroom. Don't go downstairs. I will take you home in two minutes. Firs' I must speak to Mike. Go," he said calmly but firmly.

She had sidled past him, stretching her limbs and looking even more confused.

When she had gone, Luis raised the gun and pointed it at Mike. "Carlos told me I mus' kill you."

"What? Why? I've just found his niece."

"He is part of the Cenote Syndicate. I think that you know this?"

Her heart sank. "They are Colombians and Nicaraguans."

"An' Mexicans."

"Shit."

He put the gun back in his waistband and reached for her wrists. "Maybe I missed," he suggested, unlocking her handcuffs and chains.

"How did you find us?"

"I put a tracker on your bike."

"Luis, thank you." Mike began to regain her composure. "You need to disappear out of the country – fast. Leave Angelica here with me. I will make sure that you have enough time, but please, leave now."

He nodded. "Keep Angelica out of the kitchen," he said, and then walked onto the landing.

Angelica came out of the adjoining room and hugged him. "What's happening, Luis? Why am I here?"

"Listen to Mike, but please, you did not see me. I will see you in Mexico."

***

A very short time later, Mike left a wailing and utterly exhausted Angelica on the landing. She ran downstairs into the kitchen and, avoiding the three bodies and the blood on the floor, collected her bike keys and laptop from the work surface. After grabbing her rucksack, she looked quickly in the bin for her wig, but she couldn't find it. Hearing Angelica upstairs, washing herself in the bathroom, she moved into the lounge and closed the kitchen door behind her. A minute later, she was in communication with Leonard.

"de Vries," he answered.

"Leonard, there's no time for details. Angelica is safe, and the kidnappers are dead. They were three Russians: Kiril, Ruslan and Elena."

"Fieldwork suits you," he said.

"There is no oil discovery. It was a strategy for the AGM."

"Wow! The President speaks in twenty minutes. I owe you."

She waited for his apology, but it never came.

"Catch you later," he said and was gone.

***

"Charles? It is Mike. Angelica is safe."

"I will call Maria and tell her Angelica is safe." He turned his attention back to the current circumstances. "Mike, that's fantastic news. Is she OK?"

"She will be fine. She is upstairs cleaning herself up."

"Where are you?"

"In Swindon, not far from the hospital."

"Where are the kidnappers?"

"Let's just say that they won't be doing any more kidnapping. I will get Angelica to phone you, but I need to deal with the police right now. Can you come down to pick her up? By the time you get here, she will either be at the Gablecross Police Station or being checked at the hospital. They will want to speak to her."

"We'll leave right away," he said, adding to himself, "Damn, Luis took the day off at short notice. He's never here when you need him."

***

Mike opened the front door, both to let in some fresh air – as the house reeked of a wide range of bodily fluids – and to give the police access. They were her next call now that Luis had a head start on his journey back to Buckinghamshire (and Heathrow). She went up the stairs to check what Angelica was doing and found her gargling with some mouthwash. She had found her high wedges in the bedroom and was now standing in front of a mirror wearing her soiled yellow hot pants. She had washed off the mascara that had run and dried on her cheeks. She was looking forlorn, but halfway normal.

"There's a blanket on the sofa in the lounge. You can wrap yourself in that. I have phoned your mum and dad. They're on their way." She paused as Angelica spat out the mouthwash into the basin. "May we talk about Luis?"

"Did he kill Robert and Cyril and that woman?" Angelica asked.

"Yes, but if he hadn't, things might not have worked out so well for you and me. You understand that, don't you?"

"Did they kill Belinda?"

"Yes, they gave you both a heavy cocktail of drugs, and she never recovered from hers."

Mike expected Angelica to burst into tears again, but she appeared to be all cried out for the moment.

"Bee really liked Robert," she said.

"She was meant to." Mike paused. "Angelica, may we agree that Luis was never here and that we don't know who freed us? May we agree that it was a big, unknown man who never said anything? Can you stick to that story?"

"Yes," she said in a considered tone, "Why did Luis say, 'I will see you in Mexico'?"

"He will fly out as soon as possible, probably tonight. In time, you should talk to your mother about him. He knows your uncle Carlos; that's all I'll say now." She switched tack. "Right, let's go down and get you that blanket, and I will phone the police."

They walked downstairs to the sound of considerable activity outside in the road. Mike could see a police car in the distance from the lounge window. She put her arm around Angelica, and the odd couple walked slowly out of the front door.

***

The US President, was sitting with his team when Leonard rang. He was wearing a yellow tie and very dark green suit – this was his concession to the PR team, who wanted him to look a little less aggressive than in his usual dark blue suit and red tie.

"You're kidding me. Really? This is for definite?" He listened to the details. "What? Russians? … It was the Russians trying to put pressure on me and the UK? They want this Antarctic Treaty torn up pretty bad." He listened some more and then said, "OK, thanks, Leonard."

He ran a hand through his immaculate hair and digested the news for ten seconds.

"They have not discovered oil. It's all a big hoax, and it was Russian agents who had kidnapped that girl so that her dad would announce a big oil discovery and call for the treaty to be torn up," he told the others in the room.

"We have five minutes," a speech writer said anxiously.

"There's no time. I will wing it. Highlight in red on the teleprompter the sentences about reviewing the treaty, and I will ignore them and say what I want."

"What about the PM?" someone asked.

"He's already on stage, ready to welcome you. We can get a message to him."

"And get Marine One warmed up, I want to get out of this godforsaken place as soon as I can."

***

There were huge cheers as the President walked out onto the stage, beaming and waving. He was greeted by the PM. Sophie Beardsmore was also on stage, at a table where she was acting as chair of the final afternoon session. She was still writing pencil amendments to her closing speech, trying to strike a balance that would not leave the Government in the situation where tearing up the treaty was the inevitable outcome. She had Mervyn's crib sheet at the bottom of her pile in case she needed some handy facts. He was probably still helping the police with a sworn statement on what he had heard. She felt sorry for him and would see what she could do once she was back in Gloucestershire after the conference. Her thoughts were interrupted by the President, who had finished his introduction and was beginning to speak about climate change.

"… swapping from fossil fuel to green technologies is not a problem; it's an opportunity. It creates jobs," he said, pronouncing 'jobs' as 'jabs', "America is the home of the entrepreneur. We will lead the world in the use of solar and wind power, in geothermal power and tidal barrages. The sun and the wind do not recognise national boundaries; our discoveries and products can and will be used all over the world."

Sophie's thoughts drifted back to her speech. She tuned in again when she heard the word 'oil'.

" ... there has been much talk and speculation about a recent oil discovery in Antarctica and the threat it poses to the planet, once the Pandora's box of minerals and mining has been opened. Let me tell everyone quite clearly that there is *no* oil discovery in Antarctica. The subject of mining or anything else does not arise, because of the wonderful Antarctic Treaty that has protected it, and us, for fifty years." He was ad-libbing now. "My friend the Russian President has confirmed to me that he doesn't want it reviewed either. We will all re-ratify it for another fifty years." The President's smile was mistaken in the hall as happiness at the re-ratification, when it was, in fact, an ironic smirk, knowing that the Russian President had set himself up to be blackmailed into joining in.

Both the PM and Sophie were hastily scribbling notes on their speeches. A minute is a long time in politics. It was easy for Sophie to edit her speech. She only had to remove all of the qualifying adverbs and get-out clauses, which she had hated in the first place.

Outside, the crowd was cheering while watching the large screens set up to broadcast the event. The demonstrators and protesters felt that their pressure had played its part and their involvement had been vindicated. No one had thought the President would make this announcement. This included the PM, who had only just been passed a note telling him of events in Swindon. What had the Russians got against Wiltshire? First, Salisbury, and now, Swindon. But to the PM, this meant that his re-election prospects were sky-high on the back of the successful conference; he was glad he had thought of it. He stood up to thunderous applause and began by thanking the President.

Sophie sat back and relaxed in the knowledge that the Antarctic Treaty, something she had known nothing about five days earlier, was in place for the next fifty years.

CHAPTER THIRTY-TWO

The fact that Parliament was in its summer recess may have made things fractionally easier.

After the conference, the PM and Sophie had met in London to digest what had happened and to put mechanisms in place to prop up what he called, given his public school education, the 'status quo ante'. The PM was riding on the crest of a wave of popularity from backing the re-ratification of the Antarctic Treaty, such that even the Greens were finding it hard to land punches. Quite how a summer reshuffle of key ministers and special advisers helped to maintain the previous status quo was not explained.

JHV and his friend Moss had been arrested and were waiting for the trial that would send them to prison and end their careers as parasites on the body politic. Patrick Ratoath had escaped by the skin of his teeth, but had severed all connections with the Government and had suddenly remembered a long-standing family commitment to help out on their estate in

South Africa that supplied so many of the world's crocodile skins. The fact that he wouldn't know a crocodile if it bit him was not apparently a hindrance, as was proved a year later when one took off his right arm at the elbow. This proved more of an inconvenience than he realised at first.

Russell Walker had been in government a very long time and absolutely no mud stuck to him, despite so many suspicions, tales and innuendo. The PM took everything into consideration and manoeuvred him sideways to the historic position of Chancellor of the Duchy of Lancaster, where he could collect the rents for the Queen or whatever the chancellor did – no one was sure.

As to Sophie, the PM transferred Antarctica across from BEIS to her department, together with the new area of 'Space, planets and planetary bodies', placing the emphasis firmly on the environment and its long-term protection. Territorial expansion by others and the whole geopolitical game would be monitored by a new committee that she would chair.

Sophie, for her part, kept her word and had several telephone conversations with the head of NERC in Swindon and the British Antarctic survey in Cambridge, which cleared the way for Mervyn to go back to his beloved Antarctica.

***

"Do you want the good news or the bad news?"

"Mervyn, you're a depressive; you only do bad news."

"Miles, the good news is … I am coming back to sunny Antarctica."

"Shit! And that's the good news? Please don't tell us the bad news." Miles was sporting a few weeks' growth on his face and was eating something from a spoon.

"Do you want the bad news?"

"Not while I'm eating Irish stew out of a can, thank you."

"I'm coming out in four weeks' time."

The groans could be heard even above the scraping of cutlery on the inside of a tin.

"You won't get a visa in time,"

"I don't need a visa."

"That was the best I could do with no warning."

"*Have you told your mam?*" someone off camera shouted.

"Yes, and I'm seeing her next week,"

"Has she married your uncle Cledwyn yet?" The guys in Antarctica were used to the soap opera that was his mam's life.

"No, but she says that they are going steady,"

"Mervyn, would you like some good news?" Miles was licking his spoon.

"What?"

"I don't have to wash up this spoon." He held it close to the camera.

"But I'm not coming out for a month."

"Exactly."

***

Mike Kingdom caught sight of her reflection. She had shaved off the tufts of hair completely, so that she resembled the polystyrene head on which her missing black wig used to sit. The only other change in her life was the new microwave, bought with some of the money that Charles Yelland had paid her. In fact, she had been paid three times: by Charles, who had doubled the figure on her bill; by Maria, who had felt eternally grateful for what she had done on everything from Angelica's rescue to Rod Cameron's blackmailing and to her treatment of Luis, who was now safely back in Mexico; and, finally, from Leonard, who had arranged a discretionary payment for 'services rendered to the President of the USA'.

She had not taken on any new projects; she didn't need to, as her bank balance was as healthy as it had ever been. Even though her two experiences of fieldwork had resulted in multiple deaths and injury to herself, she was coming to the conclusion that, bizarrely, she quite enjoyed it. She had always been an adrenalin junkie.

The phone rang.

"How's my favourite agent?" an American voice began.

"Leonard, I almost died … again."

"Get the failures out of the way early in your career – that's what I say. When are you coming back full time?"

"Was that what the money was for? To tempt me back?"

"You could say thank you."

"You could say sorry. And why are you phoning?"

"I have some exciting news."

"Oh great. Let me be the judge of that."

"The President has confirmed an extension of my contract in the UK by three years."

"*What?* That's the best news you can offer?"

"I asked for five years." He pretended to sound disappointed.

"Leonard, has anyone told you that you are the most exasperating boss ever?"

"Michaela … Mike," he corrected himself in a substantial concession, "he wants you and me to concentrate on this geopolitical expansion by Russia and China. It's his top priority. He mentioned you by name."

"Leonard, you are a lying asshole. Do you *actually* have a spine?"

"How do you think that I support all of this flab?"

***

In the Yelland household, it was breakfast time. Charles was alone, drinking tea and reading the paper.

Angelica came down wearing jeans and a loose linen shirt.

"What are you wearing?" he asked.

She stopped and lowered her head while still staring at her father in a mock affronted way. There was no return to normal; there never could be. "They're called jeans. You're too old to wear them … Anyway, that won't stop you." She sashayed across the kitchen to the breakfast bar and flopped onto a stool.

"Would you like some orange juice?"

"Not if it's the stuff you drink."

"I wasn't aware I drank different orange juice to everyone else?"

Since the kidnap, the bickering did not have the venom of previous encounters and was now a pastiche.

"Where's your mother?"

"She was showering earlier, but I haven't seen her since. Probably letting Larry out." Angelica jumped up and began opening cupboards in a perfunctory way before settling on the same cereal she ate most days. "Anyway, you're looking smug."

"I've been counting my chickens … and I'm very grateful. I'm trying to appreciate what I've got, not worry about what I haven't."

"I have no idea what you are talking about. Is that even English?" she said as she began pouring cornflakes into a bowl.

"I have you and your mother back safe. Everything else is a bonus."

Larry the spaniel came running into the kitchen and bounced up to Angelica. Maria followed a few seconds later, wearing a green Barbour jacket two sizes too big, which clearly belonged to someone else. She walked up to her daughter and hugged her. "What's the matter, Charles?"

"Nothing. Can't a man drink a cup of tea and read the paper in his own house?"

"I get nervous watching you read the paper," Maria said as she took off the jacket, "Please don't tell me there are more photographs of oil rigs."

"There are no pictures of oil rigs ... even ones in the South Atlantic."

"Something's up. You've organised a surprise!" Angelica slipped off her stool and clapped her hands.

"I have not organised anything. Why do you think I've organised anything?"

"What are you up to, Charles?" Maria joined the inquisition.

"Nothing. Now you are both going to be disappointed, as I have done nothing."

"You're up to something, Charles? Is it work? Have you taken over NorCarbon?"

***

Three weeks earlier, the entire board of NorCarbon had resigned and several directors were facing serious criminal charges, including that of bribing government officials. The interim chair had opened discussions with Tony, and all indications were that

Petronello's slightly lower offer would be accepted. In Norway, Charles was lauded in the media as an honest family man who had put his family ahead of business. Petronello's environmental record as one of the good guys in a polluting industry was paraded in aid of a takeover of the corrupt NorCarbon. Not for the first time, Charles was portrayed as a safe pair of hands and a visionary. His and his company's treatment at the hands of Russian state terrorism was condemned. Behind the scenes, pressure from America and the UK was ensuring that the Russian President would vote to re-ratify the Antarctic Treaty or the full extent of what happened in Swindon would be released.

The environmental movement was ambivalent. It was having trouble openly supporting anyone connected to fossil fuels, but its key spokespeople recognised the golden opportunity presented by the President's and PM's vocal support of the Antarctic Treaty. No amount of draped banners and coffee mornings was going to match this.

***

The small cuts and dark bruises on Angelica's wrists were healing, but she continued to hide them under shirt sleeves and jewellery. Belinda's funeral had been a difficult day, but since then, she had felt she could begin the long road to recovery, even though she had not left the house since. Events had brought the family together, and Maria had settled into a heavily sedated state of numbness, which would be hard to give up in favour of a gilt-edged but unfulfilling reality.

"So, have you?" she asked again.

"The takeover is going through, but it's never over 'til the fat lady sings," Charles declared.

"That's not very woke." Angelica was pouring boiling water on a bag of red leaves while reading the back of the packet.

"OK, 'til the fat man sings," he corrected himself.

"Charles, how do you get away with it?" Maria asked with no malice.

"People love a winner, and I'm a winner. I just feel like there's going to be exciting news soon," he said as matter-of-factly as is possible while breaking into a sheepish grin.

***

Lazeena left her parent's house at 5.00am. It had been built by her father on a small plot in Edinburgh Gardens that he had inherited from an uncle. She came down the outside stairs and walked into the void under the first floor, between the concrete pillars. Her heels click-clacked on each step. At the bottom, a dog came towards her with its tail wagging. Magic, the German shepherd, had come out of his small shelter and walked the length of his chain to lick her hand. Twenty minutes later, she was leaving Chaguanas packed into a minibus with ten others; its windows were open, and they were bitching about anyone not on the bus, and therefore able to defend their honour.

Throughout the day, clouds appeared from nowhere and towered upwards, forcing the pure, blue sky into a two-dimensional background role.

From his office on the twenty-seventh floor of the two tallest buildings in Trinidad, the Minister of Energy and Energy Industries, and his PPS, looked down on the container port and the urban sprawl and across to the low mountains to the north. The hydrofoil was just leaving and heading west, then north and back east to Tobago. The vultures that normally flew around in this rarefied air, which were oblivious to the high-level governmental decisions taken here, had suddenly disappeared. They had probably hightailed it to Venezuela or somewhere where they could see the ground or find shelter.

As with all corners of the Caribbean, the storm appeared in seconds and unleashed its load on every surface unfortunate enough to get in the way.

Large-leaved climbers grew up the chain link fencing that projected from the mildewed concrete walls. The rain was coming down like stair rods and pounding on the rusty corrugated-tin roofs. The roads had already begun to steam. Elegant ladies in high heels, on their way home from work, were struggling under umbrellas while trying not to step into the concrete channels on either side, which were filled with stormwater to overflowing. They were glaring at the drivers, especially those wallowing in wide American cars totally unsuited to Trinidad's roads. An old man in a Rasta beanie was staggering up the road, causing chaos but oblivious to all conversations apart from those in his head. Around the perimeter of the Savannah, the vast central green space in Port of Spain, the traffic drove clockwise in the one-way system, often more slowly than the joggers and walkers on the adjoining paths.

In a modern concrete building not far from the Savannah, on the way to the Queen's Park Oval cricket ground, lab technicians were taking off their white coats and glasses. They were all faced with long journeys home by bus, Maxi taxi or shared car. Port of Spain's roads were clogged to a standstill at this time, and July and August were often the wettest months. By the time they arrived home a few hours later, the clouds would have begun to clear, leading to a fine hot night.

Lazeena was in an extremely happy mood; it always felt good when great lengths of her core samples tested positive for hydrocarbons, and today, the results were exceptional. She was looking forward to basketball practice later that evening, where she could show off in the new kit and trainers bought by her brother Vernon. Her long nails – painted in red, white and black – made typing on her phone a slow and deliberate process. She began a message thanking him again for the clothes, mentioning her excellent day at work and signing it "Love Lazeena".

And for the first time, she added "XX".

ABOUT THE AUTHOR

DAVID JARVIS went to art college, and then ran his design and planning practice for forty years, working all over the world. He ended up planning countries. His canvases just got bigger and bigger.